By Chassie West

Killer Chameleon
Killer Riches
Killing Kin
Loss of Innocence
Sunrise

CHASSIE WEST

KILLING KIN

HarperTorch
An Imprint of HarperCollinsPublishers

This is a work of fiction. Names, characters, places, and incidents are products of the author's imagination or are used fictitiously and are not to be construed as real. Any resemblance to actual events, locales, organizations, or persons, living or dead, is entirely coincidental.

❦

HARPERTORCH
An Imprint of HarperCollins*Publishers*
10 East 53rd Street
New York, New York 10022-5299

Copyright © 2000 by Chassie L. West
ISBN: 0-06-104389-3

First HarperTorch paperback printing: October 2004
First Avon Books paperback printing: July 2000

HarperCollins®, HarperTorch™, and ❦™ are trademarks of HarperCollins Publishers Inc.

Printed in the United States of America

Visit HarperTorch on the World Wide Web at www.harpercollins.com

10 9 8 7 6 5 4 3

For Bob
1939–1998

whose light burns with an
eternal flame in my heart

1

IT WAS ONE OF THOSE DAYS WHEN NOTH-
ing had gone right. Not your garden-variety nothing, like when you're dressed to kill, looking good
and know it, and the sky opens up in a mini-
monsoon, your umbrella's at home and you aren't.
Or the first call of the day on your shift is a drunk
who barfs all over the backseat of your freshly
washed and vacuumed squad car. That's chump
change. I'm talking about the kind of rotten luck
that, by the end of the day, had me giving serious
consideration to popping in on Madam Selena to
stock up on as many talismans, charms and
chicken feet as I could afford.

This September morning had started out just
fine—crisp, clear and goose-bump chilly when I'd
left for home from the mountains of North
Carolina. I'd dressed appropriately—jeans, a long-
sleeved denim shirt with a windbreaker for good
measure. Then I hit the Piedmont, and Mother
Nature—feeling bitchy, I guess, after a downright
wimpy June through August—opened her blast
furnace and let loose the meanest, earliest Indian
summer the East Coast had suffered through in
years. So several hundred miles and twenty-plus

degrees after my departure from Sunrise, the jacket was long gone, my shirt and jeans felt like a wet suit, and I smelled like Eau de Mountain Goat. And by the time I reached my neighborhood service station in Northwest D.C., I looked and felt as if I'd been char-broiled. I was soaking wet, ass-dragging tired and not, I repeat, *not* in the mood to be bothered by any known oxygen-breathing organism that stood upright on two legs. But considering the way things had gone, I knew as soon as I saw the derelict cross the street—against the light, I might add—that he was going to make a contribution to what was already one hell of a lousy day. The way my luck was running, he'd probably want to sit down beside me.

Granted, there was room enough for him, and I had no claim other than squatter's rights to the bench outside the Mobil station where I was waiting for my tire to be patched, but all anyone had to do was look at me to know that it would be prudent to find a seat elsewhere. This guy, however, was clearly oblivious to the emanations I was giving off—in fact, oblivious to everything except the effort involved in putting one foot in front of the other without falling on his face.

I'd watched his approach from the corner of my eye. Wear a badge and you learn to see as much with your peripheral vision as you do looking straight ahead. You never lose that. He would have been hard to miss either way. He was white—I think—with the jiggly-legged gait of someone who's made alcohol or drugs a lifelong companion, his shoulder-length locks matted and snarled like Medusa on a bad hair day, his shirt and jeans streaked with dirt and who knows what else. I was familiar with most of the street people in the area, but I'd never seen this one before.

He fingered the return-coin slot of the pay phone on the corner before making his way to the Coke machine beside the rest room doors to try his luck there. Then, focusing with difficulty, he spotted me and I could swear a neon light saying JACKPOT! flared in his eyes. He'd found a mark.

I cussed under my breath as he wobbled unsteadily toward me. Stopping at the unoccupied end of the bench, he shoved his hands into his pockets and squinted at me bleary-eyed, swaying in the breeze. I waited, assuming the point of the exercise would be to hit on me for spare change. What he said instead was, "Damn, baby, you sure look bad!"

He was right, but that's beside the point. At least I had legitimate reasons for my appearance: first, the usual nine-hour drive from Sunrise that had turned into eleven and a half hours of torture, thanks to the demise of my recently repaired air conditioner a quarter of the way home and, second, a flat just over the Virginia state line. There is no way to stay squeaky clean while you change a tire on the shoulder of an interstate highway in ninety-two–degree heat. Besides, I'd had to unpack the trunk to get to the damned spare and then cram all of it back in. That took longer than it had taken to change the flat, and by the time I'd finished, the solar index had burned the toasted almond complexion I'd been born with to something closer to black walnut.

On top of all that, what with no air conditioning, I'd had to drive the remaining three hundred miles with my window open, the rushing wind drying my eyeballs, blasting silt up my nose and bugs through my hair. So I knew what a mess I was, and the last thing I needed was the unsolicited opinion of a street hustler who looked as if he hadn't seen water since he'd left his mother's womb. I took a deep breath, ready to blast him out of his filth-encrusted tennis shoes.

He interrupted me mid-huff. "Yeah, I know, the pot calling the kettle . . . uh . . . never mind. Close your mouth and act like you're digging for loose change. I've gotta talk to you." He lowered himself gingerly, as if expecting the bench to rise up and meet his backside halfway.

I stared at him, taking in his features. "Jesus, Weems, is that you?" Narcotics, obviously under-cover. Way undercover.

"Sorry, sweetcakes. Thought you recognized me. You been out of town or something? I've been hang-ing around this block for a week looking for you. And will you please stop staring at me?" He began picking his nose, and I turned my back on him in a hurry. Really, there was such a thing as taking role playing too seriously. "How've ya been doing?" he asked. "How's the knee?"

"Better," I said, wanting no reminders of the rea-son I was now Ms. rather than Officer Leigh Ann Warren. "And don't call me sweetcakes. Why were you looking for me?"

"I figured you'd be the person to ask."

"Ask what?"

He seemed to erupt with frustration. "Where the hell is Duck? What's really happening with him?"

The subject wasn't one I'd expected, so I stalled for a second. I had no idea what was happening with Detective Dillon Upshur Kennedy, Duck for short, and as far as I was concerned, a dead one, kaput, done with, numero uno on my shit list. If you get the impression I was a bit upset with him, you're one smart cookie.

Duck and I had a long history. He'd been my big brother, my buddy. That had been stage one. Then things got complicated. There's nothing like a bullet through the breastbone to put things into perspective for you. Duck had gotten himself shot—well, both of us had in an incident too dumb to mention here. But he's the one who found himself outside the pearly gates and who sweet-talked Saint Peter into letting him back on the train heading south into this life. After which, being appreciably smarter about how fast you can find yourself on that train in the first place, he'd felt called upon to take care of all unfinished business, which included formal notification of a change in his feelings for yours truly.

I'd always accepted that Duck loved me. And I loved him. Only now it turned out that somewhere during our eight-year history, his platonic affection for me had gone bye-bye. He declared himself In Love. I was a bit more ambivalent about the whole business, one of those do-I-or-don't-I things, primarily because I had to admit that every now and then the possibility of a different kind of relationship with him had crossed my mind. I put him off for a while, but face it, there's no way to resist a man smooth enough to talk St. Peter into giving him a rain check.

So we became an item—until June when, without warning, Duck went nuts and issued an ultimatum. I chose his "or else," and Duck and I were history. Weems had to know that.

"Sorry," I said. "Can't help you."

"Come on, Leigh," he whined. "What's going on? I know better than to believe the shit I've been hearing on the street, but why has everyone been acting so squirrely about him? Hey, I'm covering for him with Jensen, so you owe me."

It was too much. "I got news for you, Weems," I snapped. "I'm free, black, thirty-none of your damned business, and the only man I owe is the one I pay rent to. If you're covering for Duck—whatever that means—then he's the one who owes you, not me. Take it up with him."

"I've been trying to and batting zero. The man's gone 'poof.' No sign of him anywhere. Is he on slick leave or something?"

"Don't ask me." I hadn't spoken to Duck in three months. Sometimes it felt a lot longer, especially when it had been a really dynamite day—or a rotten one, for that matter—and there'd been no one to gloat with me or extend a sympathetic "Chin up, honey. Tomorrow will be better." Now after eight years, that was over, all of it—Duck, and the job and badge that had become as much a part of me as my skin. I'd always thought I could handle change, but withdrawal was lasting an awfully long time.

Weems shifted on the bench, stirring up malodorous currents and making me wish I were upwind of him. "Look, Jensen and me," he said, "we're buddies and all that, but Duck's his main man. He's the one should be standing up with Jensen, not me. What the hell is so important he has to back out of this wedding?"

My jaw dropped. "Duck backed out? I don't believe it." Duck and Cody Jensen had been tight for fully ten of the fifteen years Cody had been engaged to Martha Makrow. Nobody but nobody who could bribe or blackmail someone else to take his shift that day would miss this wedding, least of all Duck, who had started a pool going back in March on how many hours before the nuptials Cody would chicken out. "What reason did he give?"

"That's the point. He didn't, just left a note on Jensen's desk saying something had come up and not to count on him. Nobody's seen him since, and I mean nobody. Ask the guys at the Sixth about him, and they clam up like their jaws have been wired shut. How come?"

"I already told you, I don't know," I said, mystified. "Call his sister. Vanessa Blake. Lives—"

"Already did. Took me half an hour to convince her I was okay. And according to her, he's working undercover for a while."

With that little tidbit, I gave up on the I-don't-know-this-person charade and turned to face him. "Say what?"

"That's what he told her. Only thing is," Weems continued, "Marty did some digging on the q.t. and came up blank. And you know Marty. Put her in front of a computer, and she can dig up the date of your first wet dream. So I figure maybe he's on loan to one of the federal agencies or something. They're as spooked about this new batch of weed on the street as we are."

"What new—" I shook my head. "Never mind. I repeat. I haven't seen or talked to Duck since June."

He grunted. "This is not good. Shit." He shifted his weight, clearly uneasy. "Look, sweetcakes, can I ask you something without you decking me?"

"The mood I'm in, I make no promises. What?"

"You ever known the Duck to have a drug problem?"

I was on my feet before I realized I'd moved. "What?"

Weems backed away, hands up. "Forget I asked. I'd better get moving. If you see him, tell him to check in with me. The least he can do is let me borrow his tux." He got up, shrugged one shoulder, a farewell gesture, I guess, and started away.

"Wait a minute," I called. "How long ago did he leave the note for Cody?"

"It's been a while, some time in August. See ya around, sweetcakes. And take care of that knee." Heading for the corner, he checked the coin-return slot of the phone again, crossed the street and disappeared.

I sat back down for a few minutes longer, digging under rocks in my mind for a logical reason for

Duck's desertion. If things had gone as planned, the two of us would have been jumping the broom before the end of the year. Perhaps the prospect of Cody's wedding had been too painful for him. Right. One-tenth of a nanosecond of speculation was about all that notion was worth. That wasn't Duck's way. He'd have stuck it out regardless. Something else had to have happened, especially given the whopper he'd given his sister, Vanessa. Whatever the reason, it wasn't my business, and I was determined I wouldn't be the one to break the three months of silence between us.

Edgy now, I left the bench and prodded the kid patching my tire into speeding up his act. Loitering just inside the door of the service bay, I watched him, my thoughts elsewhere. I couldn't get over it. Duck, the most ethical man I knew, had *lied* to his sister. No way on earth he could be working undercover.

A home boy in the purest sense of the term, Duck had come up through the city's school system, had gone to college here and, after sixteen years on the force, had worked in practically every district in this city. The result was that, excluding the migrants who rode in on the coattails of each new resident of the White House and out again four years later, Duck knew practically everybody. Wherever he went, whether it was Capitol Hill, Embassy Row, the city jail, or a shelter for the homeless, he could call people by name. Walk down the street with him in certain neighborhoods and you might as well have been working your way through a reception line.

Go out to Lorton, the District's notorious "big house," and you'd think you'd crashed a meeting of the Dillon Kennedy fan club. Even the crooks he'd collared greeted him with a sheepish grin because in spite of it all, they liked him. I repeat, Duck knew practically everybody. The flip side of that is that practically everybody knew Duck, too, which rendered him completely ineffective as an undercover officer. His cover would be blown inside his first five minutes on the street. So why had he lied? And why was he walking out on Jensen's wedding?

I couldn't stand it. My curiosity had worked its way into the kind of itch you get dead center of your shoulder blades a half inch beyond the reach of your fingers. "Be right back," I told the kid, who'd finally gotten around to putting the tire back on the rim. I fished coins out of my wallet and headed for the corner phone to see if Duck was home.

No response. Not even his answering machine. I had even less luck with his beeper. It wasn't turned on. That really threw me. I'd never known him to disable the thing. I repeat, never. There were times I'd considered it as good a birth-control device as anything on the market.

More than curious now, I called his mother. No answer, in itself unusual. At his sister's, a recorded message suggested I leave one. I passed on the offer, unsure what to say. Vanessa was so convinced that eventually Duck and I would patch things up that she might misinterpret my reason for trying to get in touch with her brother. My itch hadn't been scratched; in fact, it was worse, but by now I'd come to my senses. Better to go home and keep my nose out of the whole mess.

I had the kid toss the spare into the trunk on top of its other contents, settled the bill, and drove the two and a half blocks to my apartment building. Seeing its ugly faux Gothic facade with its gargoyles hunkered down above the door was a comfort, warming me with a sense of the familiar when so much about my life seemed to be dangling like loose ends. I pulled over into the loading zone out front and sat there, dreading the ordeal to come—getting this stuff upstairs.

The car was jammed with treasured junk from my old room and the attic down home in Sunrise. I'd always accused Nunna, my foster mother, of being unable to let go of things. She had receipts for dishes she'd bought during World War II. Now that she'd married again, however—at seventy-six years of age, thank you very much—and was cleaning house, I was the one who'd raided the pile she'd collected to give to her church for a rumble sale. It was as if the souvenirs and symbols of my childhood were being tossed on the trash heap. She was about to let someone sell my roots for twenty cents on the dollar! Shows the state I was in. Now that I had it, where in hell would I put it? There was no space in my one-bedroom with den apartment.

Sighing, I got out, opened the back door and wrestled the pink rocking chair onto the sidewalk. My portable typewriter followed, a sixties model Royal which would have been more at home in a museum—or a dumpster. It wasn't even electric. But the essay that had won the Sunrise Good Citizen Award—hot stuff in my little hometown—had been typed on that Royal. I deposited it on the rocking chair and placed an old overnight case from my college days on top of it as I tried to work out the strategy for getting all this junk upstairs.

The trick would be figuring out how much I could carry at a time, given the fragile state of my knee. The apartment building was U-shaped with the front doors at the base of the U. I'd have quite a distance to go just to get the stuff to the lobby. There was also the nuisance of the car alarm. It would have to be activated between trips in case someone thought there was something here worth stealing. Nothing I'd brought back would bring more than a dollar-fifty at any respectable yard sale, but I'd ferried it almost five hundred miles, and by God, I intended to keep it, at least until the next trash pickup. And there was an unfamiliar figure, a big one, lounging against the corner of the building watching me with avid interest.

Cataloguing his particulars, I squinted at him from behind my sunglasses. Male black, thirty to thirty-five, six-five, two-fifty at least, medium complexion, bald head gleaming in the afternoon sun. He was a brown-skinned Mr. Clean in his snowy white athletic shoes, a colorful patchwork vest over a white T-shirt, sleeves rolled up to expose a weightlifter's biceps, and snugly fitted blue jeans. I had no reason to be suspicious of him other than the fact that he didn't belong. Probably just waiting for someone, I rationalized, but I'd keep an eye on him just in case.

I locked the door on the passenger side, then realized I didn't have my purse. Unlocking again, I'd leaned in to reach for the bag when the door slammed hard against my protruding backside and calves, the impact propelling me across the front seat. My forehead collided with the steering wheel, and the whole of the Milky Way danced behind my eyes. Momentarily stunned, I lay there, legs protruding as I tried to clear my head and figure out what had happened. The car wasn't parked on an incline. There was no wind and therefore no reason for that door to have closed on me. So why had it? Blinking the stars away, I levered myself onto my hands and knees and, the back of my calves on fire, scurried backward out of the car in time to see a scrawny kid, jeans hung so low that I could see the crack of his butt as he haul-assed toward the corner, my overnight case in one hand.

My reaction was automatic. I yelled, "Stop! Police!" and scrambled to open the glove box, where until recently my service revolver would have been stashed if I was off duty. The door flopped down to expose a flashlight, maps, assorted gasoline receipts, a couple of just-in-case tampons, a tire-pressure gauge and nothing else. I'd forgotten I was no longer entitled to a service revolver. I was just like everyone else out here now, an ordinary citizen. And like many another ordinary citizen, I'd just been robbed. In broad daylight. In front of my own apartment building, my sanctuary.

A blaze of fury ignited in my midsection. The nerve of the little bastard! Infuriated enough to ignore the snare-drum riff playing in my head, I slammed the door shut and darted around the rocking chair. I managed two running steps before the knee said, "Now, wait a minute, sister. We can't have this." A sparkler of white-hot pain exploded under my kneecap, and I went down, rolling as I fell so that I was back on my feet—well, one foot anyway, almost immediately. Teeth clenched and swearing under my breath, I hopped back to my front fender and leaned against it, waiting for the fireworks to subside.

I could kiss the overnight case good-bye. Why couldn't he have snatched the typewriter? Someone might have given him a dollar for that. The only thing he'd get for the contents of the overnight case would be a howl of laughter. Teddy bears were a dime a dozen these days, and a moth-eaten one in a faded Howard Bison T-shirt would be worth exactly zero.

"You okay, Miz Warren?" Cholly, our maintenance man, called to me from the double doors of the building. He'd always reminded me of Danny DeVito, except for the color of his skin, a rich pumpernickel brown. "I seen you fall. I'll be right out to help you carry your things." He disappeared into the lobby. Whether he'd also seen the theft of my overnight case was open to debate. Cholly avoided involvement in anything that smelled remotely of trouble.

I stood up and brushed off my right side, now embedded with grit from shoulder to knee. If it hadn't been for the long-sleeved blouse, I'd have had no skin on my elbow. And I hated to think what the back of my legs would look like if I hadn't been wearing winter-weight jeans.

"YOU ALL RIGHT?" a hearty basso voice boomed at me. "DON'T WORRY ABOUT YOUR CASE. I CAUGHT THE MOTHERFUCKER FOR YOU."

I turned to see the stranger in the patchwork vest approaching, my overnight bag in one hand, the little bastard who'd swiped it wedged securely, head down, in the crook of the other arm, his blue-jeaned bottom and a good deal of cheeks exposed to God and everybody. Legs flailing, the kid yelled a slew of imaginative profanity as he punched the Good Samaritan in the back of his thighs.

"Quit it!" The Samaritan jiggled his arm, apparently with a good deal of pressure. The perp whimpered and stopped wriggling. I could understand why. The biceps tucked around his waist were as big as a side of Grade A beef. All muscle, no fat.

"I'LL SET YOUR CASE RIGHT HERE," he roared at me, volume turned up to maximum, and placed the bag behind the rocking chair. "THE NAME'S TANK, MA'AM. WHAT DO YOU WANT ME TO DO WITH THIS LITTLE TURD, BUST HIM UP SOME? BE GLAD TO DO IT."

"Come on, Tank," his quarry whined. "I wouldn'ta done it if I knowed she was your lady, honest."

"You know him?" I asked. "And not so loud, please." My head was vibrating like a cymbal.

"Oh. Sorry. Yes, ma'am, I know him. How 'bout I bust a couple of fingers to teach him a lesson?" He grinned.

"Naw, Tank. Come on, now, man." The thug's voice climbed the register. He sounded younger. "I won't do it no more, Tank, swear to God. Please, lady, don't let him break my fingers. Please."

I wondered if Tank might be serious. The kid certainly thought so. "Thanks," I said. "I appreciate the offer, but I guess you'd better not."

"Well, I can take him to the Fourth District station if you want. No trouble at all."

"Hold on a minute." It occurred to me that I really didn't know what he looked like. I could probably pick his butt out of a lineup of other rear ends, but the thought wasn't very appealing. I moved around behind Tank to get a better view of him. He peered up at me, a plea in his eyes. "How old are you?" I asked, in my no-fooling-around cop voice.

"Thirteen."

I weighed the prospect of the paperwork and hours involved in dealing with this little thug against the futility of its making an impression on him and shook my head. If I thought it would make a difference, I'd have driven him to the district station myself. But I knew better. I'd served my time in Juvenile and knew he'd be home in bed long before the police had jumped through all the hoops required for someone his age.

Tank must have seen the resignation in my eyes. Grabbing the kid by the waist of his jeans, he held him in midair and shook him like a dust mop before setting him on his feet. "This is your lucky day, dummy. She's letting you off. Apologize to the lady."

"Sorry," the boy muttered, wiping his nose on his sleeve.

"All right," Tank said. "Now, listen up. I know where you live. Try a stunt like this again and your ass is mine. Do we understand each other?"

The kid nodded, humiliation blazing in his angular face. "Yeah."

"Then get on away from here."

He took off, but turned at the corner and shot Tank a finger—vertical rather than horizontal or I'd have changed my mind. Too many kids carry guns these days, and the last thing I wanted was him coming back to shoot Tank. Or me. Been there, done that. Once was enough.

"Thanks for your help," I said to Tank, and meant it. Not many would have bothered.

"NO PROBLEM," Tank bellowed at me. I wondered if he thought I was hard of hearing. Much longer around him and I would be. "NOW, LET's GET THIS STUFF INDOORS. WHAT ELSE GOES?"

This was more than I'd bargained for. I appreciated his stepping in as he had, but he was still a stranger. I pawed my brain for a gracious response. "Uh, thanks, you've done enough. Cholly will help," I said, relieved to see him coming out again, pushing a luggage cart now that it was safe.

Tank turned to look at him. "THAT LITTLE SQUIRT? TAKE YOU ALL DAY IF YOU GOTTA DEPEND ON HIM. I'LL GET THE REST OF THE SHIT OUT OF THE BACKSEAT. GOT STUFF IN THE TRUNK, TOO?"

I felt my hackles stir. All right, none of it was valuable, but I still didn't appreciate it being labeled shit, especially at top volume.

Cholly and probably everyone else within two blocks had to have heard Tank's opinion of him. Halting the dolly at the curb, he lifted his chin, jaws tight. "You can go on about your business now," he said, surprising me with this show of bravado. Turning his back on Tank, he picked up the overnight case and placed it on the luggage rack. "Whatcha want me to take, Miz Warren? This thing can tote plenty."

Tank snorted. "OH, MAN, GIT ON AWAY FROM HERE. I'LL HELP THE LADY AND DO IT IN HALF THE TIME. THAT'S WHAT I'M HERE FOR." He yanked open the back door, reached in and grabbed the two boxes wedged behind the front seat. "ANY OF THIS SHIT BREAKABLE?"

That did it. "Just wait a minute, Mr. Tank. As I said before, I'm grateful for your help with that kid. That does not, however, give you the right to call my belongings shit. They may not mean anything to you, but they do to me. Another thing: I have excellent hearing, so I'd appreciate it if you'd lower your voice. Now, what do you mean, that's what you're here for?"

He set the boxes on the sidewalk and grinned. "Sorry. My grandmother's on the deaf side, so I'm used to talking loud. And I'm sorry 'bout callin' your sh— stuff what I did. I didn't mean no harm." He stopped, brow puckered. "What else did you ask me?"

"Why did you say helping me was what you're here for?"

"Oh, that. You're the Duck's main squeeze, aren't ya?"

"Ex-cuse me?" My hackles were now boogeying big-time.

"I heard Shorty here call you Miss Warren. You're the Duck's main squeeze. I've been hangin' around, waiting for you to show for a couple of weeks. Supposed to keep an eye on you."

I spluttered, so steamed that I had difficulty forming words. I snatched a deep breath and counted to fifteen, since ten wasn't enough.

"Let me tell you something," I said softly. "One, I'm nobody's main squeeze, understand? Never have been, never will be. Friend, companion, lover, maybe. But main squeeze, definitely not. The term is demeaning, so don't you ever call me or any other woman that again. Am I clear? Two, not that it's any of your business, but Duck and I are history. I haven't seen him in months. Three, thanks but I don't need you or anybody else to keep an eye on me. It was nice meeting you. Perhaps we'll run into each other again sometime. Good-bye, Mr. Tank."

He chuckled. "That Duck, he sure knows how to call 'em. He said you had a hot-chili temper and wouldn't go for this, not one little bit, but that I shouldn't pay you no mind. He asked me to keep an eye on you, and that's what I aim to do. Now, do you want help with your stuff, or what?"

In spite of an explanation that under other circumstances would have precipitated another blowup, the fact that here was someone who'd evidently spoken to Duck, fairly recently, I assumed, effectively diluted my snit and reawakened the itch. "When's the last time you saw Duck?"

"Right after my birthday, August tenth, maybe eleventh. I been looking for him to tell him you hadn't shown up yet, but I guess he's gone."

"Gone where?"

Tank shrugged, setting off enough muscular ripples to make a body seasick. "Said he had to split town on important business. Didn't know when he'd be back."

This was news. "Back from where? Where was he going?"

"Don't know and don't care. Duck's my main man, my home boy. Nothing I wouldn't do for him. He say to keep an eye on you, I'm stickin' to you like maggots on road kill." With that he took the car keys from my hand, opened the trunk and removed the tire, leaning it against the fender. "Here, Shorty, you can take the light stuff," he said, loading luggage onto Cholly's cart. "I'll handle the rest. We should be able to make it in one trip."

Cholly eyed the contents of the trunk and must have decided to bury his pride. "Well, if it's all right with you, Miz Warren. And 'fore I forget," he added, looping elastic bands around his load. There was an officious quality in his tone. "It's against the rules to change your lock without giving me a key. Management don't care what kind you use long as me or Neva got a key for emergencies."

The mystery of Duck's important business and my alarm at the thought of Tank as my guardian angel for the rest of my natural life added to my annoyance that Cholly had picked this moment to play Company Man. "I know the rules, Cholly. What's your point?"

"You didn't give us a new key, is the point. I figure you got busy getting ready for your trip and forgot, so I didn't report you. Could have lost my job if management had found out."

He had my full attention now. I trusted Cholly, but his wife, Neva, was another matter. More than one tenant suspected that she poked around in their units while they were out. "Just how did you come to the conclusion that I'd changed the lock?" I asked.

I never got an answer.

"Girlfriend!"

I turned around and found myself in the Opium-scented embrace of Janeece, my next-door neighbor. There's a lot to Janeece, physically and mentally, though she tends to camouflage the latter with a line of D.C.-block-girl lip. "'Bout time you got your skinny behind back here! Hey, Cholly. Who's your tall, dark and handsome friend here?"

"He ain't my friend," Cholly grumbled.

Playing the flirt, a role she'd mastered, Janeece flashed a laser-bright smile at Tank, who gaped at her awestruck. I doubted seriously he'd ever met a woman who could see the top of his clean-shaven head without standing on a ladder. Janeece was six-four and a half in flats, which she rarely wore, and had a figure that had caused more than one rear-end collision on D.C.'s streets.

"Girlfriend." She draped an arm around my shoulders, which meant my head was on a level with her left nipple. "You been holding out on me?"

"This is Tank," I said, since he had yet to close the distance between his bottom jaw and the rest of his face. "Tank, this is Janeece Holloway."

"M-m-ma'am." Tank bobbed his head, his greeting practically a whisper, for him anyway.

"Tank, huh? You're well named, I'll say that for you. Sorry I can't stop and chat. Got an appointment to get my wig waxed." She patted her mile-high French roll. "This stuff ain't been washed in two weeks. Bet there's cooties up there. Just so you know," she directed at Tank, "I live right next door to Leigh, here. Apartment 503, hint, hint. Speaking of that, girlfriend, the next time you're gonna be gone this long, empty your damned garbage before you leave. I'd have done it for you, but I couldn't get in. Ta-ta, y'all." Executing a hundred-and-eighty-degree about-face on her four-inch heels, she strode toward the far corner and disappeared.

"Gawd a'mighty," Tank rumbled. "That's a lotta woman. She married?"

To tell the truth, I couldn't remember. Janeece and her husband had tied the knot twice that I knew of. I wasn't sure whether the last one had been officially snipped or not. "Ask her yourself," I said, and picked up the Royal as a reminder of what we were supposed to be doing. It worked, and after another ten minutes spent deciding who would take what, the three of us headed inside, Tank carrying an incredible load under each big arm and balancing the upside-down rocking chair on his bald pate like some bizarre pink headdress.

As the elevator whined its way to the fifth floor, fatigue settled around my shoulders, shattering any illusions I had about unpacking and finding space for the additional clutter I'd brought with me. This was one evening I was going to do as much of nothing as I could, except for standing in the shower until I was as wrinkled as a prune. Any messages on the answering machine would have to wait, unless Duck had left one. I wanted to talk to him in the worst way, if only to get on his case about siccing Tank on me. Chuck Ross might have called, too, wanting to know if I planned to take him up on his offer to work part-time for him while I was out on disability. I didn't. So aside from Duck, the only call I planned to make was to the Chinese restaurant for carry-out, after which I would slide between the sheets and stay there until tomorrow. That fantasy lasted all the way up to the fifth floor and halfway down the hall. That's when my nose began to twitch.

Cholly noticed. "Ain't my fault," he said. "I guess your disposal's backed up again. Got several complaints from Mr. Tucker and Miz Wickham. I'd have taken care of it, but like I said, with that new lock you got, I couldn't get in."

"Got news for you, Cholly," I said, holding up my key. "I haven't replaced the lock. Maybe you used the wrong—"

"Holy shit!" Tank, dropping his load beside my door, lifted the rocking chair from his head. Fanning his face with a ham-sized palm, he stepped back, eyes watering.

I didn't catch the full brunt of it until I was directly in front of the door. Tank was right; it was pretty bad—in fact, worse than he imagined. This was trouble; I knew that smell. Once you've encountered it, you never ever forget the stench of putrefying human flesh.

2

I FELT LIKE CAPTAIN KIRK FINDING HIMSELF in an alternate universe on a starship that appears to be the *Enterprise* he knows but isn't quite. This was my apartment, my door—at least it was when I left. The hallway looked like mine—bland charcoal carpeting and stingy sixty-watt bulbs in ceiling fixtures badly in need of a good cleaning. The door of 501 was a twin of my own, right down to the gouged-out spot near the lower hinge where a moving man had bumped into it with my filing cabinet. Only it couldn't possibly be the same bit of real estate I'd left more than a month ago, not if there was a corpse behind that door somewhere, and I knew without a doubt that there was definitely a corpse behind that door somewhere.

An annoying metallic clamor finally snapped me out of it: Cholly rattling the batch of keys he kept on a giant ring secured to a belt loop. In the world I inhabited they were his sceptre, his symbol of power, his theme song, like the ominous two-note warning that preceded the shark in *Jaws*. So any alternative-universe theory had to be a crock. It was time for me to get a grip and deal with reality.

"Cholly, call the police," I said, rooting in my purse for something to hold over my nose. I'd exhausted my supply of tissues mopping sweat for three hundred miles.

"The police?" Cholly's expression suggested I had lost my mind. "For a backed-up disposal? Management ain't liable, Miz Warren. Ain't my fault I couldn't get in to fix it."

The key business again. Giving up my search for Kleenex, I pinched my nostrils closed and went down on the good knee to peer at the lock and the area around it. No signs of forced entry, no visible scratches. The wood of the door and the metal frame were untouched.

Gingerly I tried my key. It turned easily, the tumblers doing whatever it is tumblers are supposed to do. I gave the door a gentle nudge. It didn't open. Using the key for leverage, I pushed a little harder and met continued resistance.

Suddenly a new thought slithered in from left field. Sure, the lock might have been picked, but there was also a possibility that whoever was on the other side of that door might have used a key. Aside from Cholly, Janeece and me, the only other person who had a key to my apartment was Duck. He'd left me the one on his key ring the night of our blowup but had never returned a second copy he had. According to Weems, Duck hadn't been seen in roughly six weeks, about the same time Tank had last talked to him. What if Duck had never left town after all? What if. . . ? My stomach plummeted.

"Cholly, damn it, call the police. We've got to get this door open!"

"Shoot, Miss Warren," Tank said. "Don't need no cops for that." He lifted his leg and slammed the sole of his snow white Nike against the door, the sound of the impact reverberating with explosive force in the confined space of the hallway. The wood cracked, split and surrendered its hold on the lock, leaving it secured to the frame. The door, with a jagged rectangular hole where the lock had been, flew open and crashed against the wall behind it. Inside, several long, mahogany-colored dowels rolled across my carpet, coming to rest against the skirts of the sofa and love seat. I squinted at them and groaned. They were the backs and legs of one of my kitchen chairs. It must have been wedged under the knob. Doors popped open down the hall, and neighbors stared at us with alarm. But I felt a smidgen of hope—and anger. Duck wouldn't have done something like this, only someone who didn't belong here.

The stench, no longer contained, was suddenly overwhelming, slamming into us as if it had mass. I stepped back, trying to escape it, a waste of energy since I knew from experience that it would be days before my nose would be clear of it. It would never leave my mind.

"Management ain't payin' for that!" Cholly squawked. "Management—" He stopped, face contorted. "Gawd almighty, Miz Warren, what did you put down the disposal? I ain't never smelled nothing this bad."

I swung around on him. "That's not garbage," I said, jaw clenched tight, "that's a body, as in corpse. Now call the police, goddamn it!"

Cholly's rich brown skin turned the color of the hall carpet. He swallowed, eyes bulging. "Yes, ma'am. 9–1–1. I'm callin' right now." Keys jangling, he scurried away.

"And you," I said, rounding on Tank, "don't move a muscle again without checking with me first. Kicking that door in has compromised a crime scene." That was a bit of a stretch, since as far as I could tell, there'd been no actual break-in, but I had to put a leash on Tank before he laid waste to anything else.

He looked chagrined. "Sorry, Miss Warren. I was just trying to help." He shrugged out of his patchwork vest and held it out to me. "Cover your nose and mouth with this if you want. It's clean. Why don't I stack your boxes on top of one another so you'll have somewhere to sit while you're waiting for the police?"

"I'm not waiting," I said, accepting the colorful vest. "I'm going in."

Tank peered at me sidewise. "You sure you oughta do that, Miss Warren? Whoever it is ain't gonna be a pretty sight, not the way he smells."

"Can't be helped." I jammed the vest against my nose, relieved at its fresh, clean scent. "I need to know for sure."

"Know what, ma'am? Somebody's dead in there, ain't no doubt about that."

"No, there isn't," I agreed. "But before you

kicked it in, there wasn't a mark of any kind on that door. It wasn't jimmied. Whoever's in there could have used a key. The only other person with a key to my apartment is Duck."

A second passed before the horror of realization filtered into his eyes. "Naw, Miss Warren." He shook his head, a gesture of denial. "I mean, just 'cause I couldn't find him doesn't mean . . . Naw. He's left town, that's all. Besides . . ." His face cleared and he began patting his behind as if it had caught fire. "I forgot. Where did I . . . ? He gave me your key to give to you. Here it is."

I felt pounds lighter with relief until he levered the key from a back pocket. One glance and the fear returned, its bite even sharper this time. "This isn't my key, Tank, it's his. I mean, to *his* apartment. He gave you the wrong one, so I've still got to go in there, just to be sure."

"Then I'm going with you." Yanking his T-shirt free of his jeans, he pulled it off and covered his nose with it. Under other circumstances, I might have whistled in amazement, or even drooled. Tank had the physique and muscle definition of a bodybuilder. I wondered how many hours of the day he spent in a gym, and what he did for a living, then nudged the thought aside. There were more important things to contend with.

"Don't touch anything," I warned him.

"Not likely," he muttered.

"And if you feel like you're going to throw up—" He snorted. "Not likely. Let's get this over with." I stepped into the living room and saw that except for the mangled dining room chair, there wasn't all that much to complain about. It was pretty much as I'd left it, in other words immaculate. I'm not by nature a neatnik, but whenever I'm about to travel, Nunna's warning about wearing clean underwear in case I'm hit by a bus kicks in, only on a different level. Before I go away, I attack the apartment as if the health inspector's due. Should the worst ever occur while I'm gallivanting, whoever's stuck with clearing out my apartment can assure Nunna, "That child of yours, she sure kept a clean place." And all things considered, it was still clean, except that anything that could be opened had been—the drawers of the desk in my diminutive den that looked out on Georgia Avenue, the file cabinet, the doors and drawers of the wall unit to the left of the mortally wounded door. Oddly enough, it looked as if the contents of them all had been pawed through but not removed. The television, VCR and stereo were untouched, although the glass door of the storage tower containing my videotapes and CDs stood open. Now I was sure it wasn't Duck, who couldn't leave a drawer open if you paid him.

I glanced down the hallway that ran the length of the unit. The bedroom door at the end of the corridor was closed, exactly as I'd left it. I wished now that I'd left it open. The intruder might be in there. A shudder rippled along my spine at the thought of a corpse in my bedroom. Or in my bed. My brand-new queen-size bed. If it was, there went nine hundred dollars down the drain because damned if I'd ever sleep in it again.

I edged toward the kitchen, grateful that I hadn't stopped to eat on my way back from down home. My stomach was on the verge of rebelling, my mouth flooding with a foul taste that on principle I forced myself to swallow. I would probably know a few of the faces who'd be responding to Cholly's call. It was bad enough Tank had killed my door. If I barfed in here and ruined possible evidence, I'd never live it down. The prospect of that humiliation gave me something else to focus on as I approached the doorway of the kitchen.

The increasing intensity of the stench convinced me we probably wouldn't need to go any farther. Breathing as shallowly as I could despite the bass drum pounding against my lungs, I stepped into the doorway. It was a galley kitchen, little more than a narrow corridor with refrigerator, counter and sink against the right wall, a shallow pantry, more counter space and the gas stove against the left. The alcove at the window wall contained a dinette table barely big enough for two. There really hadn't been room for all four of Nunna's captain's chairs, but I had squeezed them in just because she'd given them to me. It was less of a crunch now that there were only three of them, with a distinct possibility that there would shortly be just two. One was going to the dump as soon as I could arrange it.

He was in it, his back to us, listing to one side, his right elbow hooked over the front edge of the sink as if reaching for the half-filled glass of water under the tap. He'd obviously made himself at home; I certainly hadn't left it there. And that arm over the sink was the only thing holding him up; he was slouched so low in the seat that it's a wonder he hadn't oozed right out of it onto the floor under the table. A good part of him had already started; from the looks of things his bladder had released its contents early on, and evidently he'd been there long enough for bodily fluids to begin to leak from blisters that had formed on his skin. That meant he'd been there several days at least.

"God, Miss Warren," Tank wheezed behind me. "If this is what happens to you, Grandma can sell my plot right now. I wanna be cremated."

It was bad, yes, but not as bad as it could have been. I hadn't seen his face but didn't need to. Thank the Lord and all the saints, it wasn't Duck. Even bloated, this guy was too skinny, the hand and fingers dangling in the sink too long, the hair, thinning at the crown, too coarse to be Duck's. He had probably been darker than Duck, too, but I couldn't be sure; the Grim Reaper washes us in hues of its own choosing. Whatever color he had been, he wasn't any longer. Who was he and what the hell was he doing in my kitchen? Smoking pot at that. I glared at the half-smoked roach in one of my for-company-only saucers on the table, my temper edging toward blowup. The nerve of the bastard!

"Don't you move," I warned Tank, and inched up behind the body, being careful where I stepped. But there was no way to squeeze around the left end of the table to get a better look at him without jarring him or the table.

I leaned forward as far as I could, but still couldn't

see much more than his profile. It was completely unfamiliar—I think. Chances were, his face bore little resemblance to the one he'd worn in.

Whoever he was, he hadn't been much of a thief. So far nothing seemed to be missing, at least not the kind of things I would have expected a burglar to take—the TV, VCR, stereo. Except for the drawers left open in the living room and the chair, which I could lay at Tank's door—or more correctly, mine—the apartment was much as I'd left it.

This didn't make sense. The only things out of place in here were the saucer, the glass in the sink, and the toaster, now on the table with a jar of Nunna's peach preserves and the dried-up remnants of a loaf of bread I'd left in the freezer. The slices he'd put in the toaster bore little resemblance to any grain product known to man. They wore a furry coating of olive green mold, the crusts black and charred. I felt a surge of malicious satisfaction. I'd stashed the toaster on top of the refrigerator because the last time I'd tried to use it, it had spat and smoked until I'd pulled the plug. Cholly had offered to look at it for me, but I'd kept forgetting to give it to him.

I'd had enough. "Out," I said, backing into Tank. "You got it."

We retreated, Tank leading the way. As we passed the telephone table in the hall, I spotted the light burning steadily on the answering machine. The fact that it wasn't going blink-blink to indicate there was a message waiting meant that the tape had jammed again. Duck couldn't have left a message if he'd wanted to.

I made tracks for the sanctuary and less polluted air of the hallway, reaching it just as the elevator doors opened and a pair of uniforms burst from the car, Cholly trotting behind them pointing in our direction.

"Take your time," I said to the newcomers. "He's not going anywhere." The aroma hit them, and the younger one turned an interesting shade of brownish-green.

"Who the hell busted down the door?" the older one barked, scowling.

"I did." Tank, pulling on his T-shirt, spoke up before I had a chance. "Miss Warren couldn't get in. We thought the lock was jammed or something."

"You couldn't detect that stench before you did it?" the uniform demanded.

"Yeah, but Cholly there just figured the sink had backed up."

I debated the ethics of allowing this line of reasoning to go on record unamplified. Tank hadn't lied, but he'd skirted the whole truth by a wide margin. I didn't want that to come back to haunt him later.

"It's my fault," I said, lowering the vest. "When we first detected the smell, it did remind me of the one time I stumbled across a body—"

"Oh?" he interrupted.

"I was a D.C. cop for seven years. Had to turn in my badge because of a bum knee."

"Thought you looked familiar. If you were a cop, you should have known better."

I chomped on the inside of my cheek, resenting

his tone. Unfortunately, he was right. "Look, I've been out of town for over a month and just got back. I'd already run into the two people who have keys to my apartment, so I knew they weren't in there. Besides, there were no signs the door had been jimmied, so I figured I was wrong about the smell because the garbage disposal had been acting up before I'd left. It wasn't until Tank kicked the door in and we got a snoot full that I knew my first instinct had been right."

He gave me the fish-eye, but it was a reasonable explanation, so he grunted his acceptance. "Anybody been in there?"

"I went in just to be sure. It's in the kitchen, to your right. Don't worry; nothing's been touched."

"Better not have," he said. "Is it anybody you know?"

"It's kind of hard to tell, but I'm pretty sure it isn't."

"Terrific," he grumbled. "Come on, Lister. Let's get it over with."

They went in. Ten seconds later, Lister came barreling out, hand over his mouth. He sprinted toward the elevator but didn't make it, losing his lunch a couple of steps before he reached it.

Cholly looked down the hall at the mess he'd made, shook his head tiredly and said, "Aw, shit!"

"You've got to admit, Ms. Warren, the whole thing's kind of weird. This guy you claim not to know shows up while you're out of town and lets himself in with a key; he had two and one of them fits. He props the chair under the doorknob, sort of as a just-in-case, but it looks to me as if he knew he had no reason to hurry. He doesn't go for the usual—TV, computer, or any of the stuff a burglar would normally steal. No, he pokes around in your desk and file cabinet and dresser drawers, as if he's looking for something specific. Then he settles down in your kitchen, smokes a little pot while he's making himself a bit of breakfast."

"Don't remind me," I said, still smarting over the abuse of my good saucer.

"There's not a single piece of ID on him. The only things in his pockets were some pot, a lighter, eleven dollars and change, a Metro fare card and the keys. How'd he get yours? He might have been a parking lot attendant, a hotel bellboy, someone in a position to get to your keys and make a fast copy. You're absolutely positive you've never seen him before?"

I'd been sitting on the boxes in the hall for the last three hours, watching the parade in and out of my apartment—uniforms, plainclothes, technicians, a photographer, medical examiner, ambulance attendants. Minute by minute I'd felt the gulf between myself and the mob inside grow wider and wider. Not only was I no longer a member of the brotherhood, I was now one of those anonymous citizens whose life had become circumscribed by a roll of yellow crime-scene tape.

I'd given my statement several times already, first to a uniform and then to this plainclothes pain in the butt with the unfortunate name of Tristan. I was way past fatigued and, despite the stench, famished. I have the kind of constitution that demands fuel every four hours I'm up or I get very, very ugly. Having the same question asked yet again pushed me over the edge.

"How the hell can I be absolutely positive I've never seen him before?" I demanded. "You saw his face. His own mother wouldn't recognize him now. All I can say—and let me tell you, buddy, I'm saying it for the last time—he wasn't familiar in any way. Look, I don't know how he got a key to my apartment or why he went through my desk and file cabinet. I've walked through the whole place with Margione and checked the contents of the drawers he left open. Nothing's missing. So I don't know what he was doing in there, but he's been in there long enough. Get him the hell out of my kitchen!"

The plainclothes pain in the butt gave me a bemused smile. "Testy, aren't we? Come on, you've been on this side of the situation. You know the drill. It takes time. But . . ." He jerked his head toward the attendants wheeling John Doe through the living room. "Here he comes now." He stepped aside, handkerchief over his mouth as they came out into the hall with their bagged quarry. We watched in silence as the cortege headed for the elevator. My fifth-floor neighbors, who'd been milling about at the other end of the hall, heads together, beat a hasty retreat.

"One last thing and I'm done." Tristan flipped the page of his spiral notebook. "I'm gonna want to talk to the people you've given keys to."

"Janeece Holloway. Lives in 503. She's tutoring tonight, won't be home until eleven."

"You trust her." He phrased it as a statement, brows hoisted as if it had been a question.

"Yes. We go back a long way. The manager also has a key."

"Cholston Burns," Tristan said, checking his notes. "Well, at least he's around—or was. Nick." He stepped into the living room. "What happened to Burns? Apartment manager?"

"The little guy with all the keys?" I couldn't see Nick but could hear the chuckle in his voice. "In the john tossin' his cookies. Claims he'd never seen the dude before."

I groaned. First my kitchen, now my bathroom. I'd be cleaning and scrubbing until after the turn of the century.

"We can talk to him again later. I hesitate to ask," Tristan said to me, a sly smile playing at the corners of his mouth, "but that wouldn't happen to be *your* stash the John Doe came across while he was poking around in your freezer, would it?"

It took a second for the implication to register, perhaps because I was tired. Once I realized what he meant, I exploded. "I have never, I repeat, *never*, smoked pot or anything else," I said, furious. "I have never sniffed, snorted, shot up, or turned on with illegal drugs of any kind. I was a good cop, Tristan, and I resent the question."

He grinned. "And I'm a good cop, so I had to ask. Anybody else ever have a key?"

Behind me, Tank cleared his throat—a reminder, I assumed, of the conversation we'd had while waiting for the technical types to appear. As far as he was concerned, there was no reason to mention the fact that Duck still had a key. "This has to be an inside job," he'd insisted. "Otherwise, how'd that dude know whose door the key would unlock?"

"You're saying Cholly's involved?"

I'd rejected that. I'd lived in the building long enough to know Cholly well. And even though I trusted his wife, Neva, about as far as I could throw her two hundred fifty-plus pounds, the only thing I suspected her of was the occasional foray through a unit to see what kind of furnishings you had. Neva had a thing about furniture and could tell in a minute whether you'd done your shopping at Macy's or Kmart. The bottom line was that I really didn't think she or Cholly had had anything to do with the intruder. If the police thought otherwise, it would be up to them to prove it. As for Duck, despite our differences, I had to give him the benefit of the doubt. I had no idea how the John Doe had gotten the key, but I was certain Duck had had nothing to do with it.

Which was why, in responding to Tristan's question, I fudged. "Only one other person has had a key, the guy I was engaged to. Dillon Kennedy."

Tristan's brows jumped toward his blond hairline. "Duck?" I saw his opinion of me rocket upward. His whole demeanor changed. "How is that turkey?" he asked, his tone probably as close to warm as it ever got. "Haven't seen him in ages."

"Neither have I," I said, taking the main chance. "We broke up, and he returned the key he had."

That nudged me back down a notch. "Too bad.

A good man. What about Big Foot there?" He jerked his head toward Tank. "He your new man of the hour?"

"No, he's not." I wasn't sure what Tank had told them, since we'd been questioned separately, so I stuck as close to the truth as I could. "He's a friend of Duck's. He saw me out front unloading the car and volunteered to help me carry things up. And when I couldn't get the door open, he kicked it in."

Tristan eyed the damage. "Couldn't have done a better job with police equipment. Okay, that's enough for now." He turned to go back into the living room and collided with the rotund figure of Crosley, from the medical examiner's office, coming out. "What's the word, Cros?" Tristan asked.

Crosley's bloodshot eyes swept past me and settled on the plainclothes detective. "You know it's too early to—"

"Oh, can it, man. You must have been able to tell something. It's all right to talk in front of her. She used to be one of us. Just went out on disability. Engaged to Duck, too."

"No kidding." Crosley's hound dog expression lifted, and he beamed at me. "Be damned."

I started to put the past tense on Tristan's explanation, then slammed my mouth shut. It was obvious my association with Duck carried a hell of a lot more weight with them than my previous years in uniform. I resented it, but if it enabled me to get the inside dope on my uninvited guest, it might be worth it.

"Well, I gotta tell you, you are one lucky little lady," Crosley said, rising up and down on the balls of his feet.

"Lucky?" I protested. "I come home and find a corpse growing mold at my kitchen table and you call me lucky?"

"Cut the crap, Cros." Tristan scowled at him. "What do you think?"

"I think it's a good thing this little lady's apartment is on the north side of the building, where it's a bit cooler, or he'd have been in a lot worse shape than he is. He's been in there a good five days, maybe longer."

The thought made me queasy. Suddenly I wasn't quite as anxious to take possession of my apartment.

"Five days more or less," Tristan said, scribbling on his spiral pad. "What did him? He seems kinda young for natural causes."

"Well, unless I miss my guess, death by toaster." Crosley grinned.

No doubt someone who deals with the dearly departed on a daily basis develops an offbeat sense of humor, but I was in no mood for it. "Excuse me?"

"Like I said before, you're lucky. My guess is that he had a hand on the toaster when he reached to turn on the tap with the other. The toaster must have arced—you should see those filaments—and he became a perfect conductor. Burn marks on his fingers."

I felt the skin across my cheeks constrict. "You mean he was electrocuted? By my toaster?"

"'Fraid so. Insulation must have worn off. Had it been working?"

I shook my head, not a smart idea, considering that it was empty of blood. I willed myself not to keel over. "It really killed him?"

"That's a preliminary finding, of course. I'll be able to say for sure once I open him up. Look at it this way: it could have been you. If he hadn't been in there, it wouldn't have happened to him, so it's not your fault." He checked his watch. "Gotta go. I should have been in Southeast half an hour ago. I'll be in touch, Tristan." He trotted toward the elevator, making a wide berth around the souvenir Lister had left.

"Listen to the man," Tristan said, palming my shoulder. "It wasn't your fault. You are not responsible."

I appreciated the sentiment, but it was my apartment, my kitchen and my toaster. Why hadn't I just trashed it? I could have blown a few dollars on a new toaster. How could I not feel some responsibility for the man's death? And how could I forget that it damn well could have been me at that table? I slumped back down on the stack of boxes. What else would I have to face today?

One of the technicians, whose name was vaguely familiar, came out, removing the mask over his mouth and nose with one hand, holding a couple of evidence bags in the other. "I'm done," he said to Tristan. "How 'bout taking these with you? We've got another crime scene waiting for us."

Tristan sighed. "Give 'em here. Something tells

me I'm gonna be late for dinner again tonight." He reached for the evidence bags, and I almost lost it. In one bag was a handful of marijuana and a couple of wrinkled joints peeking out of white tissue paper, the lot secured in plastic wrap with a rubber band around it. In the second plastic bag were several soggy-looking greenbacks, an equally soiled Metro fare card and a metal key ring shaped like Wile E. Coyote with two keys on it—Duck's key ring with the blue spare key to his apartment and the tacky red spare key to mine.

3

THEN ALL HELL BROKE LOOSE. THE ELEVA-
tor doors creaked open, and one of the uniforms
stepped out, eyes wide. "Lieutenant, we gotta go!
All units! A 10-13, Georgia and Alaska Avenue!
Officer down, two others trapped by a sniper!"

Tristan backed away, cramming his spiral pad
into a breast pocket. "I've got enough from you for
the time being," he said, his color high. "I'll be in
touch." Turning, he sprinted for the steps, the technician with the evidence bags right behind him.

For the second time in one day, I found myself
reacting like the retired police dog that's raring to go
every time his owner puts on his uniform. Bum
knee forgotten, I was halfway down the hall after
them, heart pounding, mouth dry, before I remembered that the call for officer needing assistance was
no longer my concern. I had no right to take up
space in any of the squad cars speeding to the scene.
Three of my brothers—correction, my former
brothers—were in peril, and I wasn't entitled to
help. I was a civilian, an outsider, my assistance no
longer needed or welcome.

Until now the fact that that stage of my life was
over had sidled up next to me now and then as a

stray thought, or in waking moments in the middle of the night. Being in Sunrise and having to focus on my foster mom's wedding plans, busy work completely unrelated to my former routine, had provided enough of a distraction to render those pinpricks of awareness fleeting and bearable. But I was home again, back among the familiar, where I'd accepted that sooner or later the full brunt of my separation from the Department would hit me like a speeding freight train. The corpse in the kitchen had delayed this moment for a while. Now, thanks to the 10-13, it had run me down and flattened me. I didn't even have the luxury of going into my apartment, shutting the door behind me and letting myself bawl like a baby. My apartment was still off-limits because of the blasted yellow tape. Even if I'd been able to, there was no door to shut.

I stopped and leaned against the wall, over-whelmed by a sense of isolation, purposelessness and lack of direction. I'd taken a month-long dip in the toilet after the shooting I'd been involved in the year before, but this was worse. There'd be no job in which to bury myself until I'd climbed out of that cesspool of self-doubt, at least not the job I'd loved for the last seven years. There'd be no Duck to . . .

Duck. That silly Wile E. Coyote key ring. I latched on to that as if a lifesaver had been tossed to me. How had that key ring found its way into the John Doe's pocket?

"You all right, Miss Warren?" Tank.

I sighed, having forgotten about my guardian angel. I pushed myself away from the wall, turning to find him towering over me, eyes blurred with concern. "Tank, that key ring the technician had, that was Duck's, the spare keys to his apartment and mine."

A vertical line etched its way between his brows. "You sure? Duck ain't the kind of dude would give your key to a sleazebag who'd go into your place and look through your things like he did. Reckon that guy stole 'em?"

"I almost wish he had." I slid down the wall and sat down to think. "But the fact that he turned up here means Duck must have told him which key was mine. For the life of me, I can't figure out why he'd have done that. For that matter, why'd he give you the key for me?"

Tank squatted beside me and extended legs so long they almost reached the opposite wall. "Got me, Miss Warren. I was so freaked out that he trusted me that much that I didn't think to ask."

"What exactly did he say when he gave them to you?"

He slid a very large hand over his bald head. "Well, we were coming out of the Adult Ed Center, and he asked me to walk with him to his car. When we get there, he says he's leaving town. I get a funny feeling because of the way he says it, so I ask if he's talking about for good. He says if he does what he's setting out to do, he probably won't be coming back. Then he gives me the key off his key ring and says I should give it to you because it was yours now."

I pried the key out of my back pocket. It was silver with the letter D stamped on it, the one he carried every day. The John Doe had had the spare. Unless Duck had a third one I didn't know about, he couldn't get into his own apartment.

"Why," I muttered, mostly to myself, "would he send this to me and why now?"

"Got me." Another technician hurried out of my apartment, and Tank folded his legs under him lotus-style so the tech wouldn't trip over them. "He said it was all he had left to give you and that I should keep an eye on you since he wouldn't be around to do it. So here I am. Whatcha want me to do now?"

Scram is what I wanted him to do. It wasn't until Duck and I were engaged that I'd realized how deeply his protective streak ran; it was the reason for our big blowup. For him to assign a deputy, however, was going a bit far, even for Duck. And as invaluable as Tank had been today, I had no intention of having him dog my every step. Convincing him of that would be a challenge, one that would have to wait. It was more important that someone know that the keys in John Doe's possession had been Duck's spares.

I directed Tank to the basement storage room and asked him to stash the things cluttering the hallway. As he left, arms piled high with boxes and cases, the last technician backed out into the hall and peeled the crime-scene tape from the frame of the doorway.

"All yours," he said, removing his mask. "You know, it's gonna be ripe in there for a while."

"Don't remind me," I grumbled. "Will you be seeing Tristan any time soon?"

"Can't ever tell. Something I can do?"

I hesitated. I wanted to pass along the info about Duck's spare keys to Tristan myself. I wanted to gauge his reaction, find out what he thought. But first I'd hit the Sixth District, Duck's stomping grounds, and collar a few of his buddies, ask a question or two. Somebody there had to know what he was up to. They might not tell Weems, but they would tell me. I thanked the technician, and he hurried away.

After a couple of deep breaths to prepare myself, I stepped into the living room and grimaced at the splotches of black now decorating practically every surface J. Doe might have touched. The combination of the odor and the prints he'd left made his invasion that much more intrusive. Even after all traces of him had been erased, I doubted I'd ever be able to sit at my desk at bill-paying time without wondering if he had touched this or moved that. Something told me that the memory of the corpse in the kitchen would probably hover in every room from now on.

Which was why I practically wet my pants when Cholly, still faintly green, came out of my bathroom. "Jesus, you scared me! You okay?" I asked.

"Yes'm," he said, clearly embarrassed. "Never seen anything that awful in my life. Tell me something, Miz Warren, your bathroom always that clean?"

I took that as a rhetorical question and ignored it, tackling the problem of my door instead. We wasted the next few minutes arguing about who was going to pay for it, a debate that wasn't settled until I resorted to a bit of blackmail regarding his wife's inclination to come visiting when no one was home. His reaction was a dead giveaway, confirming that our suspicions about Neva were true. Suitably chastened, Cholly scurried off to arrange for a carpenter and locksmith.

I was almost sorry to have won the argument, because now I was alone and, for the first time in my life, downright uneasy about it. I resented that. An only child, I was used to being by myself. One of the reasons I'd never suffered the Hitting-Thirty-and-Still-Single panic was because I was so comfortable being alone. If I'd experienced any panic at all, it had been at the thought of becoming Mrs. Leigh Ann Kennedy—or Mrs. Leigh Ann Anybody for that matter—and losing the solitude I valued so highly. Like Garfield the cat, I needed my space. And as much as I loved Duck—and I did love him— I knew it was a need he'd have tried to respect but would have never been able to understand. He might have even come to resent it. Now that that particular problem was no longer a concern, I found myself with every single nerve twanging like a banjo string at the realization that I was all by my lonesome in this apartment.

"Miss Warren."

I whirled around, my heart exploding in my chest. "Tank, please, don't ever sneak up on me like that!"

He looked wounded. "Sorry. Everybody says I'm kinda light on my feet. Here's your storage room key. I got everything in there nice and neat. But you can't stay here, not the way it smells. I'd offer the spare room at my grandma's but . . . well, Grandma's an old-fashioned glory-hallelujah Baptist and she just wouldn't go for it. And if Tina ever found out . . ." He shuddered.

I had to meet this Tina. Any female who could make someone as substantial as Tank shudder was a female worth knowing. "Thanks for the thought, but I'll probably stay with Janeece for tonight. I'll worry about tomorrow tomorrow."

"Oh. Okay, but what are we gonna do until she gets home?"

I looked at him sidewise. "We?"

"Yes, ma'am. I'm not leaving until I see you settled for the night."

I wondered if he also planned to tuck me in and read me a bedtime story. "Tank, I was a cop for seven years, so I can take care of myself. Besides, I'm sure Duck didn't mean that you had to stick with me twenty-four hours a day. You've got a life, too, things you've got to do, a job, don't you?"

He hesitated, then shook his head. "No, ma'am." My cop's antenna began to vibrate. Tank was lying. "Duck trusted me to keep an eye on you, and that's what I aim to do."

Claustrophobia slithered in around my shoulders. "Now look, Tank—" I stopped, tugged at the reins of my temper, which was close to galloping off the deep end. Duck was the one I should be mad at, not Tank. Who was this guy, anyway? "How'd you meet Duck?"

"Grandma was taking a ceramics course he was teaching at the Adult Ed Center a couple of years ago, and I used to come pick her up after class. We got to talking one night and kinda hit it off. Been buddies ever since."

That was entirely feasible. Duck was like a magnet. People gravitated to him and then stuck like glue.

"How old are you?" I asked.

"Me? Twenty-eight."

Younger than I'd pegged him, fooled by the shaved head, I guess. "Well, I'm not that much older than you are, so I'd appreciate it if you'd stop with the yes-ma'ams."

He gnawed on his bottom lip. "I'll try, Miss Warren—"

"Leigh," I corrected him.

"Uh, okay . . . Leigh. The thing is, it's habit. Where Grandma came from, you say yes, ma'am and no, ma'am, no ifs, ands or buts except mine, which caught it if I forgot. So it don' t . . . doesn't have nothing to do with age, it's just the way she brought me up."

"All right," I said grudgingly, understanding perfectly what he meant, since I'd undergone similar indoctrination in Sunrise. "But if we're going to be on a first-name basis, I'd prefer to use your real one, not Tank."

A muscle twitched in his jaw, and his eyes wandered to a point just above my head. "Tank's good enough, Miss, uh, Leigh. That's what everybody calls me. It's okay, honest. I'm used to it."

Terrific. Not only had Duck saddled me with a bodyguard who intended to stick with me like a body cast, he'd picked one for whom it was more expedient to say he had no job when I was sure he had, and who wouldn't give me his real name. I reexamined the scenario with the kid who'd snatched the overnight case and Tank's offer to break his fingers. He had certainly seemed serious about it, and the kid had definitely thought he was. Perhaps Tank was a collection agent for a dealer or a loan shark, a knee smasher to encourage a debtor to pay up. There were all sorts of possibilities, none of them particularly appetizing.

I didn't need this. I certainly didn't need a shadow, especially one who might have an out-standing warrant on file somewhere. I had to pry him loose for the time being until I could figure a way to get rid of him permanently. Thanks to a growling stomach, a condition which made me more perverse than usual, an idea occurred to me.

"All right," I said, as if giving up on the matter of his real name, "Tank it is. If you're planning to hang with me, let's get moving."

He smiled, worry clouds dispersed. "Where we goin'?"

"Fourth District headquarters," I said, unearthing my car keys. "I want to make sure they know about the spare set they found on the corpse."

"Er . . ." Tank shifted uneasily, and I bit back a grin. As I'd suspected, he would probably have pre-ferred to go to Philadelphia. Or failing that, Mars.

"Miz Warren." Cholly, out in the hall, knocked at the door frame. "Everything's taken care of. Got a carpenter on his way to replace your door.

Management's picking up the tab." He seemed very pleased with himself. "Shouldn't take him more than an hour or two."

The carriage clock on my etagere tinkled five o'clock. If I waited for the carpenter, then waited for him to finish the door, I would miss everybody on Tristan's shift.

Tank, apparently seeing a way out of a trip to the police station, jumped at it. "I can stay here while you go, Miss . . . Leigh. I know this and that about carpentry. I can watch him, make certain he does a good job."

I wasn't sure about this. Hey, I'd just met him, knew next to nothing about him except that Duck had trusted him. But could I? Once again it came down to my confidence in Duck. As much as I would have liked to bash him over the head with a two-by-four at the moment, the fact remained that my faith in his instincts was still unshaken. If he'd trusted Tank, so could I.

"You're on," I said. "Get a chair and camp out in the hall if you want. I'll be back as soon as I can." He was visibly relieved at not having to go with me, and made no effort to hide it. One thing for sure, Tank was no poker player.

I grabbed my purse and left, Cholly trotting after me down the hall toward the elevator.

"You sure about leavin' that dude in there with your valuables, Miz Warren?" he asked. "I don't like the looks of him. He might clean you out."

"As bad as it smells in there," I responded, "he's welcome to anything he wants. I wouldn't worry about it, Cholly. I'm pretty sure he's okay."

Cholly groused all the way down to the first floor. The way he was griping, you'd think he had joint ownership. He walked with me to the car and, as I locked the door and reached for the seat belt, said, "I'll go back up, sort of keep an eye on things. Miz Warren, I feel real bad about that man breaking into your apartment." He shifted from one foot to the other and looked away, like a kid caught with his hand in the cookie jar. "I can't figure out how he got past both me and Neva. You know one or t'other of us always try to keep an eye on the front door."

Cholly could be an officious pain in the butt sometimes, but he took his job seriously and seemed to have genuine concern for the tenants. I didn't want him to think he'd slipped up.

"There's a distinct possibility that guy came in through the basement door," I said.

"Uh-uh. No, ma'am." He straightened, fixed me with his I-know-whereof-I-speak stare. "I've checked that door every morning and every night. No jimmy marks or nothing."

"There was no need for him to jimmy the door." I released the emergency brake. "He had a key to my apartment in his pocket."

Cholly blinked. "Did? How'd he get a hold of it?"

"Good question. When I find out, I'll let you know," I said, and pulled away from the curb. And I definitely intended to find out.

4

HALF A BLOCK FROM HOME, I DECIDED TO
eliminate the obvious first. Just because Tank and
Weems hadn't seen Duck since early August didn't
mean he wasn't holed up in his apartment, working
on a new pot or bowl or searching for just the right
mixture of glazes. Aside from the job, and at one
point me, the only other things Duck was passionate
about were the potter's wheel and baseball. I'd
known him to take valuable vacation time and
spend it trying to perfect a technique on the wheel.
Granted, six weeks might seem excessive to the
ordinary person, but if there was one thing Duck
wasn't, it was ordinary.

It was still rush hour, which in D.C. means that
all the main arteries turn into parking lots from
around three o'clock to seven, so I snaked my way
through a maze of side streets and managed to get
from upper Northwest to Southwest in thirty-two
minutes. I circled the block around Duck's building,
the scent of the Potomac following me and nudging
the humidity that much higher. After two round
trips it occurred to me that I might be burning gas
for nothing. If Duck had really left town, there was
no need for his reserved parking slot to go to waste.

Now, if the boy hadn't changed the code to raise the gate . . .

I punched in my birthday on the key pad at the entrance to the underground garage. The metal grille twitched upward inch by agonizing inch, the first bit of luck I'd had all day. I found Duck's slot empty, but that meant nothing; his car spent more time in the shop than on the street anyway. I slipped into the space, grateful that I'd be able to take the elevator from the garage instead of running the gauntlet of The Four, a quartet of wicked little ladies, retirees long since who camped out in the lobby to watch the comings and goings through the front door, as effective a security system as anything Wells Fargo or Brinks could install. No one escaped their scrutiny, whether they were elbow deep in a game of Pitty-Pat, cups of suspicious-smelling herbal tea at their elbows, or shaking their heads at the machinations of the current villain or vixen on their favorite soap operas.

I wasn't anxious to run into them. I had to be on their shit list; they thought Dillon Kennedy was the best thing since Ben-Gay, a product with which they claimed to be intimately familiar. And not one of them would ever see the back side of seventy again. It occurred to me they might know if Duck was playing hermit, but considering the way my day had gone, I wasn't up to facing those beady, probing eyes quite yet.

Upstairs, my luck was still holding. The sixth-floor hall was empty. I walked quickly to 608, inserted the key, and Lady Luck said "Gotcha!" The door of 609 directly opposite flew open, as if Duck's key was the Open Sesame to spring Mrs. Luby from her apartment as well. Since she was one of The Four, I'd expected her to be downstairs in the lobby with her cohorts, but there she stood, swathed in a wispy lavender peignoir, her white hair decorated with matching lavender plastic curlers.

"Leigh!" she exclaimed above the Hawkins choir shouting hallelujah from her kitchen radio. "Well, child, it's about time! Gracious, girl! What in the world have you been doing, changing your oil?"

"Close," I said, encouraged by the warmth of her welcome. "Had a flat. How're you, Mrs. Luby?"

"Couldn't be better," she responded as I turned the key to the right, back to the left, then farther left, then to center. Duck had blackmailed a locksmith who thought himself in danger of imminent arrest to rig it to work like a combination lock. I felt the dead bolt retract. "Got me a date this evening," she continued, to explain the curlers, I guess. "Sure glad to see you. It's been right sad, not hearing Dillon coming home at all hours. When are you moving in?"

The question puzzled me. She had to know our engagement was history. The Four knew everyone's business, from a job not going well to the condition of a given resident's troublesome hemorrhoids. "When's the last time you saw Duck?" I asked, sidestepping her question.

"Let's see. Had to be the first of August. My arthritis was bothering me, so he mailed my condo fee for me. Lord, we miss him. We were just saying—" She winced as Tramaine Hawkins hit a particularly piercing note. "Let me turn that thing down." She engaged the kickstand Duck had installed so she could prop the door open, and disappeared into the kitchen.

I considered slipping into 608 while she was gone, but didn't have the nerve. Given her status as one of Duck's groupies, it was a miracle that she was speaking to me at all, so I didn't want to foul up now. Pocketing the key, I stepped across into her doorway to tell her I would talk to her later, when my focus locked onto the figurines of baseball players from the old Negro League in the decorative case on the opposite wall.

Mrs. Luby returned to find me staring at them in disbelief. "Aren't those. . . ?" I began.

"Dillon's?" Her pale brown features drooped, etching lines across her forehead. "Yes, they're his. He gave them to me. He knew they'd mean something special to me, since my brother played for the Grays way back when. You don't mind, do you?" She looked pained. "Don't tell me he promised them to you before y'all broke up?"

"Oh, no. I . . . I was just surprised to see them." And shaken. Duck considered ceramics made from commercial molds as beneath him. Yet he'd flipped over the figurines made of a combination of crushed pecan shells and resin, then formed in a mold. He'd driven all the way down to Denton, North Carolina, and back in one day to purchase them unstained so he could finish them himself. Once he had, he'd spent weeks to find a display cabinet that suited him—the shadow box now hanging on Mrs. Luby's wall. Yet he'd given it all away. A sick feeling crawled into the pit of my stomach.

"Leigh?" Mrs. Luby touched my arm, and I jumped, startled. "What's ailing the boy?" she asked. Anguish pinched the corners of her mouth. "I figure it must be something really bad for him to give that set to me. Tell me the truth now. Is it fatal?"

"I doubt that's the problem," I assured her. "He passed his last physical with flying colors." But, I reminded myself, I hadn't seen him since June. A lot could happen in three months. "He looked all right to you, didn't he?" I asked, needing assurance myself.

She gazed at the baseball figures, thinking. "He seemed fit enough, just . . . not himself. Hadn't been for a long time. It was like something was eating at his soul. You, mebbe." She cast a withering glance in my direction. "You weren't stepping out on him, were you?"

"Me? No!" I could just imagine her and her buddies downstairs consigning me to the ranks of every hussy they'd ever known. That didn't sit well with me. I wanted to set the record straight. "We broke up because he issued an ultimatum. I had to choose: him or the job."

"He didn't!" Her eyes widened, the pale ring around her dark pupils standing out in ghostly relief.

"He maintained he couldn't do his job effectively if he had to worry about me out on the streets. He ordered me to quit."

"And you told him to kiss your fanny. Good for you!"

I found myself treacherously close to blubbering. I'd never known Duck to do any wrong in her eyes. She was the boss of The Four. Whichever direction she swayed in the wind, the others leaned right along with her. To have her side with me was such a relief that I turned away to hide the sheen of tears in my eyes.

"Don't know what that child could have been thinking," Mrs. Luby said, folding her arms under an ample bosom. "As far as I'm concerned, he was asking for it. I gotta tell you, Mr. Luby notwithstanding—may he rest in peace—all men are dogs."

I stood there with my mouth hanging open. She was right! He *had* been asking for it. How could I be so slow to see it? Duck had set me up! He knew how much being a street cop meant to me and what my choice would be. Evidently he'd wanted to dump me and had known just what buttons to push so that I'd do the deed for him. And I'd walked right into it!

I turned and crossed the hall again, hoping, praying that he was hiding out in there. Somehow I managed a civil tone as I opened Duck's door. "Maybe I'll see you later. Thanks, Mrs. Luby."

"Don't be too hard on him," she said, behind me. "Lord knows why he acted like a jackass, but the child must love you an awful lot to sign over his unit to you. That oughta mean something."

"What?" I spun around. "What do you mean, he signed over his unit to me?"

"Isn't that why you're here?" Squinting, she

peered at me. "Didn't you get his message? He said he left it on your answering machine."

Which wasn't working. Suddenly Tank's report of his conversation with Duck began to make sense. "He sent the key to me, but I didn't know why."

"Well, it's yours now. Did it all legal, too, with a lawyer and everything. So whatever's going on in that pea brain of his, you must still mean a lot to him. Let me know when you're moving in, and me and the girls will fix you a little something to eat so you won't have to worry about unpacking your pots and pans to cook right away. Now, you're gonna have to excuse me, darling. Gotta get dressed for my date. I'll talk to you later. Leigh?" Her gaze caressed my features. "I'm real sorry about the way things worked out." She backed into her apartment and eased the door closed.

I stood there for a moment, feeling layer upon layer of warring emotions: anger, hurt, confusion, concern. Nothing had made sense today, this least of all. And if Duck really had signed over this condo to me, it put a considerable dent in the rage I'd harbored against him. I resented that. That anger had kept me going, had given me the impetus I'd needed during endless hours of physical therapy, the mind-numbing sessions on the stationary bike, the treks up and down step units to rebuild weakened muscles. Duck had wanted me off the force, and I was damned if I'd give him the satisfaction of seeing his wish come true.

In the end, the anger hadn't been enough to repair the knee, and that had fueled my rage at him even more, because he'd gotten precisely what he'd said he wanted. I was no longer in uniform. If he'd made the slightest overture to me after I went out on disability, I'd have cold-cocked him. The fact that he hadn't, aside from flowers he'd sent after my surgery, said to me that it really was over. Now this. I repeat. Didn't make sense.

Idly I polished the doorknob with my palm, stalling. I had the feeling that once I crossed the threshold, things would never be the same again, that using Duck's key signaled acceptance that he wouldn't be back. I wasn't ready to believe that yet. But I couldn't stand out in the hall indefinitely, and going home to my apartment with its splintered door, the pall of death and Tank waiting for me was an option that held absolutely no appeal. Turning the knob, I surrendered to circumstances and went in.

Chez Duck looked much the same, yet felt very different. He'd left his furniture, which didn't surprise me. He'd bought the apartment because he maintained he had to live somewhere and there was no point throwing away good money on rent. But he'd been maddeningly indifferent about what he put in here, refusing to become emotionally attached to any of the furnishings. He'd said flatly that he wanted to be able to walk away from all of it without a backward glance, an attitude I'd never understood. As a result, his decor gave a whole new meaning to the word eclectic. The rooms contained a hodgepodge of styles, everything from French provincial to Shaker, Colonial to country, every last bit of it picked up at yard sales or passed along to him by his mother or sister. As luck would have it, Duck had a real flair for mixing periods, patterns and colors, so the finished product, while unorthodox, was still as polished a decorating job as any professional could have pulled off. It was infuriating. If I'd tried cabbage rose upholstery and gingham checks in the same room the way he had, it would have looked like a model home for Raggedy Ann and Andy.

There were important things missing, however. The living room walls had been stripped of the collages he'd collected, the Yoruba masks, the Gullah baskets, and, of course, the Pecan collection. A tour through the other rooms confirmed my initial impression; he'd cleared the apartment of all the artworks, the only things he'd really cared about. Even his kiln and potter's wheel had been removed. He'd left his desktop computer, but I couldn't find his laptop, and a deep hollow completely unrelated to hunger invaded the pit of my stomach. It was true. Duck was gone. But where? And why?

Okay, he'd fibbed to his sister, Vanessa, about going undercover, but I couldn't imagine him lying to his mom. Duck swore she was a walking lie detector. Whether she'd tell me what she knew was another matter. I started dialing her number and stopped halfway, puzzled by the fat brown envelope under the forties model phone. I picked up the old-fashioned base and saw BABE, a name Duck knew I hated, in bold block letters. Perching on the mahogany bench he'd picked up at a yard sale, I opened the envelope, removed the contents, scanned them quickly, and felt as if I had plummeted into some bottomless pit. The deed to the condominium. And Duck's will.

I had read through them both, the will especially, four or five times before I discovered the single sheet of paper folded and tucked in the bottom of the envelope. After the cold, impersonal typeface and legalese of the deed and will, the bold, fluid strokes of Duck's handwriting loosened the knot in my throat. I read it several times before taking it out onto the balcony to go over it once again. It seemed an appropriate place to do it, given the message Duck had left.

Babe,

I made a promise to myself years ago, something I've got to do, even though it means walking away from every good thing I've ever done. It also means walking away from you, and that's the most painful sacrifice of all.

I love you, Babe, always have, always will. I wanted to leave you something special to prove it. I know how much you've loved my balcony. Can't detach the damned thing, so you'll have to take the apartment along with it. The condo fee's paid through the end of the year, and the mortgage payments are just about what you're paying for rent. See Reed Sellars. There'll be things for you to sign. And don't give the son of a bitch one red cent. I've already paid him.

Think of me now and then. I was a good cop, Leigh. I never dishonored my badge. Not once. Believe that.

All my love,
Duck

A P.S. was added in an impatient scrawl.

Will you please *get your damned answering machine fixed!*

I collapsed onto a dust-covered chaise, the note plastered against my chest as if his words were a decal I could press across the contours of my heart. I hadn't felt his presence in the apartment; with the walls stripped of the things he'd valued most, the rooms had no personality. It could have belonged to anyone. Out here on the balcony, however, I could close my eyes and swear he was sitting beside me on the chaise. This was still his place. The exterior of the building had all the personality of a stack of bricks fresh out of the kiln, but the view from his balcony looking out over the Washington Channel and National Airport more than made up for the sterile and unimaginative design of the outside. I loved this balcony.

But so did Duck. Summer or winter, it had been his retreat, the first place he went when he got home and the last place he'd go, if only for a minute or two, before leaving for work. We'd spent countless hours just sitting, listening to the murmur of the Potomac and trying to spot incoming planes while they were still mere pinpricks of bright light above a distant horizon. This balcony had taught me the meaning of *covet* as nothing else could have, perhaps because it reminded me of balmy summer evenings in the front porch swing down home in Sunrise, bare feet tucked underneath me, a bowl of snap beans in my lap. Only now instead of snap beans, it was a big brown envelope containing the deed and his will weighing heavily across my thighs.

After what Mrs. Luby had told me, I hadn't been surprised to find the deed to the apartment. But I had not expected to find the will. I'd known that he'd made one. Making a will, he'd said, was part of his responsibility to see that his mother, widowed since Duck was twelve, would be taken care of if he died. But this was not the one he'd told me about several years back. It was new, appointing me executrix and heir to half of his estate. I assumed at first this had been done while we were engaged and he hadn't gotten around to amending it. The date, however, proved otherwise. Signed and witnessed on August 8. Roughly six weeks ago.

I lay back on the chaise, closed my eyes and forced myself to breathe slowly, deeply, in an attempt to empty my mind of all the questions, all the turmoil. As many times as I'd tried, I'd never mastered meditation. Nine times out of ten, that humming business tickled my throat and I'd find myself struggling to keep from breaking out in giggles. Deep breathing nudged me as close to a tranquil state as I could get, and I reached for it now, tossing errant memories of the day aside one by one.

It almost worked. After several minutes, the tension in my muscles began to ooze through my pores and evaporate in the early evening air. I felt the skin across my forehead smooth, relaxation ironing out the frown lines. My hands became limp, and I let them dangle at my sides, sensing the blood pooling in my fingertips. Gradually my brain settled down, not the calm emptiness I'd hoped for but more than comfortable with the tidbit left lurking in a far corner: the picture of the first time I saw Dillon Kennedy.

I was in law school back then, engaged to his partner, Josh Mitchell, who'd dragged me away from a study session to meet the second most important person in his life. Duck was sitting in Ben's Chili Bowl, peering down at the sandwich in his hands as if he'd just reached the gates of paradise. At first glance there was nothing special about him, just your basic black brother with nothing more on his mind than eating his way to paradise. It wasn't until Josh was killed after walking in on the botched robbery of a mom and pop grocery store that I'd really gotten to know Duck. We'd grieved together and had gradually become buddies in the purest sense of the term. When I was accepted at the police academy, giving in to a dream I'd had practically all my life, it was Duck who'd assured me there was no higher calling. He'd tutored me, supported me, always there through good days and bad. We'd carpooled together before he'd moved here. We'd nursed one another through everything from head colds to food poisoning and a few hangovers on the side, as at ease with one another as a pair of ratty old slippers.

Then last year we were both shot by a really nice kid delivering pizzas who thought Duck, who'd walked up behind him, was about to rob him. I'd barged onto the scene unaware what had happened and took a bullet, too, since the kid assumed I was an accomplice. For Duck, it had sounded a wake-up call. That's when he'd told me he loved me and it was time I realized I felt the same. From that point everything changed.

Suddenly we were lovers, then engaged. Life went on much as it had before for me, except for a sense that things were off-kilter, not quite right, but I couldn't figure out how. The question had plagued me, the answer always just out of reach. Now I shrugged and gave up for the umpteenth time. What was the point? Not only were Duck and I unengaged now, Duck was gone.

Detecting the distant burr of a jet approaching the airport, I opened my eyes and sat up, scanning a clear, cloudless sky until I spotted it coming in from the southwest, a tiny diamond chip of light. Had Duck been here, I'd have demanded that he pay up, because I'd detected the plane first. That's when it all came together, the source of my uneasiness the whole of this past year: I missed my best friend. Bedmates were a dime a dozen, but best friends were rare and priceless.

Not that he hadn't filled the bill in his new role as lover and fiancé; he was as good in bed as he was at everything else he did. The difference boiled down to his change in attitude toward me. Whereas before we'd been equals, a pair of cops who could relate to one another by virtue of the work we did, once we became engaged, Duck's protective streak where I was concerned flared to life and became a conflagration. The days when he would have commiserated with me about what was a normal part of being a D.C. cop were gone. He worried about me, stewed over assignments that put me in more than usual jeopardy, fumed whenever I had to pull overtime because it might tire me out, slow my reactions, dull alertness. I appreciated his concern, but it made me feel less an equal and I resented it. It ate at me. Which was probably why my explosion when he demanded that I quit made the eruption of Mount St. Helens look like an impolite burp.

But he still loved me. I held the proof in my hands. I could lay any doubt about that to rest. But the note he'd left dumped one great load of questions in my lap. What promise had he made to himself that required him to pull up stakes this way? And where had he gone? Would anything he'd left here give me a clue?

It wasn't long before that was answered. Duck rarely did things halfway. His closets were empty. The dresser and desk drawers yawned at me, with not so much as a blob of lint or paper dust in them. They couldn't have been cleaner if he'd vacuumed them. He'd even emptied the shelves in his workroom of all the pots and vases he'd thrown, except one, a tiny bud vase finished with a dark pink and mother of pearl glaze. The front was slightly indented, and he'd pressed his thumb in the middle of the depression, a signature of sorts. The whorls of his thumbprint seemed to repeat the manner in which the soft white swirled through the more dominant deep rose. He hadn't been completely happy with the glaze, which under normal circumstances meant that the vase would have been trashed. I'd pleaded for its life, so he'd kept it as a reminder to try again. And he'd left it for me. I ran a finger around the lip and over the thumbprint, then replaced it, swallowing against tears, and moved on to the kitchen.

It was the one room more or less intact. All his dishes and flatware were in their usual places and the few small appliances he'd acquired. The Calphalon pots and pans, however, were missing, no surprise. Duck knew they'd be wasted on me. If not for prepackaged foods and microwaves, I'd have starved years ago. I hadn't really thought I'd find anything in the kitchen that would shed light on where he'd gone, but it would have bugged me if I hadn't looked.

I'd left his computer for last. I plugged it in and hit the power switch, watching the tower as it chugged to life and launched into its warm-up exercises. Once it was finished, it sat, fan whispering quietly, the monitor blank except for eight letters: PASSWORD. I swore, crossed my fingers, and tried the last one I remembered him using: Satchel. My chances for success were slim to none, since he'd set up his system so that the password had to be changed every quarter. And of course, Satchel was a bust.

I typed in every one I could recall he'd used—baseball players past and present, his birthday, his mother's name, her birthday, his sister's, his niece, Tyler's, mine. None worked. His desktop was in effect a twenty-five-hundred-dollar paperweight. Why would he leave it for me without disabling the password?

Frustrated, I turned the thing off and opened the carousel in which he kept his diskettes. Duck religiously backed up any work he did on two diskettes, one which remained here. The other he'd use in his laptop. I ignored the program disks and picked out those containing data of any kind. If Duck had saved anything, chances were they were on these diskettes somewhere. Thanks to the kind of work she did, Janeece had a computer for home use. I would try these out on hers.

I rooted around in my purse until I found a big enough envelope to hold the diskettes, secured it with a rubber band and took one last look around. The place felt so different without Duck roaming through it. Lord, I didn't want to stay here, not without him. I glanced at his bedroom door, which I'd closed, unable to stand the view of his big brass bed. It had the most comfortable mattress this side of heaven, but the thought of sleeping on it, alone anyway, wedged a lump in my throat. There was, however, his couch, a sleep sofa. It wouldn't be as comfortable as his bed, but it would do.

I closed the blinds, locked the balcony, my thoughts bouncing off one another. Somebody he worked with had to know what he was up to.

Obviously Cody Jensen didn't, since Duck hadn't specified a reason for backing out of being his best man, other than that something had come up. But Cody wasn't the only close friend Duck had at the Sixth. There was Eddie Grimes. I hadn't seen him since June and wasn't even certain he'd open up to me if he knew anything. If Eddie would just tell me that Duck was all right, I might be able to live with that. My curiosity wouldn't be satisfied, but somehow I'd manage. I checked my watch. Almost six. I needed to hurry if I was going to catch Eddie before I tracked down Tristan.

I tried Mrs. Kennedy's number one last time and again got no answer, then checked to see if Tristan had returned to the Fourth. He hadn't. Probably still at the stand-off with the sniper. After one last look around, I opened the door to leave and almost ran over Mrs. Luby, her fist raised to knock. She was in scarlet, unrelieved by any color other than the white of her hair and the cocoa butter brown of her skin. I wondered where in God's kingdom she'd managed to find scarlet panty hose.

"Mercy, child," she said, "you almost scared me out of my Victoria's Secret drawers. You leaving already?"

"A couple of errands to run. You're going to knock your date's eyes out." Well, I had to say something, and that was the truth. "Did you need me to zip you up?"

"No. Found one of those zipper pulls." She frowned. "What did I want, now? Oh, yes, you be sure and have that lock changed. No tellin' how many friends Dillon gave a key to. I certainly didn't like the looks of the ones stopped by here last week."

Remembering my initial impression of Tank, I could understand her reaction. "A tall guy, shaved head?" I asked.

"No, indeed. First one was a skinny little weasel, head full of those wiggly things. Deadlocks? He said Dillon had sent him to pick up something. He had Dillon's key, but he couldn't get it to work right. He—"

"Just a minute," I said. My toast-making intruder had worn dreadlocks. "Was he wearing a striped T-shirt and overalls?"

"That's him. Didn't know people still wore those things. Except farmers, maybe."

"And he was trying to get in here? How did you happen to see him?"

"Me and the girls were late getting together that day. The power had gone off the night before, so everybody's clock was slow. I opened the door to leave and there he was, twisting the key in the lock like he'd been at it awhile and was getting mad because he couldn't get in."

"What makes you think it was Duck's key he had?" I asked.

"Well, who else's could it have been? I know that little coyote key ring when I see it. Anyhow, I said good morning and asked if he was having trouble and he said yes, that Dillon had sent him to get something—"

I interrupted her again. "He called him Dillon?

Or did he say Duck?" Aside from his groupies and his family, the only people who called him by his first name were those who hadn't known him very long.

She surveyed the ceiling, thinking. "I honestly don't remember. I asked him how Dillon was doing and he said fine, and he kept turning the key all wrong. I started to show him how it works, only I didn't think it was my place to do it, it being your apartment now, so I told him to get in touch with you."

"He knew who I was?" I asked.

"He did after I gave him your name and address. I have it in my book in there. And Dillon told me about your mama getting married, so I warned the feller you might still be out of town. I figured he could leave his name and number with your resident manager so you could call him. The second one who came looking for Dillon was a white boy who looked like he needed a good shampoo."

That was probably Weems, and she was being diplomatic to have stopped with a shampoo.

"Now, you're gonna have to excuse me," she said. "I've gotta take my medication before I go. Don't want to be late for my date." She waggled a couple of fingers at me and went back inside.

I gaped at her closed door, vacillating between exasperation and relief. I hadn't wanted to believe that Duck would give someone access to my apartment. Now it appeared that the John Doe probably hadn't had the slightest idea to whom that second key belonged until Mrs. Luby obliged by quoting him chapter and verse. Thank God she didn't know my Social Security number or she'd have given him that, too. This was something else Tristan would need to jot down in his little spiral notebook. I looked at my watch and took off for the elevator. If I didn't move it, I'd miss both the guys I wanted to see about Duck, and probably miss Tristan, too.

5

I PLAYED HAVOC WITH THE SPEED LIMIT heading for the district station Duck had been assigned to for the last year, slipped into a slot one point eight seconds after it had been vacated by a cruiser, and hurried inside. Without thinking, I'd started up the steps to the second floor when my knee reminded me that the elevator might be a better idea.

It's amazing how much we take for granted joints that behave the way they're supposed to, and how difficult it is to adjust when they don't. Back in late June I'd been forced to execute a somersault to get out of the way of a drunk driver who'd mistaken the sidewalk for a right-turn lane. I'd have walked away scot-free if it hadn't been for the fire hydrant in my way. My knee slammed into it, and I rolled to the side gasping with pain just as the car hit it and a geyser erupted. And I couldn't move. By the time a passing Samaritan scooped me up, I was soaked, and my knee looked like a basketball. Shattered patella, torn cartilage and ligaments, you name it, I'd done it. Now after orthoscopic surgery and weeks of the cast and crutches deal, plus the legal torture called physical therapy, I could walk with just a hint of a telltale limp most of the time.

The problem was how unpredictable the knee could be. On one day the pain might be bearable; the next would be one of teeth-gritting agony, requiring a cane if I could walk at all. I kept the cane in the car, which was why I was in moderate pain most of the time. I preferred to grin and bear it. Dumb. Go figure.

On stairs I was reduced to a toddler's tactics, step up with the good leg, crank the bad one up to join it. And I couldn't run. Or carry more than twenty pounds without setting the knee on fire. Or pass the physical that would release me from limited duty. In other words, the street was definitely off-limits to me, and the street was where I wanted to be, where I felt I could do the most good. A single week of desk duty had demonstrated the effect that sitting on my fanny for any length of time would have on the knee. If I didn't get to my feet every ten minutes to work out the kinks, I walked like a ninety-year-old once I did get up. So I'd opted out, preferring to survive on two-thirds salary so I could concentrate on rehab in hopes I might be able to come back on my own terms, fit and ready to fight if I had to.

My orthopedist had warned me there was a possibility that day might never come, that too much damage had been done. An artificial knee was not an option yet; I was too young. So I'd try intensive rehab. But could I handle Duck's mortgage on reduced wages? I hadn't thought of that.

I took the elevator. At the second floor I stepped out and ricocheted off the rotund midsection of Captain Ray Moon, Duck's superior.

"Sorry," he rumbled, his brows bunching together in a frown as he peered down at me from above tortoiseshell half-frames perched on the end of his broad nose. He was average height but had the biggest feet this side of the Potomac. The toes of Moon's shoes preceded the rest of him through a doorway by a good dozen inches. "Warren, isn't it?" he asked, holding the door open with one hand.

"Yes, sir." I was surprised he knew my name. His rank put him light-years above mine, and I'd only met him once, years before. I had liked him immediately. More important, Duck liked him and trusted him. "Do you have a minute, sir? I'd like to talk to you about Duck . . . I mean, Detective Kennedy."

The deep grooves in the skin of his walnut brown forehead disappeared. "That's where I know you from. I'm on my way out. Haven't seen my wife since day before yesterday, so any talkin' we do will have to be done between here and my car."

"Yes, sir." I stepped back onto the elevator and he followed, something about his expression making it clear he was unwilling to begin our conversation about Duck with others in the car. "Any news on the sniper situation?" I asked to fill the time between floors. We were on the slowest elevator east of the Pacific.

"We got him. He's at the Hospital Center with a bullet in his butt, which is fitting, since that's the same place he shot our guy." When the door opened, he nodded me out. "Okay, Warren, how can I help you?"

We started for the exit, my knee twinging as I

hurried to keep up with him. Outdoors and away from the parade of foot traffic, I stopped him at the corner.

"Look, sir, something's come up and I need to get in touch with Duck. No one's seen him in a while, but I figure if anyone knows where he is, it'll be you. If he's working deep undercover, I'd appreciate it if you'd tell me. It won't go any further; I would never do anything to put him in danger. But it's imperative that I talk to him or I wouldn't ask."

He looked around, squinting. "Didn't I hear you two were engaged?"

I considered my answer and did some judicious editing. "We had a misunderstanding, and until we straighten it out, the engagement's off."

He nodded, but turned the corner and didn't respond until he stopped beside a faded silver Taurus. Leaning against the passenger door, he gazed at me speculatively. "Look, Warren, the only reason I'm talking to you is because Duck's one of my best men and we go back a long way; he rode with me his rookie year. And what I'm going to tell you is confidential. If I hear it anywhere else, I'll know where it came from. Duck walked into my office about six weeks ago, put his badge and gun on my desk, and said he was quitting."

For a moment I ceased to function, my brain on hold. Then Duck's strong squared-off letters scrolled behind my eyes. *I never dishonored my badge.* "He—he quit? Why?"

"Wouldn't say, refused to discuss it. After what you've told me, I assume you're the reason. And considering the rumors circulating about him, I admit I'm relieved you're the reason."

"What rumors?" I asked.

"No point in going into that. I didn't believe them anyhow. This makes a lot more sense. So love's been the problem all along."

I shook my head, both to reject what he'd said and to get the synapses firing again. No. No way. Duck loved me, but he loved being a cop more. "He wouldn't quit because of me," I said. "Besides, we broke up back in June. If it had hit him that hard, why'd he wait another month and a half to do this? Uh-uh. I mean no, sir. Something else must have happened. Maybe he was just burned out."

He exchanged sunglasses for his tortoiseshells. "The dude who walked into my office didn't look burned out to me. Burnin' up, maybe. Mad as hell. But not rantin' and raving the way he usually does when he blows his top. Composed, deathly calm." Moon moved around to the driver's side and unlocked the door. "He was a walking iceman, and I gotta tell you, little lady, he was scary. Okay." He heaved a deep sigh. "Okay. His badge and gun are still in my desk, and I've taken care of his absence with the higher-ups until he works through his problem. I'd damned sure appreciate it if you two would straighten things out. The Department needs him. He's too valuable a man for us to lose. Now, you'll have to excuse me, little lady, or I'm gonna be paying alimony for the rest of my natural life."

I thanked him and stepped back from the curb, only vaguely aware of my surroundings as he maneuvered into traffic and sped away. Backing up against the building, I stayed put for a moment, trying to reassemble the world I'd left six weeks before, an imperfect world, sure, but one that made sense. This one certainly didn't. I looked around, still fuzzy-headed, trying to remember where I'd left my car, when someone grabbed my elbow and spun me around. Eddie Grimes.

"Where the hell is Duck?" he hissed, his dark eyes spitting fire.

That slapped me back into the here and now. "I don't know," I snapped, and yanked my arm free. I liked Eddie, but I was in no mood to be manhandled, and he could overdo the aggression sometimes, perhaps because of his stature. Everyone swore he'd worn sandbags in his shorts to meet the Department's weight requirement. "You don't know where he is either? Honestly?"

His lips tightened, and concern replaced his anger. "Come here a minute," he said, and nudged me farther from the corner. "I have hit every fast-food place and restaurant in this city, the Adult Ed Center, the skating rinks and basketball courts, every one of his favorite hangouts with the kids. Nothing. I've had my snitches scouring Sixth District neighborhoods, talking to any and everybody. Nobody's seen him, I mean nobody. You've got to find him and tell him to get in touch with me. I ain't covering for him much longer."

"You, too?" I asked, annoyed at hearing this line from yet another person, as if I manned a complaints counter. "What's the matter? Have you been stuck with throwing the bachelor party or something?"

"Huh?" He squinted at me. "Oh. The wedding. No, Harvey's doing that. I'm talking about keeping the fool out of jail."

"Excuse me?"

He moved in even closer, one eye on the proximity of passersby. "First, he walks off with evidence and—"

"Wait a minute, wait a minute," I said, nearing overload. "He what?"

"Remember when Toulouse Archer cracked up in the Explorer?"

"Sure." No one was likely to forget it. There'd been an all-points out on him as a suspect in a drive-by shooting. Jimmy Archer, nicknamed Toulouse, had saved the District the trouble of footing the bill for a trial by smashing into a retaining wall at ninety miles an hour. The rear of the stolen Explorer had been packed with enough heroin to net him a mint on the streets. "Are you saying Duck filched some of the smack?" I asked, disbelieving.

He hesitated until there was no one within earshot. "Weed," he said, his lips barely moving.

"Weed?" My head began to spin. "I thought there was just heroin in the car."

"There was also a couple of baggies and a piggy bank filled with weed. We figure it was Toulouse's private stash."

"But why do you say Duck kept it?"

"He signed the inventory. Only now it looks like all he turned in was the smack and the two baggies.

He kept the bank. And now it turns out the baggies are full of oregano instead of mary jane. We know Duck pulled that switch. Wilkies saw him with them. Duck made out like it was evidence from some other case."

"That's bullshit," I protested. "You know how by-the-book Duck is about things like that. And as fouled up as things are in the evidence warehouse, the bank could be anywhere out there. What else would he do with the pot anyway? It's not as if he'd smoke it. You know him, Eddie. He hates the stuff and what it does to people—marijuana, coke, crack, smack, all of it."

Eddie looked decidedly uncomfortable. "That's what I always thought. Only—"

"Only what?"

Pain intensified the creases around Eddie's mouth. "Look, Leigh, the only way I can do this is to say it straight out. Word on the street is that Duck spent the summer doing business with dealers, buying weed as if he planned to set up shop himself."

An icy finger slithered across the back of my neck, and Weems's voice whispered in my ear. *You ever known the Duck to have a drug problem?* "Working Narcotics, you mean."

"Uh-uh. Word is our boy has picked up a habit, that he's on the take to feed it."

"No!" I shook my head, couldn't stop shaking it. "No. That's not possible. No, no, no."

"I don't want to believe it, either, but what am I supposed to think? Why keep Toulouse's stash? And why freak out over a stupid piggy bank?"

"What do you mean?"

"It was weird." Eddie's eyes focused somewhere beyond me. "At first he was real cool, like usual, joking around like the rest of us to keep from tossing our cookies. Toulouse looked like he'd gone through a meat grinder. And all these bundles of heroin had spilled out the back, so we knew we'd hit the jackpot. Then Foster found the baggies under the front seat. Me and Duck went up to the passenger side to watch Foster. That's when we spotted the bank. It had fallen out of the glove compartment. Duck froze, stared at it like it was a snake or something. I mean, for a minute there I thought the dude was gonna pass out."

"Because of a piggy bank? What was so special about it?"

"Aside from the roach sticking out of the slot, nothing. But he didn't turn it in. And later he goes back to the evidence warehouse and the baggies disappear for a couple of weeks. Voilà, oregano! I don't want to believe he's turned, Leigh, but it's getting harder and harder to think anything else. And if he's turned, honey, Eddie's gonna have to turn, too. If there's any question what happened to the shit that's missing, I'm gonna have to give him up."

"You wouldn't," I stammered.

"Find him. Tell him to get his black ass and that stuff back here because Eddie Grimes ain't losin' his job over no goddamned piggy bank. You tell him, okay?" He cocked his finger at me as if aiming a gun, and headed back around toward the front door, leaving me with my arms pebbled with goose bumps. The bottom had dropped out of a part of my world.

There are some things that you can safely take for granted: the sun will always rise in the east, set in the west; after Monday comes Tuesday, then Wednesday. And Dillon Upshur Kennedy would always be the consummate cop, trustworthy, rock solid, rock steady. Whether we were speaking or not, it would never occur to me that that might change.

Go bad? Succumb to a habit? Duck? It was unimaginable, like trying to grasp the concept of eternity. It was just as unimaginable that Duck would turn in his badge and leave the Department. But he had. Something had knocked him off his foundation. The question was what form the wrecking ball had taken and how much damage it had done.

I walked slowly around to the front of the station, reluctant to leave the area and its tenuous connection to Duck quite yet, despite the parking ticket I could see under my windshield wiper for using a cruiser space. Unable to make sense of everything I'd heard about and from Duck today, I reviewed our last few months together without the haze of angry red that had colored my memory of him since June.

When we'd first returned from Sunrise, where Duck had tracked me down to declare everlasting love last summer, everything had seemed fine between us—weird, in that the physical intimacy was new, but otherwise fine. Then slowly things had changed back in the early spring sometime. He'd seemed distracted, self-absorbed, forgetful, which had made me wonder if he might be having second thoughts about having proposed. When he'd assured me that it was the job and the latest assignment bugging him, I'd accepted it, since Duck could be part terrier, refusing to let go of a case until he'd either solved it or had shaken it until there was no life left in it.

Now with hindsight, I realized that in the eight years I'd known him, I couldn't recall another time when he'd been so consumed with the job that his family had come second on his list of priorities. I'd never known him to forget their birthdays or anniversaries. They were a big deal to him, the only time he really enjoyed shopping, the hunt for that very special and unique gift. But he'd almost forgotten his niece's birthday. I stopped at the curb, dug into my bag and found my appointment book, flipping pages until I located the notation I was looking for. March 16. "Tyler's birthday." And Duck had almost missed it. That lapse took on even more importance now.

I went back into the station, winding my way through hallways and the squad rooms in search of Eddie again. I found him with his phone glued to his ear as he tapped an impatient finger against his blotter. When he saw me, his brows shot up with surprise and he signaled that he wouldn't be long. Uh-huhing to the person on the phone, he tugged at the front of his shirt, a finger under the top button, and pulled it away from his chest, as if trying to cool off.

It occurred to me it was the first time I'd seen him without a tie. Eddie always appeared to be in his Sunday-go-to-meeting clothes, complete with jacket and matching pants, starched shirt, tie, and shoes that gleamed like freshly Windexed mirrors. He took a lot of teasing about it, but as far as he was concerned, being a cop was a profession and being in plain clothes was no excuse to look other than professional. It also camouflaged what a bantamweight he was.

He'd taken a lot of teasing about that as well until a fellow officer who'd probably been a bully as a kid took the teasing one step too far. Eddie invited him to the gym out of sight of superior officers and put a whipping on the guy that from then on had eliminated Eddie as the butt of jokes about being skinny. Duck knew he had been lifting weight for years, but felt his buddy should handle the heavy-handed teasing himself.

"You okay?" he asked, hanging up.

"No." I perched on the edge of his desk. "Eddie, when was the accident? Toulouse's, I mean. What was the date?"

He grunted. "That's one I don't have to look up. March fifteenth. Why?"

His phone rang, saving me the trouble of coming up with a reason, since I hadn't made up my mind just how forthcoming I should be. I cleared the chair beside his desk of a stack of papers and sat down, filing the date in the mental folder labeled The Trouble With Duck. The Ides of March, the day before Tyler's fourth birthday.

The party had been practically over before Duck arrived at Vanessa's, saying he'd been tied up with paperwork about the accident. And he'd turned down his sister's offer of the plate she'd put aside for him, another reason to remember that day. Duck loved food. Proprietors of restaurants serving all-you-can-eat buffets stared mournfully into the face of bankruptcy any time Duck crossed their thresholds. But even Tyler, who could get him to do practically anything, hadn't been able to entice him with a slice of her birthday cake. He'd claimed he wasn't feeling well, and we'd accepted his explanation without question because another of our truisms was when Duck didn't eat, Duck was definitely sick. But had he been? Or had there been something else on his mind? A bumper crop of pot, for instance?

Eddie slammed down the receiver and kicked the corner of his desk. "God protect me from snitches. As if I've got fifty big ones to pay for a tidbit worth squat. Hey, who's the dude answering your phone? You found a replacement for Duck already?"

"You called me?" I wasn't sure I was comfortable with the thought of Tank taking messages for me, but all things considered, he had to be better than an answering machine that didn't work. "What did you want?"

"To leave my pager number in case you heard from my man. Here," he said, scribbling it on the back of a card.

I dropped it into my bag and looked him straight in the eye. "Eddie, give it to me without the histrionics. Are you absolutely certain Duck kept the pot?"

He opened the lap drawer of his desk, rooted under an assortment of flotsam and retrieved a large brown envelope. He emptied the contents into his hand, then fanned a dozen or more Polaroid shots across his blotter. One clear view of the photo nearest me and I averted my gaze. I'd seen enough carnage at accident scenes that I was a trifle hardened by them, but this was something else again. Toulouse had really done a number on himself. Eddie examined several before passing one to me. There was no need for explanation.

The shot had been taken from the passenger side, showing clearly the glove box, its door mangled and flopping from a hinge, and half in, half out of its interior, two Ziploc baggies of marijuana, and the one completely incongruous element, the bank. Showing little signs of damage, the piggy bank was a pale pink with what appeared to be a rough-textured finish dotted by small, deep pink and blue flowers. One large blue flower decorated the snout, another its head, like a floppy hat, giving it a whimsical air. Protruding from the coin slot was a twist of ripped paper, undoubtedly part of Toulouse's makings, bits of dark leaves spilling from it.

Eddie leaned in toward me, lowered his voice. "You know how I feel about Duck. But every day that goes by that he doesn't show up, I'm less and less sure about him. All I do know is if push comes to shove, Duck's ass is grass. Duck's, not mine, am I clear?"

I couldn't blame him. Eddie had a wife and four kids to worry about. "Does Captain Moon know about all this?" I asked.

"About the missing evidence? Hell, no!" He leaned closer. "Just me, Foster, Tap and Wilkies."

I groaned. Wilkies had no love for Duck. He was lazy, did sloppy work, and Duck had called him on it more than once.

"I know what you're thinking." Eddie reached over and squeezed my hand. "Don't worry about Wilkies. He knows if he rats on Duck before it's absolutely necessary, he'd better transfer because his next call for backup might never be answered. We'll cover for Duck as long as we can. But come D-Day, we're gonna have to give him up, honey."

His anguish was palpable. He and Duck had been friends since childhood. It occurred to me that since he knew Duck as well as anyone, picking his brain might help.

"Did you notice any change in Duck over the last few months?" I asked, hoping it wasn't a leading question.

He nodded, sitting back, his hands locked behind his head. "Something was messin' with his mind. I know now it was taking the pot, but back then I figured it was you, especially after y'all broke off the engagement. Except nothing really changed afterward. He was as, well, not there as he'd been before. Then for a while . . ."

He hesitated, stalling by restacking the pile of photos. I prodded him. "What?"

"Well, I thought maybe it was another woman."

"Who?" I demanded, green demons cavorting before my eyes.

"Somebody named Evie Artis. Might be short for Evelyn or maybe Eve."

Something shriveled inside me like overcooked bacon. Perhaps this woman was a first love, he'd promised to find again? "How'd her name come up?"

"It's scribbled all over his blotter. You know the way he doodles when he's thinking. And he asked Marty to check out the name on CIC and any other database she could think of. Came up blank, so Marty says. I asked him about it, and he sort of brushed it off, said he'd heard it somewhere. But he still seemed to be in a fog. Almost got us killed a couple of months ago, too. That really shook him up. The next thing I know, he's gone. No note, no call, nothing. You really haven't heard from him, Leigh? Honest?"

It was time to piss or get off the pot. Considering Eddie's history with Duck, he was the only person I dared trust with the truth.

I looked around. No one was paying the least attention to us, but I was still edgy. Too many ears. "Outside, okay? I'd rather not talk here."

His eyes blazed with curiosity. "Hey, Riggins, watch my phones for a few minutes?" he asked the guy at the desk behind him. Picking up the envelope, he reached for the photo I held.

I glanced down at it. It was another tenuous connection to Duck, and I didn't want to give it up. "Can I borrow this one for a day or two?"

He tilted his head to one side. "For what?"

"I'm staying at Duck's place," I said. "It doesn't make sense he'd leave the missing stuff there, but I can check."

"Keep it. Well, now." His smile was wicked as he closed the clasp on the envelope and shoved it back into the drawer. "Bunking down in one dude's place while another stays at yours. Yes, indeedy, I do want to hear about this." Taking my arm, he led the way to the stairs.

"Elevator," I said, pointing at my knee.

"Sorry, I forgot. How's it coming along?"

We discussed knees, physical therapy, exercise regimens and over-the-counter painkillers until we were out on the street. "Want to walk or something?" he asked. "It'll do you good and I'll go slow."

The approach of the meter maid decided the matter for me. "Mind if we sit in the car? One ticket a day's my limit."

He chuckled. "Lead the way."

"How long have you known Duck?" I asked as we headed for Old Faithful.

"I was eleven, he was almost thirteen when him and his family moved next door. Hit it off from the first day. And he was nuts about my dad, probably because his had died the year before and he was still grieving. Couldn't even talk about him. We've been tight ever since. Shit, I'm a cop because of him," he added, climbing into the passenger seat. "He's always been my hero. Tell anybody I said that and I'll find an excuse to shoot you in your good knee."

If I'd had any doubts about coming clean with

Eddie, hearing the affection coloring his explanation eliminated them for me. So I told him everything, about Weems, Tank, my toasted intruder and the keys he'd had. Eddie seemed more and more baffled. When I showed him the will and the note Duck had left, all the air seemed to go out of him.

"A promise he made to himself?" he demanded. "What promise? What the hell's he talking about?"

"I was hoping you'd have some idea."

Eddie rubbed his eyes and pain settled around his mouth. "Whatever the problem is, why didn't he come to me? I mean, he knows there's practically nothin' I wouldn't do for him. Even if he's picked up a habit, I'd help him kick it. Damn it, Leigh, I thought I knew him! But this note he left makes it sound as if he really has gone bad."

Panic punched me in the midsection. Granted, it wasn't the only way to interpret Duck's words, but given the circumstances, it rose to the top of the list of possibilities.

"I don't know what's happened to Duck," I admitted, "but I can't believe he's hooked. It's something else, and it sounds to me as if it started the day of the accident. Right?"

He sat back and finally nodded. "As far as I can remember, everything was fine before then. Jesus, Leigh, I'd like to help, but I don't know what else I can do. I've looked everywhere I can think of. On top of that I'm working umpteen cases, late home half the time. Marilyn's pregnant again—"

"You're kidding!" He'd sworn number four would be their last. "Congratulations!"

"Congratulations, my ass! I'm getting a vasectomy next week. Do you know how much it costs to feed and clothe four kids, not to mention five? What I'm saying is that I'm gonna have to start moonlighting. I won't be able to help you find him." He squinted at me. "You are gonna try to find him, aren't you?"

I wasn't sure what I was going to do and said so. "I'll keep you posted. That's all I can say at the moment."

"Well, now wait." Eddie sat up straight. "One thing I can do is keep tabs on whatever they come up with on your John Doe. Who handled the call?"

"The senior man was a character named Tristan."

"Good." Eddie's head bobbed up and down. "I can work with him. Tris is okay, once you get to know him. I'd better get back inside." He unlocked the door. "You have my numbers. How long are you staying at Duck's?"

"At least until my place airs out. After that . . ." I shrugged. "We'll see."

"Okay. God, what a mess. Stay in touch, Leigh." He leaned over and gave me a quick hug, then got out, stopping on his way to the door long enough to engage in a short exchange with the meter maid, who looked at me long and hard before coming over to remove the ticket from under my windshield wiper. She gave it to Eddie, who grinned, waving it at me, and then sprinted indoors.

I knew better than to think he'd fixed it. He was too straight-arrow for that. That little weasel was going to pay it himself. I got out, asked how much the fine was and made a mental note to send him a check. With four little crumb snatchers at home and one in the bun warmer, he needed the money worse than I did.

I started back toward Northwest, grateful to have Eddie in Duck's corner. But Eddie was typical of Duck's friends. Any man who could earn that kind of loyalty couldn't possibly have gone bad. Duck? A dirty cop? A cop with a habit? No way.

Then I remembered. As far as Duck was concerned, he wasn't a cop anymore.

6

I NEEDED A TIME-OUT, A BREAK, RECESS. I drove aimlessly, wandering up one street, down the next with no particular destination in mind. The sun had given up its dominance, the sticky, cloying heat of the day gradually yielding to more temperate breezes whispering across the city. I wound up on Capitol Hill and immediately began to relax, stress loosening its grip on the muscles of my neck and shoulders.

As an undergraduate student at Howard University, I would occasionally cut class, hop a bus or two to the Capitol and just walk the area, past Senate and Congressional office buildings and the Library of Congress. I loved the way the midday sun bounced off the marble facade of the Supreme Court building, rendering it one white-hot glow of such intensity you had to squint to look at it. I loved the way the setting sun painted the Washington Monument and Lincoln Memorial in a soft orange wash, the sun itself reminding me of a scoop of Mandarin sherbet melting on the horizon. In spite of ever present tourists and ubiquitous government workers, for me there was something serene and calming about this part of town, a permanence, amazement that despite the glitches, bumps and hiccups, the system still worked.

If I needed an infusion of energy, I'd head for Florida Avenue, my part of town, and walk west on U Street toward Fourteenth. Granted, scars of the 1968 riots still remained there, a shameful reminder of the madness that had followed the assassination of Martin Luther King. But the affected neighborhoods had begun to rally and regain a sense of community. The streets swarmed with people—locals rather than tourists, going about their business with an obvious sense of purpose, imbuing the city with a different brand of permanence, the sort that came with calling D.C. home. I'd coveted their sense of belonging here. I'd wanted to call it home, too.

It had seemed a sensible goal, especially for someone heading for law school in a city jam-packed with lawyers. But after passing the bar just to prove I could, I'd applied and had been accepted into D.C.'s police academy, my affection for the city so deeply ingrained by then that I wanted to help protect it, but from the streets, out here among the people, as opposed to the rarefied atmosphere of a law firm. Now for the first time since I'd settled in Washington, I felt as if I'd lost my moorings. Not only did I have no job and therefore no purpose, I'd lost my anchor. My apartment was no longer solely my own.

I'd been so content there, surrounded by things I valued because I'd chosen them with great care. How Duck could feel no attachment for his belongings was the only facet of his personality I'd never understood. Now, however, I envied him that detachment because I knew that I could never feel the same about my apartment again. I'd have an invisible roommate: John Doe.

I kept imagining him walking through my rooms, fingering this, poking through that, looking at my belongings with his stranger's eyes. I envisioned him opening my refrigerator, my freezer, rambling through cabinet drawers for a knife to spread Nunna's preserves, removing a saucer from the stack on the shelf. The mental picture of him making himself comfortable at the kitchen table, lighting his roach, inhaling and holding it in, then releasing those stinking fumes, poisoning *my* air, filled me with fury.

And in spite of the fact that he had no god-damned business being where he was, I would always feel responsible for his death because I hadn't been able to bring myself to drop that toaster down the trash chute. It had been one of the first small appliances I'd bought after I'd moved in, one of those must-haves that would make my kitchen homey, like Nunna's. Now I would never be able to see my kitchen without him in it. I didn't want to live there anymore.

But I didn't want to move into Duck's condo, either. I'd stay there temporarily, balcony or no, because I had little choice, but I didn't want it on a permanent basis, especially not this way. I drifted slowly past the Lincoln Memorial, then along Hains Point, Duck's building in plain view from the spit of land opposite National Airport. Seeing it reinforced how reluctant I was to return to that empty condo. I didn't want to go home, either, but guilt at the thought of Tank stuck like a faithful retainer in my smelly apartment finally drove me back to Northwest D.C.

I found him dozing out in the hall, his back against the wall next to the door. He came to with a start and scrambled to his feet, a sheepish grin on his lips. "Hi, Miz—I mean, Leigh. I was just resting my eyes. What did the dude say about Duck's keys?"

"I never got to tell him. It's a long story," I said, fiddling with my own keys. "What's the matter, the smell get to you?"

The sheepish grin deepened, and he focused on the toes of his snowy white Nikes. "Well, yes, ma'am. I've been popping out ever so often to get some air; only this last time, I sorta forgot and let the door close behind me. Locked myself out. I went downstairs to look for the little fella with the keys, but I couldn't find him."

"You should have gone on home," I said, and stuck my key in the lock, praying that something might be out of alignment and I wouldn't be able to get in. The key turned easily and the door opened. The smell wasn't quite as bad, but that wasn't saying much. John Doe was still here. I couldn't stand it.

"You hungry?" I asked Tank.

He shrugged. "A little."

"Good. Let's go eat." It took every ounce of grit I could dredge up to cross that threshold. I grabbed the suitcase of dirty clothes I'd brought back from

Sunrise, added enough odds and ends to last me a few days, and left the apartment to the ghost of my pot-smoking intruder. He could have it.

Tank took my suitcases, and we started for the elevator, speeding up when we heard the door begin to wheeze open. "Hold it, please," I called.

"I'll get it." Tank sprinted toward it just as a chocolate-colored Tasmanian devil hurtled out of the car as if she'd been shot from a catapult, a tote bag slung over one arm, a thick three-ring binder under the other.

"Uh-huh! Caught ya!" she yelled.

"Aw, shit. Tina." Tank's rich brown skin took on an ashy hue, like a chocolate bar a year past its sell-by date.

Dropping the tote bag, she sailed into him, whopping him over the head with her notebook at a tempo Sheila E. would envy. It was the first time I'd seen a three-ring binder used as a lethal weapon. "Thought (whap!) you could (whappity-whap!) step out (whappity-whappity-whap) on me, didja?"

Tank tried to fend her off with my bags, yelling, "Wait-a-minute, wait-a-minute!" but her arms were windmills spinning at triple speed. He had to be twice as tall and three times her weight, but that gave him no advantage. She was a little tornado, faster than he'd ever be.

Finally he dropped the luggage and managed to grab her wrists, backing as far as he could out of shin-kicking distance. Something told me it was a move he'd learned to perfect due to previous encounters. "Tina, baby, will you please calm down?"

Doors at the far end of the hall had opened again, my neighbors peering at us with consternation. I edged to one side, giving serious consideration to retrieving my bags and leaving them to it.

"Don't you baby me!" Tina spat, struggling to free herself. "Now I know why you were hanging around on that corner outside!"

"You been watchin' me?" Tank demanded, so astonished that he forgot himself and let her go. "Followin' me?"

"You betcher sweet ass I've been followin' you! Saw you meet her downstairs and carry her stuff in. Woulda been up here a long time ago, but I had to wait for that big heifer on the first floor to stop watching the front door."

Neva. With Cholly occupied elsewhere, she'd be keeping an eye on who came in and out.

Tina whirled around to grace me with one of those head-to-toe looks and back up again. "You mean you been stepping out on me with this bitch?" Her lips curled in a sneer, a trick I'd been trying to master since sixth grade. Tina had it down pat. "How old is she anyway, forty?"

"Now, just wait a damned minute." I'd been faintly amused before, but she'd just crossed the line.

"Wait nothing." She hurled the binder to the floor. "I'm gonna show you what happens to bitches who mess with Tina's man. I'm gonna kick the shit outta you." She took a boxer's stance, fists raised.

"Uh, Tina—" Tank began.

Her fist shot toward my chin and I grabbed it, bending it backward.

"Listen, little girl," I said, stepping in so that we were nose to nose. "I was a D.C. cop for seven years. Do you understand what that means? I could stomp you so flat it would take a vacuum cleaner to separate you from this carpet. Now, back off. I'm tired. I haven't eaten in almost twelve hours, and when I'm hungry I can be your worst nightmare. And, little lady, nothing riles me more than one sister calling another bitch. Now do you still want to tangle with me?"

Our gazes locked. She blinked. "Well, maybe not."

"Smart move." I released her fist but kept my guard up in case she wanted to be stupid.

"I ain't been steppin' out on you," Tank said, aggrieved. "This is Miz Warren, Duck's main—I mean, fianceé. He's out of town and asked me to keep an eye on her."

"Oh." Tina eyed me warily, then Tank. "Why didn't you say so before?" She waggled the offending fist back and forth, shaking off the discomfort I'd caused. Then with an impish grin, she extended her hand. "Tina Rae Jones."

We shook. Cautiously. "Leigh Warren."

"Pleased to meetcha. Your hallway always smell this bad? Smells like somebody's cookin' last month's garbage."

Tank tried to shush her. "That ain't food, Tina, that's—"

"How 'bout we talk about it later?" I cut him off.

"We're on our way to get something to eat. You coming, Tina?"

"You buyin?'" she asked me. Seeing little alternative, I nodded. "Then what y'all waitin' for? I'm starving."

"That's my Tina." Tank chuckled. "Get your stuff, baby."

This wasn't quite what I'd had in mind. I'd figured the least I could do was feed my protector and, while we ate, convince him that his services weren't required. I needed to be able to move around the city and ask questions about Duck's activities in the days before he disappeared. That would be awkward with Tank in tow, considering the way he idolized Duck. Tina was a third wheel I hadn't anticipated.

On the other hand, Tina might be my ace in the hole. I was certain she wasn't happy about the role he'd assumed. It was also apparent that in this relationship, Tina called the shots. With her along to nudge him in the right direction, there was every possibility that by the time I paid the check, I'd be seeing the last of Tank and Tina. This meal might be worth whatever it cost me.

Right.

Over a buffet dinner at a local restaurant, I presented what seemed to me to be perfectly logical reasons why I had no need for a baby-sitter.

"I haven't been able to give this knee the attention it needs, so I'll be spending the next few weeks in rehab, going from the clinic to my apartment and back again. There's no reason for you to hang around, Tank. You'd be bored silly, stuck out in the waiting area with nothing to do. So you can go back to spending your day at whatever it is you normally do and feel that you've kept your word to Duck. Okay?"

"You got a point. That does sound boring, all right."

Tina managed an affectionate smile between mouthfuls of the second plate she'd loaded with so much food it resembled Mount Kilimanjaro. "Nothing my Tankie hates worse than being bored."

The name was so ridiculous that something went down the wrong way and I spent the next thirty seconds or so trying to avoid spraying macaroni across the table as I coughed my lungs out.

Tank pounded me on the back with such gusto I'd be bruised for life. When I'd finally regained a semblance of composure, he wiped a big mitt on his jeans. "She's right. Don't like sitting around with nothing to do. Oh, well. Think I'll get another slice of that coconut cream pie." He headed for the dessert table, and I breathed a sigh of relief. Cutting him loose had been easier than I'd thought.

"Don't worry about him," Tina said while he was gone. "He'll get over it. He's pretty pragmatic when you get right down to it."

Pragmatic. It wasn't a term I'd expect her to know, and I gave myself a mental kick in the pants for drawing superficial conclusions about this little fireball.

Tank demolished another piece of pie, and Tina worked her way through a chunk of cheesecake the size of a cement block before declaring that she thought she'd had enough to last until she got home.

Pleased that I had accomplished what I'd set out to do, with, all things considered, very little input from Tina, I paid the bill and offered to drop them off at a nearby Metro stop.

Tank shook his head. "No, ma'am. Got to see you back to the foxy lady's apartment."

"What foxy lady?" Tina demanded.

"Tank, I told you—" I started.

"Yes, ma'am, you did. But I gave my word to Duck to look after you, so that's what I'm gonna do. What time you got to be at the clinic tomorrow?"

I turned to Tina in exasperation.

She shrugged. "Don't look at me. He gave his word. Where's this foxy lady"—she squinted at Tank with an expression just short of a silent death threat—"live? I hope it ain't far. I got a class tonight. Don't want to be late. And in case there's any doubt about this arrangement," she directed at me, "wherever Tankie's goin' now, Tina's going, too."

Terrific. I gave up for the moment, and they rode with me back to my apartment building. With them dogging me every step of the way, we went up to the fifth floor, where I let myself into Janeece's, praying they wouldn't remember that my bags were still in the car. We arranged to meet in the morning, and I watched from the window until they'd disappeared from view, a comical couple, six-foot-three and four-ten or -eleven walking arm in arm. But there was no doubt who jumped through whose hoops. Tank had it bad.

I gave it fifteen minutes, then hit the streets again, trying to think of somewhere to go. As good a friend as she was, I didn't want to stay with Janeece. I needed solitude. Granted, she wouldn't be home until eleven, but Janeece was a night person and would want to stay up and talk. I had neither the inclination nor the energy. Besides, two hours with Janeece was like four in a room full of people. She had the kind of personality that would leave me drained in no time flat. Duck called her a walking firecracker.

Duck. The only leads I had to his motives for walking away from everything he valued were the John Doe, whose name I might never know, and la femme, Evie Artis. I wondered if his mother or sister had heard him mention her. It was still fairly early, and the only way to find out would be to ask.

The decision as to which of them I should talk to first was made for me as I approached an amber light at Georgia Avenue and Colesville Road. I wasn't sure how long it had been yellow, but a precautionary glance in my rearview mirror convinced me that there was no way the bumper-riding jackass behind me could stop in time if I played good citizen and didn't run the red light.

I'd noticed the beat-up old Volkswagen bus when I'd crossed the District line a few blocks back, and he'd been following too closely ever since. Someone I knew, perhaps from the job, playing with me? Sometimes a skewed sense of humor and playing practical jokes were the only things that kept a cop sane. But no one I knew owned a VW this old. And if it was someone I'd arrested or had had to give a hard time for whatever reason, someone bearing a grudge, this could get ugly. The traffic signal was still amber, but it was do something now or get stuck by the red light in a second. Gunning the engine I'd kept fine-tuned in case I ever needed it on the job, I shot into the intersection and turned right onto Colesville, grinning as brakes squealed behind me. Pedestrian traffic would hold him up for a while. Served him right.

In the interim, I headed for the Beltway, then Route 95 toward Baltimore and Vanessa's house. Even if Vanessa wasn't home, the drive up to Catonsville would kill some time. If she was there . . . I felt a surge of hope, remembering her vacant guest room. If I played my cards right, I might be able to delay going back to Duck's for a day or two. My luck was about to change. I was sure of it. Right. Again.

The driveway was empty. So was the garage. No sign of Vanessa's Toyota or Rich's BMW. Shit. I got out and went to the door anyway, just in case. No response to the doorbell. Still, no newspapers out front or mail in the mailbox, a good sign. They weren't out of town—unless the mail and newspapers were being held. But that wasn't likely. Everything was as pristine as usual. If they'd been away for any length of time, there'd be a layer of dust on the porch. The highway, the bane of Vanessa's existence because of her allergies, was too near by.

I dug into my bag for pen and paper so I could leave a note asking her to call me at her brother's, and was about to drop it in her mailbox when the roar of an approaching car in dire need of a new muffler distracted me. Vanessa's battered Corolla, nearing its thirteenth birthday, turned into the driveway, shuddered loudly for a moment, then died. The ensuing silence, as the saying goes, was deafening.

Vanessa climbed out. "Leigh! Girl, am I glad to see you!"

"Thanks," I called down to her, "but not as glad as the Midas man will be to see you. How long have you been driving around sounding like a freight train?"

She slammed the door and hurried up to the porch. "Since yesterday. Muffler went blooey, and replacing it's going to be way down on my list of priorities for the moment. Hey, sugar." Throwing an arm around my neck, she pecked me on the cheek. They were a family of kissers—she, Duck and her mother. It had taken me a while to get used to that.

Pudgy and not the least bit concerned or self-conscious about it, Duck's sister was his feminine counterpart in that, at first glance, there was nothing remarkable about her. Round face, skin the color of October leaves, dark eyes with the same lustrous lashes and brows as her brother's. But a few minutes in her presence and you were struck by a warmth, openness and lack of pretension. You liked her immediately, felt as if you'd known her for a long time and could talk to her about anything.

It was the same quality that made Duck such a success at interrogation. Witnesses volunteered information eagerly. Perpetrators, lulled into carelessness by his easy and unthreatening manner, tended to slip up and, with very little encouragement, would eventually spill their guts to him, coaxed by a sense that in spite of what they'd done, Duck knew how it was. He'd understand. With Vanessa, friends and acquaintances tended to unload to her, too, one of the reasons she was such an effective counselor. If she'd opted to go on to med school and specialize in psychiatry, she'd have been rich.

She gave me another quick hug. "Come on in. I'm just here for a second. Mom's in the hospital, Leigh. She had a heart attack last night."

"No!" Suddenly the reverses I'd suffered today seemed like trifles. Mrs. Kennedy, a petite woman, fragile as a hummingbird, was second only to Nunna, my foster mother, in my affections. "How is she?"

"Stable, but things were real dicey for a while. We're just lucky she was here when it happened and not home by herself."

She unlocked the door, and I followed her in, immediately envious of the decorating flair she and her brother shared. Vanessa's colonial looked like something out of *House and Gardens*, as warm and welcoming as she was.

"Mom hadn't been feeling well," she was saying, "so Rich went and brought her over for dinner with us, but she wouldn't eat, just wanted to lie down. Then later she started complaining of a tightness in her chest."

"Which hospital?" I asked, trailing her through her slate blue and mauve living room into the rear hallway.

"University of Maryland. Rich's brother is a cardiologist there, and we know he'll keep an eye on her. This is the first chance I've had to come home. Gotta clean myself up. I positively stink. Then I've got to go to Mom's and pack some things for her. Looks like she'll be there a while." Her bottom lip quivered for a second, but only a second. She began unbuttoning her blouse, her features composed again. "I need to get in touch with Dillon. He doesn't know, and she keeps asking for him."

Oh, God. What could I tell her? To stall, I peppered her with questions about her mother's condition while she showered and changed into a pair of navy slacks and a short-sleeve chambray top. By the time she'd finished, I felt positively upbeat about finding a corpse in my kitchen. As gross as the experience had been, it couldn't have been worse than witnessing your mother suffer a coronary.

"Anything I can do, 'Nessa? I'm not just asking to be polite."

She eyed me, thinking. "Would you mind taking me to Mom's place and then to the hospital? The thought of a squad car pulling me over because of my muffler gives me palpitations."

"Consider yourself chauffeured," I said, relieved at being able to help. Vanessa had never taken sides after my engagement to her brother bit the dust. Neither had her mother. I might never marry Duck, but these people were still as close to family as I had this far north. "Where's Tyler?" I asked as she set the security alarm and locked the front door.

"At the hospital with Rich. I don't know what I'm going to do about her."

"What do you mean?" I asked, unlocking the passenger side for her.

"Good Lord," she said, getting in. "Who have you been ferrying around? Somebody a helluva lot taller than my brother, that's obvious." I helped her push the seat forward, not quite sure how to explain the Tank phenomenon. I needn't have worried. Vanessa had her daughter on her mind. "Ty's in day care until noon, but unless there's room enough for her to stay all day, we've got a problem."

"Why?" I asked, wrestling with my seat belt.

"I really don't want to come home again until Mom's out of the woods. Rich is supposed to fly to Chicago tomorrow, and it's really important that he go. Betty next door would keep Ty, but she's away and won't be home until day after tomorrow."

"Then your problem's solved," I said. "I'm on disability."

"Oh, Leigh, I'm sorry. Your knee?"

I nodded. "My schedule's pretty fluid. I can take Ty to day care, go to the clinic for physical therapy, then pick her up and bring her home so her routine won't be completely upset. I can even stay overnight if you need me to." I had the decency to feel ashamed of myself, given the hidden agenda I'd arrived with, but it looked to me as if the arrangement might solve one of her problems, to say nothing of several of mine.

A few of the clouds left Vanessa's face. "Oh, Leigh, would you? That would be terrific." Twisting awkwardly in her seat, she reached over, both arms extended, and hugged me with the usual Kennedy enthusiasm. It was just as well we were still in her driveway; she practically yanked me from under the steering wheel. "The house is yours. There's fresh linen in the bathroom closet and freshly baked—well, yesterday anyhow—gingersnaps in the cookie jar."

It was that simple. I had a roof over my head, one with no miasma of death. No Tank. No condo with faint whiffs of Duck. Just the company of a sweet little girl and a giant canister of home-baked ginger-snaps. Man, I was in clover.

Mrs. Kennedy's snug apartment reminded me of my foster mother's house in Sunrise—unfussy but com-fortable well-worn mahogany furniture, plump chairs and sofa backs laced with antimacassars. Knickknacks of indeterminate age were clustered on end tables. Duck in a brand-new uniform and shiny badge smiled down from one end of the mantel, Vanessa in cap and gown, diploma held high, from the other. Color photos of plump brown-skinned babies and gap-toothed school pictures spanned the space between. And not a speck of dust anywhere. Everything gleamed. Vanessa had come by her housekeeping habits honestly.

I'd wanted to wait in the car. I was no stranger to Mrs. Kennedy's apartment, but the thought of being here without Duck caused an uncomfortable ache to my midsection. There was no saying no to a

Kennedy who'd made up his or her mind, however, so now here I was perusing the photos while Vanessa packed a suitcase for her mom.

Neither Duck nor his sister had changed much over the years. Vanessa had had her Bugs Bunny teeth nudged into line by braces, but other than that, both were clearly identifiable. There were a few snapshots of a second little boy, probably a cousin since he shared the Kennedy round face and infectious grin. I wondered what Duck's father looked like; there were no pictures of him. None of Mrs. Kennedy, either, but I knew her to be camera shy.

Polaroids of Tyler filled in the gaps on the mantel. With Rich's hazel eyes and fair complexion, she was her dad's miniature, with braids and the giggles. I sighed and moved to the window, surprising myself by wondering what a child of Duck's and mine might look like. I had to get out of here. Mrs. Kennedy's apartment was playing head games with me.

"Vanessa," I called to her, "all my stuff's in the car. If there's nothing I can do to help here, I'd rather go back out and wait."

"You can come in here and keep me company," she responded, sounding uncharacteristically lost. I followed her voice to a neat, sparsely furnished room containing a single bed, glass-topped mahogany dresser, chest of drawers, bedside table and one straight-back chair. A braided rag rug covered the floor. There were few frills here, and it contrasted a good deal with the plump upholstered pieces in the living room. "I can't figure out how many gowns to pack," Vanessa was saying. "Or which robe. It's cold in her hospital room. Maybe the chenille. Oh, God, Leigh, I hate this!" Her hands trembled like frightened birds.

"How about I do it?" I suggested, unnerved at seeing her losing control. "You can tell me where things are."

She pressed her lips into a thin, hard line. "No. I should do it. Five gowns to start with," she said, composed again. "She hates those things with the backside out. And I should take panties. Mom wears panties to bed." She rooted in the drawer of the dresser, pulling garments out and folding them neatly before tucking them into a blue Samsonite bag.

I sat in the chair beside the bed, scanning the arrangement of pictures above the headboard, the only decorative elements in the room. These were more formal portraits of the family—Duck, Vanessa with Rich and Tyler, and a third portrait, an obvious blowup of a smaller snapshot filled with the brilliant smile and chubby cheeks of the child I'd seen in the living room. He must be someone special to deserve a place with the others. My curiosity got the best of me. "Vanessa, who's the little boy?"

"Hmm?" Distracted, she looked around. Her smile softened. "Christopher. Our little brother. Duck never mentioned him?"

Their little brother? "I had no idea. To tell the truth, I don't remember him talking about his childhood much. What happened to Christopher?"

"He died when he was six." Faint lines of pain

radiated from the corners of her mouth. "He was asthmatic, the sweetest kid in the world. Duck never got over his death. There were six years between them, but they were really close."

So were Duck and I, I'd thought. It was damned disconcerting to find out how many important elements he'd left out of our heart-to-heart discussions during the years we'd been best buddies. A baby brother he'd lost. A promise he'd made to himself. What else hadn't he told me?

"Slippers," Vanessa muttered, dropping to one knee and rooting under the bed. "Oh, Lord, and denture cup." She disappeared into the bathroom.

"All these pictures," I said, my gaze fixed on the eyes in Duck's pictures. They seemed to look back at me, open, trusting. "Why none of your parents?"

"You couldn't get Mom to sit still in front of a camera if you gave her a winning lottery ticket," Vanessa said from the bathroom. "As for Dad ... well, there were a few, but I haven't seen them in years. I'm not sure what happened to them." She hurried from the bathroom carrying a denture cup and adhesive, which she tucked into a pocket of the suitcase. After stuffing a robe in on top, she closed and engaged the locks. Halfway out the door, she took one last look around. "I should unplug her TV and VCR. God, her list. Look under the phone and get that piece of paper, please. It's got all her important phone numbers. Did you see her Bible in the living room?" She disappeared.

Picking up the telephone on the bedside table, I reached for the folded paper beneath it. Under the glass top, hidden by the telephone, was a Polaroid snapshot. I tilted my head to peer at it. Why put a snapshot of Duck there? And when had he learned to drive a big rig? The photo had been taken just outside the front seat of a semi, considering the number of gear shifts visible at the bottom edge of the shot. I stooped to get a closer look. It wasn't Duck. The face wasn't quite as round, the skin a shade darker. This was obviously Duck's father. He grinned at the camera, a cloth in his hand, as if he'd been polishing the steering wheel.

"Leigh. You coming?" Vanessa called from the living room.

"On the way." Lifting the glass carefully, I eased the picture out, turned off the light and hurried to the living room, where Vanessa stood, door open, keys to lock it in her hand. I held up the snapshot. "Do you think your mom would want this, too? I found it under the telephone."

She squinted at it, her chin dropping slowly. She put the suitcase down. "Under the telephone? Why, that sneaky old lady! That's Dad." She took it, an odd expression in her eyes. "My God, this was taken the day he bought the truck. How could I have forgotten this?" She handed it back, snapping off the light and retrieving the suitcase. "Hold onto it. I'll ask her if she wants it. You really dug up some memories with that one. Let's go."

I followed her out, and she locked the door. Shoving aside my reluctance at probing into family affairs, I delayed asking more questions only until we were back in the car and headed for Baltimore.

"Vanessa, it's none of my business, and you have every right to tell me so, but why would your mother keep a picture of her husband under the telephone—as if she were hiding it?"

Her response was a snort. "She was, from Dillon. If he'd seen it, he'd have ripped it up and tossed it in the nearest trash can. And as far as I'm concerned, you're family, so I don't mind your asking. Take the Parkway," she directed. "The hospital's practically a straight shot from there."

I maneuvered my way over to Route 295, the forty-mile stretch between D.C. and Baltimore, and settled down to an even sixty. Traffic was fairly light. Rush hour was over, a relief, since I found it difficult to concentrate on driving. "I don't understand, 'Nessa. According to Eddie Grimes, Duck adored his father and was so broken up over his death that he couldn't talk about him."

Vanessa was silent for so long that I glanced at her to be sure she hadn't dropped off. "You might as well know," she said finally, her intonation flat, as if denying its importance. "It's pure fabrication, Leigh, Dillon's coping mechanism. Dad didn't die. He walked out on us and never came back. And Duck's hated him ever since."

7

"WAIT A MINUTE. JUST . . . JUST HOLD ON A minute." Eddie Grimes squinted at me from across the booth at Wally's, an after-shift hangout in the shadow of the Sixth District station. "You're telling me Duck's dad never died? The whole thing was a lie?"

"Well," I said, hoping to soften the blow, "Vanessa called it a coping mechanism. Duck idolized his father. But he left one day and never came back. I don't know whether that was before or after Christopher died. It's obviously a painful subject for them all, so I didn't push."

"Christopher? Who's Christopher?" Eddie demanded.

I winced. I'd just assumed he knew. "Their baby brother. He died when he was six, a severe asthmatic. 'Nessa said Duck was twelve then, so both things must have happened around the same time."

Eddie looked off, lips pressed into a straight line. Without warning he slid out of the booth. "Going to the can," he said, and left.

I cradled the mug of coffee I had yet to drink and settled down to wait for however long it took for Eddie to pull himself together. I felt bad for him. It had been two days since Vanessa had dropped the bomb in my lap, and I had yet to recover myself. The rest of that evening had been as close to an out-of-body experience as I cared to live through. I'd operated on automatic pilot, doing what had to be done, but my memory of those hours was like lace—wispy, fragile, more holes than fabric.

I know I drove into Baltimore to the hospital without incident, parked in the underground garage on Redwood, went in with Vanessa, came out with a sleeping Tyler in my arms, and left again after paying an attendant three-fifty for the privilege of taking up a parking space for perhaps a quarter of an hour.

I know I took my godchild home, put her to bed, and had a vague memory of listening to her ask God to bless her parents, her grandmother, me, her Uncle Dillon and the fuzzy brown thing that lived in the corner of the garage, after which I went out and moved my car onto the street. That I remember clearly.

I phoned Cholly to let him know I'd be staying with a friend, asked him to pass that tidbit along to Janeece and to Tank when he showed up. I collapsed onto the bed in the guest room fully clothed and at some point got up when I heard Rich come home. I had an aural memory of his fatigue-coarsened voice relaying that Mrs. Kennedy was in guarded condition and being watched very closely. From that point the rest of the night was a blank. The sleep of the dead is a phrase that comes to mind.

The last couple of mornings I'd let Tyler pick which of the lethal-looking rainbow-colored cereals she wanted for breakfast, bathed and dressed her, and took her off to day care. While she was there, I spent the next couple of hours on rehab and wasted the remainder of the morning in a halfhearted attempt to find out where Duck had gone. I'd even hit all the ceramics shops he frequented and had stumbled onto the place that had bought his kiln. I'd assumed he might have loaned it to another ceramicist friend, but nothing drove home his determination to cut all ties as much as discovering that he'd actually sold the kiln. That brought me to my senses, awakened the part of my mind that, thanks to my preoccupation with taking care of Tyler, had been absent without leave. Knowing that Vanessa's neighbor would be home tomorrow to take over for me allowed my brain to report for duty again and let me in on what it had been doing. It had been busy.

I was past the point of trying to convince myself that I was wrong about Duck, adding two and two and getting six and seven-tenths. A week before, I'd have sworn on a Bible there was no way the Duck I knew would intentionally break the law, no way he'd withhold or tamper with evidence. That fairytale view no longer existed. The Duck I thought I knew, Mr. Ethics, Mr. By-the-Book, had been a figment of my imagination.

And now mine were the ethics being put to the test. I was the one withholding, if not evidence, then at least knowledge that there was a connection of some sort between Duck and the squatter in my kitchen. Letting Tristan in on that bit of information would mean he would try to get in touch with Duck to verify that the keys were his. That would bring to Tristan's attention that Detective Dillon Upshur Kennedy was unaccountably absent. So I still hadn't told him. I would. I swore to myself I would, just not quite yet.

Make no mistake, I was one mad, steam-coming-out-of-my-ears pissed mama, especially when I replayed all the heart-to-hearts we'd had over the years, and counted all the beers we'd blubbered in spilling our guts and innermost secrets to each other. That was a laugh. How many gaps had there been in Duck's story? Evidently more than a few. Our whole relationship had been a big fat sham, all eight years of it. And that hurt. Because along with being the closest to a big brother as I'd ever have, then an alleged best friend, then lover, Duck had been my role model. I'd looked up to him, strived to be like him both as a person and a professional. He'd failed me, he'd failed the Department.

In spite of all that, I was still having problems believing that Duck had become an addict. But he'd been up to something in the weeks before he'd disappeared. And although it was obvious I hadn't known him as well as I'd supposed, I did know how he worked, how he attacked a problem. So if anyone could find him, I could. The question was, should I bother?

Was he worth the effort? Should I waste valuable rehab time on Duck or spend it in the clinic and the gym as I'd planned? I'd needed a sounding board. So I had called Eddie and wondered now if he was ever coming back.

I'd questioned the wisdom of trying to talk here at Wally's, considering that the place was about the size of a bus station men's room and there were bound to be at least a dozen guys who'd just changed shifts and had stopped for coffee and a few minutes to wind down before heading for home. Aside from the counter, which sat eight, and a pair of booths, there were only six tables squeezed so close together there was no way to get between them if the tables were occupied and your hips were any larger than twenty-eight inches around. On most days you couldn't buy privacy or solitude with a hundred-dollar bill.

It was not most days. Only three cops hunkered at the counter in a fatigue-induced stupor, cradling heavy white mugs with both hands, which meant they were in bad shape. Wally's coffee had been known to remove oil-based paint. None of the tables were occupied.

Eddie finally returned, his jaw tight with anger. "Sorry to be so long," he said, grabbing his mug of inky black java as he slipped into the booth. "But I had a lot to think about, and the john's where I do my most serious thinking." He flipped two sugars at me. "I'll tell you what I've decided in a minute. Here's the info you asked for related to the accident. And I guess it won't hurt to let you know they've identified your uninvited guest. James Braden Thomas Jr. No fixed address." Pulling a sheet of paper torn from his notebook, he slid it across the table. "Not all that much on his rap sheet—tres-passing, vagrancy, that kind of thing up in Frederick

County, and that was a couple of years ago.
Nothing since."

A vagrant? Why would Duck have given his keys
to a vagrant?

"No B and E? No connection with drugs?" I
asked, glancing at the slip of paper. Something
about the name pinged faintly in a shady corner of
my brain.

"Probably never got caught at it," Eddie was saying.

I folded the sheet in half, folded it again, then
again. I wasn't sure what else to say to him. Eddie's
illusions had been completely shattered. He seemed
to have shrunk by a couple of inches and several
pounds, neither of which he could afford to lose.

"Goddamn it!" He pounded on the table, setting
both mugs dancing. Behind the counter, Wally
peered over his glasses at us, beetle brows kissing
each other above his broad nose. I forced my lips
into a placating smile, and he waggled a fat finger at
me, a warning that I'd better take my charge in
hand. The cops sipping coffee didn't even turn
around.

Eddie slumped in the booth. "He could have told
me the truth, Leigh. He knows me. Didn't he think
I'd understand?"

I could sympathize with Eddie's need for time to
digest the revelations and deal with the hurt, but it
was a luxury we didn't have. "Come on, Eddie.
You've been around long enough to know you never
can tell how a person will react when they feel
they've been betrayed. Vanessa said he and his dad

had been practically inseparable, did everything together. When his dad left, the charade that his father was dead became the only way he could handle it. After a while he probably began to believe the lie himself."

Eddie ground his knuckles against his eyelids. "His dad left—what?—twenty-something years ago. Seems to me that's time enough for him to get over it. How'd the subject come up to begin with?"

I explained about finding the photo in his mother's apartment. "In fact, I still have it." I dug it out and handed it to him. "Duck's a dead ringer for him."

After examining it for a couple of seconds, Eddie nodded and slid it back as if it was too painful to look at. "You're right. A dead ringer. Okay, that's it, Leigh. I'm butting out."

"What do you mean?" I'd been dreading this moment since he'd returned from the rest room and crossed my fingers under the table that he wouldn't go to Moon.

"I mean just what I said. I thought I knew him. Turns out I didn't. He's not the dude we thought he was. So I'm out of it. If you're smart, you'll butt out, too, honey."

"Eddie—"

"The last couple of months have been hell, Leigh, trying to come up with reasons for what he did, for not hearing from him, the whole bit. Nothing I thought of made sense. But I was willing to give him the benefit of the doubt based on twenty-five years of friendship—hell, brotherhood. I shared my father with him, considered him blood kin." His eyes watered, and he wiped them away. "The will he left you and the note say he's gone off the deep end, and I don't swim so good. As for Moon, I haven't decided whether to come clean with him yet. I need more bathroom time before I make up my mind about that. Whatever I do, I'll let you know, for old times' sake. But I . . . I've had it." He leaned across the table and kissed my forehead. "Good luck, honey. And take care of that knee, okay?" He went to the counter, slapped a couple of dollars in front of Wally and left.

In shock, I sat there for a moment, watching his retreating back as he crossed the street in the middle of the block, almost getting creamed by an approaching squad car, his mind obviously elsewhere. The uniform in the squad car slowed, then shook his finger at Eddie before pulling over to park behind a rust-pocked Volkswagen bus of sixties vintage.

I felt a prickling at the nape of my neck. I do not believe in coincidences, and I clearly remembered the old VW bus riding my bumper my first day back. Granted, they'd been popular family vans and hippie transportation when I was in my teens, but had long since been replaced by a more clean-cut version. The rust marks hadn't been visible in my rearview mirror on Monday, so I couldn't be sure it was the same one.

I moved closer to the door and squinted at it, but couldn't make out the driver; the window was closed and in sore need of a bottle of Windex. The squad car behind him must have made him edgy. He gunned the engine and pulled out of the parking space, slipping into traffic and disappearing. I shrugged, vowed to keep an eye out for it from now on and went inside to decide what to do.

I hadn't counted on Eddie's reaction. I'd assumed he might be hurt, even angry, but it had never occurred to me that he'd give up on Duck altogether. Thank God I hadn't told him about Duck quitting the Department, or Eddie'd be in Moon's office right now. I glanced down at the photograph that had apparently broken the camel's back for him and understood immediately. I might as well have been looking at Duck, the same mask, full cheeks and infectious smile. If this had been taken against the interior of a squad car instead of the cab of a tractor trailer—

Something caught my eye, and for the first time I concentrated on the background instead of the face. I'd missed it before, and still wasn't certain I was seeing what I thought I was. The camera had been focused on the foreground, so the scene behind Mr. Kennedy was far less precise. On the dashboard of the cab was what at first appeared to be a pale pink blob I'd assumed was a buffing cloth, since Mr. Kennedy held a can of wax in one hand and a rag in the other. Now, peering at the pink blob more closely, I saw I was mistaken. The shape was wrong, and there was nothing soft or fluid about it.

I wiggled out of the booth. "Wally, do you have a magnifying glass?"

Wally McKiver had been in the business long enough to be unaffected by much of anything.

"Dumb question," he said, digging under the counter. "Have to keep one on hand to check for counterfeits." One of the uniforms huddled over coffee at the bar took it from him and, without turning, extended his arm back toward me.

"Thanks." I took it, sat down and, holding my breath, examined the old photo. There on the center of the dashboard, and reflected against the windshield behind it, was a piggy bank. Scrabbling in my purse, I found the Polaroid Eddie had given me. I didn't need the magnifier this time. There was no mistake. It was the same bank, decorated with the same pink and blue flowers on its sides, the blue flower on its snout and the one across its head like a hat. This was the catalyst that had sent Duck spinning out of his orbit. And I'd been carrying it around since Monday.

I had no explanation for the presence of a piggy bank in the cab of a tractor trailer. I did recall Duck saying that his father had introduced him to ceramics, a hobby he'd picked up while recuperating in a VA hospital after his return from Vietnam. Whether he or one of the kids had made it was immaterial; the point was it had been in Mr. Kennedy's possession on an important enough occasion for Vanessa to remember as soon as she'd seen the photo. It was the day he'd gotten the truck. If she remembered it, Duck would, too. That's why he'd kept it. And now some of the things he'd done began to make sense.

I had to talk to Vanessa, and that presented a problem. The use of cell phones on a critical-care unit was strictly forbidden. I did the only thing I could do. I called the unit and asked the desk clerk to have Vanessa phone me. She responded almost immediately, fueled by panic that something had happened to Tyler.

"She's fine," I assured her. "She's still at day care. I didn't mean to scare you, but I needed to get to you and this was the only way I could think of to do it."

She exhaled with relief. "Thank God. Okay, what's up?"

I wasn't sure how to pose the question, but there was nothing to be gained by pussyfooting around her. She was too astute a counselor not to recognize diversionary tactics. "Vanessa, I promise I'll explain why I'm asking, but please answer my questions first. Were you serious when you said Duck hates his father?"

Bless her, after a silence loaded with speculation, she responded. "Perhaps I'd better sit down. Hold on." There were footsteps, then rustling sounds. "I'm back. And I was deadly serious. You have to understand, Leigh, our family went into crisis after Dad left. Mom did the best she could without him, but there were so many bills, especially Christopher's medical bills, that things gradually went to hell. We were evicted, our stuff stacked on the curb. People just picked it up and walked off with it as if they'd paid some invisible cashier for it. That's why Dillon refuses to become attached to things. He knows what it's like to lose them."

"My God." I'd never have guessed. "And you haven't heard from your father since?"

"Not a word. It's just as well. Dillon blamed him

for Christopher's death. We lived without heat for days before we were evicted, and I'll never as long as I draw breath forget that bone-chilling cold. Chris caught pneumonia and wasn't strong enough to fight it off. As far as Dillon was concerned, it was all Dad's fault, and he worked up a colossal hatred for him. All someone had to do was mention him, and Dillon would blow up. So we stopped talking about Dad and prayed he'd never come back. If he had, Dillon would have killed him."

"You don't mean that."

"The hell I don't." There was no hesitation, no equivocation. "And don't think that's changed, honey, because it hasn't. I know, I know," she said, forestalling my protest. "He's an adult now. But I can't tell you how hard Dad's leaving was on Dillon. In the beginning he made up all sorts of excuses for him. His truck broke down. Or he'd been hired by the government to ferry a secret shipment somewhere and couldn't get in touch. I'll never forget him shrieking that fairy tale to the guys who came to evict us, trying desperately to get them to believe him. Then Christopher died, and Dillon swore if he ever saw Daddy again, he'd be a dead man."

"But that was then," I argued. "You'd expect that kind of threat from a wounded child."

"A wounded kid who grew into a wounded man, when it comes to anything related to our father. Now, and Lord knows I'm terrified of the answer, why did you ask?"

"The piggy bank in the picture of your father, the one I found on your mother's nightstand—"

"Cordelia," she said immediately. "Dad made it for Mom, then raided it to play a number. This was before the lotteries. He hit it big enough to make the down payment on that cab, so he mounted it on the dashboard. It disappeared when he did. Why?"

"Because Duck found it at the scene of an accident back in March."

Her gasp was audible and full of terror. "Oh, my God! I knew something was wrong. So did Mom. He's never gone this long without at least calling her. Leigh, you've got to talk to him, make sure he's not thinking of doing something stupid."

"Like what?" I asked.

"I hate to say it, but when he first joined the Department, I wondered if he'd done it because being a cop might make it easier for him to find Daddy. It sure as hell would make it easier to kill him. Because he meant it, Leigh. He meant it then, and if he's got Cordelia, he still means it. He'll kill him, Leigh. He'll kill him without a second thought."

8

I WAS THOROUGHLY SHAKEN, AND IT MUST have shown. Without a word, Wally ambled over and exchanged my cold coffee for another mug. "On the house," he said, and returned to his cash register. And I was in such bad shape that I actually drank it. I longed to trot around to the Sixth to tell Eddie what I'd learned, but knew I couldn't chance it. There was no way to know what he'd do. Besides, if I'd found out the reasons for Duck's aberrant behavior too late to stop him, I would have made Eddie an accessory after the fact. This was something I'd have to do alone. And fast.

Several minutes later, when the caffeine had kicked in and I could think again, I unfolded the papers Eddie had given me and focused on the name of my intruder again. James Braden Thomas Jr. I was certain I'd never met him, so why did the name ring a bell? I scanned my memory bank and came up empty. It would emerge eventually. I just hoped it wasn't important and wouldn't pop into my consciousness when it was too late to do any good.

Flipping through the pages, I squinted at the information Eddie had supplied about the accident and Toulouse. Since Toulouse had the piggy bank, I had to start with him. I groaned. He had five sisters. I would rather talk to them than their mother, but there was no telling how long it would take me to track them down. Mrs. Archer, however, lived about ten blocks away, in public housing, which surprised me. Her son had been dealing long enough to have put her up in a mansion. Now that I thought about it, I was even more surprised that he'd been living with her at all.

I sighed and gave up. I had to talk to Mrs. Archer, and with Eddie trying to make up his mind whether to spill the beans, I couldn't afford to put it off. Before leaving the booth, I checked in with Cholly again.

Neva answered. "Hey, Miz Warren. Cholly ain't here. He's working on the toilet in 202. Want me to give him a message?"

"Just ask him to keep an eye on my apartment. I've been kinda busy but will be contracting with a cleaning company to go in and do what they can. I'll call you beforehand so you or Cholly can let them in."

"Hmph," she grunted. "Whatever they charge you won't be nowhere near enough. Your place is pretty bad. By the way, that big bald dude was here the past few mornings looking for you. Cholly told him you'd found someplace else to stay and wouldn't be back for a few days, so he left. When you gonna pick up your mail? You've got a whole shoe box full."

I'd completely forgotten that. And since the telephone and utilities bill had been due the first of the month, I'd better pick them up. At least I didn't have to worry about avoiding Tank.

"Thanks for the reminder, Neva. If I don't get there today, I'll be by first thing tomorrow."

"I'll be here," she said, and hung up. Neva never said good-bye on the phone. I punched the End button, stashed the phone and aimed for the home of Mrs. Anna May Archer.

"You're a friend of my Jimmy?"

She was older than I'd expected, somewhere between sixty and seventy, and wore the souvenirs of years of backbreaking toil on her coarse, roughened hands. But her thinning gray hair, as short as a Marine recruit's, was neatly trimmed, her faded blue-checked dress as crisp as a dollar bill fresh off the press. She stood as straight as her rounded shoulders allowed, chin lifted. Yet there was a sweetness about her as well, an openness in the deep-set eyes that regarded me with warmth as she stepped aside to let me in. I'd expected anything but a gracious invitation and hung back for a moment, puzzled by something about her I couldn't put my finger on.

"I hope I'm not keeping you from anything," I said, finally crossing the threshold. "I should have called first, but—"

"If you had, I'd have said, 'You come right on, honey.' Jimmy's friends are always welcome, but they don't come around much since he left. Here, sit right down. Can I get you something? It's so hot. I like iced tea when it's hot like this."

I declined, taking a seat and glancing around. Three of the four walls were jammed with paintings, matted rather than framed—still lifes, portraits, abstracts. They were interesting, some quite good. If Toulouse had done these, his nickname made sense. Other than the artwork, the living room was spare but immaculate, slipcovers camouflaging upholstered easy chairs that had seen years of hard wear, considering the sag of the cushions. The lamp tables gleamed despite scratches and chipped veneer. But it was her windows that did it for me, announced that this was no hit-or-miss housekeeper who vacuumed and dusted only when company was expected. The glass was so clean it was damned near invisible. Mrs. Archer and my foster mother were soul mates. Once a month Nunna's whole house in Sunrise smelled like one big fat pickle, thanks to the vinegar she used to polish those windows.

The wall space above Mrs. Archer's sofa was a montage of photos of her six children. I tried not to stare at the picture of Toulouse. I'd seen only mug shots of him, typically unflattering when in actuality, if these photos were any indication, he'd been lip-smacking gorgeous, with large dark eyes, lashes to kill for, almost male model handsome.

But I was surprised to find no evidence of the money he'd made dealing crack. No monster television and VCR, no fancy entertainment center, in fact, no new anything. If he'd bought jewelry for his mother, she wasn't wearing it, only a plain gold band her husband had probably put on her finger on their wedding day.

She sat down across from me, arranged the folds of her dress around her knees primly and gazed at me, a pleased smile subtracting years from her seamed face. "I can't tell you how nice it is to have company. The house gets so quiet. I play the television, but after a while it gets on my nerves, so I turn it off and clean. I like things to be clean. But there's only so much of it a body can do. I just finished washing two or three little things and was thinking about ironing, but it's too hot. I was flat out of ways to keep myself busy, so I'm really glad you came."

"Uh, thank you," I said, suspecting she wouldn't be for long. Determined to get this over with, I launched into the speech I'd rehearsed on the way. "First, Mrs. Archer, let me express my sympathy. You must miss Jimmy a great deal."

"Can't tell you how much," she said, shaking her head. "It just don't feel right with him gone. Not so bad during the daytime, but it takes me forever to fall asleep a-night, 'cause I'm waiting for the sound of his key in the door. Used to come in at all hours, though. I didn't like that. You sure I can't get you something? There's juices in the refrigerator."

"Thanks, no. I'm fine. What I'd like to ask—"

"Don't even have to say it," she cut me off with a chuckle. "You want to know when that rascal is going to bring his tail back home. I— What'd you say your name was?"

I frowned, the hairs standing up on the back of my neck. "Uh—Leigh Warren."

"Funny. I don't remember you coming around before. I'll tell you, Leigh." She sat forward on her chair, her expression earnest. "Much as I miss that boy, I pray he stays up home because he won't be around no drugs. And if anyone can turn him around, Big Sis can. I thank the Lord every day that I sent him to her. Vangie don't take no stuff, never has. So—"

A key rattled in the lock. The front door opened, and a statuesque young woman with skin the color of maple syrup and hair as shiny as black patent leather backed in, a garment bag in one hand, a whopper of a suitcase in the other.

"Sorry I'm late, Mama," she said, nudging the door shut. "The bus was—" Turning, she saw me and stared, lips parted. "Who the hell are you?" She dropped the bags. "Mama, how many times do I have to tell you not to open this door to nobody when I'm not here. Did you sign anything? Did you?"

Mrs. Archer looked hurt. "No."

"Thank God for that." She rounded on me, her manner threatening. "Whatever you're selling, she ain't buying. She's not responsible. Now, you get outta here." Stepping back, she opened the door.

"You got no call to talk to her like that, Malinda," her mother chided her, clearly embarrassed. "She's a friend of Jimmy's. Came by to find out when he's coming back."

"Oh, did she." In spite of the snarl contorting her mouth, Malinda was baby-doll pretty, the resemblance to her brother very strong. "If she was a friend of Jimmy's, she'd know he ain't coming back. He's dead. So she can just take her narrow ass outta here."

"Jimmy's dead?" Mrs. Archer gazed at her daughter in confusion.

Malinda took a deep breath and shook it in resignation. Not one single strand of hair moved, gelled to a fare-thee-well. "Yes, Mama, Jimmy's dead. He died in the car accident. We buried him, don't you remember? Right next to Daddy. We went out last Sunday and put flowers on both their graves, remember?"

Abruptly her demeanor changed, and she turned to glare down at me. "A friend of Jimmy's, huh? Well, we don't want your kind around here. You can leave on your own or I can kick you out. Your choice."

I held up a hand. "Look, Malinda, I'm sorry. I didn't realize your mother . . . had a problem. And she misunderstood. I never actually met your brother. I knew about him, though. I was a cop."

She reared back. "A cop. I mighta known. Well, what could you possibly want now? You figure we took over the business or something? Sorry. Ain't no dealers left in this family. He was the only one. He shamed us, and I don't care if he was my twin, I still hate him for it!" Just like that, tears flooded her eyes.

"Malinda, why you cryin', honey?" her mother asked, getting to her feet. "Your stomach hurt? Let me fix you something. Milk of magnesia or something. That's what you need, a little milk of magnesia. I'll be right back." She hurried out.

"Oh, God." Malinda watched her go, and flopped into the seat her mother had vacated.

"What am I gonna do about her? How can I go to work and leave her by herself if she's gonna be opening the door to every Tom, Dick or Harry who knocks? She can't be doin' that in this neighborhood."

"Is that why your brother lived here with her?" I asked. "So there'd always be someone with her?"

She blinked, startled. I think she'd forgotten I was there. "That's none of your goddamned business. Jimmy's dead. Isn't that enough for you? He's out of y'all's hair. And I'll tell you and anybody else wants to know, he got what he deserved, for bringing that shit into this house, putting our mama in danger. If y'all had come bustin' in here, who'd believe she didn't know what was goin' on? You would have tossed her in a cell without a second thought. Well, that's all over. Ain't no crack in this house. Just me and Mama and memories, and even they are slipping away from her. Now, for the last time, go away and leave us alone." There was little energy behind her words now, only fatigue and resignation.

I gazed across at her, shame nipping at my heels. I'd come here with strongly biased notions about these people and what to expect, and I'd been way off base.

"Look," I said, rooting around in my bag until I found my notebook and a pencil. "Call this number. It's the Adult Ed Center over on Bladensburg. Ask for Troy Burdette. She's an okay sister, and she can hook you up with a day-care center for senior citizens like your mother. Don't worry about the cost," I added, forestalling the protest I saw forming on her full lips. "You pay only what you can afford."

Suspicion danced across her face. "What's the catch?"

"No catch. Call her. Tell her Leigh Warren referred you. Now, before I go, I need to find out where your brother got the drugs he had with him when he died."

She sat up as if she'd been jabbed in the back, lightning bolts arcing from her eyes. "We don't know nothin' about where he got that shit from! Damn him!" She jumped up, began to pace. "Swear to God, if he hadn't killed himself, me or one of my sisters would have done it for him before long."

"Malinda!" Mrs. Archer filled the doorway, indignation and righteousness lending her twice the stature of moments before. Wherever her mind might have been when I arrived, it was at this moment in the here and now. In spades. "I won't have you talking like that. That ain't how I raised you. Vengeance is mine, sayeth the Lord. Jimmy did wrong, but he was your brother."

"Why are you still taking his side?" Malinda demanded with equal parts anger and anguish. "It's not fair! You raised him in the church just like you did us; only he turned rotten and that's the truth. Wasn't like he needed the money. Y'all always gave him whatever he wanted, and if you couldn't get it, the rest of us came up with it. Armintha bought him that fancy twelve-speed he just had to have. Vangie gave him her car. Gave it to him. Nothing we wouldn't have done for that boy. Know why? To please you, hoping that one day you'd look at one of us as if the sun rose and set on us the way you did him. He was your favorite from the day he was born. He had everything! There was no reason for him to start selling that shit! There was no need!" She finished on a wail, her fury spent.

"Watch your mouth," Mrs. Archer spat. "Yes, we spoiled him. And we never meant to slight the rest of you. But you have to understand, he was the only boy, his daddy's image, after Elijah had just about give up on someone to carry on his name. So Jimmy tended to get a little extra. And I don't know why he turned his back on the Lord and went against his raising. No matter. He was still your twin. Your brother." She turned and moved from the room with regal grace.

I gathered my belongings. "The choice was his," I reminded Malinda. "And he wound up paying for it. It's over now. You've got your mother to concentrate on. But I still need to know where your brother got the drugs he had in the car he was driving."

Her outburst had evidently sapped what spirit Malinda had left. "Told you, I don't know. The last time we saw him was a couple of weeks before he died. He was on the run, scared to death but wouldn't say why. Begged Mama for enough money to go up home for a while. Mr. Big-shot drug dealer beggin' for bus fare, can you believe that? Anyhow, Mama gave it to him. Next thing we know, cops knocking on the door saying Jimmy done smeared himself all over South Capitol in a stolen car. Aunt Vangie said he never showed up, so for all we know, he never went nowhere." She wiped her eyes, blew her nose and peered at me. "You said you was a cop. What happened? Get caught with your hand in some cookie jar?"

I bit my tongue. "No. I'm on disability."

"Then why do you care where he got the stuff from?"

I decided on the truth, perhaps to atone for the expectations I'd arrived with. "I stand a good chance of losing someone who means a great deal to me unless I can find out where your brother spent the last days of his life."

She squinted at me. "Your man hooked? Or is he a dealer? I ain't helpin' no scumbag dealer."

"He hates the drug trade," I said, truthfully. I had to present something she'd respond to. "I think he's after the supplier, plans to kill him. Sure, it would be no great loss, but if he does it, his life won't be worth the price of a roll of toilet paper. You know those people. They won't tolerate his interference. They'll have to show that no one gets away with snuffing out a member of their organization. I've got to find him and convince him to let the police take care of the supplier." Malinda snorted, but I plodded on. "I can't lose him, Malinda. He's all I have." I ran down, out of breath and half-truths. Whole ones, too.

Her gaze turned inward for a moment before she aimed it at me. I felt like an onion being peeled layer by layer and fought off the urge to fill the silence by saying something, anything.

"What'd you say your name was?" she asked. I told her and she nodded. "I wish you the best of luck, Leigh Warren. If I knew where Jimmy was before he died, I'd tell you, 'specially if it meant it might get rid of one more turd out there poisoning folk left and right. But I can't help you."

I recognized the truth when I heard it and gave up. "Okay. Thanks anyhow. Better go see to your mother." I started for the door, then realized I'd be stupid not to ask. "Exactly where is 'up home'?"

"Western Maryland. But I told you, Aunt Vangie said he never showed. Just as well, too. If he'd turned up in Sanctuary with drugs, she'd have kicked his ass from here to January."

"Sanctuary? That's the name of the town?"

Malinda managed a wry smile. "Ain't that a bitch? It really is kind of a safe place, though, tucked back up there in the mountains, so out of the way it takes a bloodhound to find it." She sobered. "He shoulda gone. He'd have been right at home up there with all those artsy-fartsy folks. He did all these." She nodded toward the paintings. "Yeah. He shoulda gone. The fool might still be alive." She shook herself and stood up. "I'd better get moving. I bet Mama hasn't packed a thing."

"She's going away?" I asked.

Malinda smiled, and I saw how pretty she really was. "Me and my sisters are taking her to Disney World for a week. She's wanted to go for years, so we're taking her." Despair washed over her face. "And two days after we get back, she won't remember a thing about it. Nice meetin' you, Miss Warren." She opened the door for me. My visit was over. "Good luck finding your man."

9

THURSDAY MORNING AFTER A DOUBLE
session of physical therapy, I circled my block a couple of times, checking to see if the bald protector
might be lurking somewhere, waiting to ambush
me. One good thing about Tank, however: when he
was around, he was so big there was no way to miss
him. Even if you didn't see him, Lord knows you'd
hear him. To my relief, all the faces in the vicinity
were familiar. Several young mothers from my
building pushed strollers and carriages along the
front, traveling in tandem, soaking up adult companionship while the getting was good. Boots and
Sadie, twin Scottish terriers, were walking their
owners, the Filby twins, sweet little ladies approaching the century mark, frail and tottery mirror
images of each other. It was a toss-up as to which
pair was older, the women or the dogs. Cholly
swore the Scotties were way past their puppyhood
when he'd moved in fourteen years ago.

I parked in the lot behind the building, cased the
basement entrance and scooted in, darting past the
laundry room and the elevators to take the steps up.
Hugging the wall, I edged the door open and
scanned the lobby. Mr. Ives and a fairly new resident

whose name I didn't know sat in easy chairs reading newspapers. Mrs. Ives perched at the end of the sofa opposite, rocking back and forth, humming tunelessly and endlessly, as relaxed as she ever was, which meant that Tank was not camped out in the corner I couldn't see. An unfamiliar face would have sent Mrs. Ives scurrying back up to her apartment. The fact that she was down here at all meant that for the moment anyway the coast was clear.

Waving a hello, I crossed the lobby and hurried up the four steps to the first-floor landing. As usual the door of 102 was ajar so that Cholly or Neva could see whoever came up the stairs to go to a first-floor apartment or use the elevators. With Cholly it was an extension of his protective nature about the building and its tenants. With Neva it was nosiness, pure and simple. Whatever their motivation, they made us feel more secure than we were—witness J. B. Thomas, who'd not only made it into the building but up to the fifth floor and into my apartment without being seen.

I suspected it would be a long time before Cholly got over that lapse. He'd been lobbying the management for years to keep the front doors locked so that a tenant would have to use a key to get into the building. Now that he'd seen how ineffective that would be, he'd probably upgrade his recommendation to a keypad that required a code to gain entry to the lobby, something I'd suggested to him when I first moved in. I wished Cholly well. Someone else would be punching in a code for apartment 501. It damned sure wouldn't be me.

I tapped at Cholly's open door and immediately heard the flop-flop-flop of Neva's bedroom slippers. A portable phone growing out of one ear, she hove into view wearing a turquoise and blue-flowered muumuu large enough to serve as a canopy for a garden party. Granted, Neva was a sizable woman built as solidly as a Land Rover, but there was enough fabric in her dress to make two garments. She fluttered the fingers of her free hand in greeting but otherwise never missed a beat holding up her end of the conversation, a series of "You don't mean to tell me," "Get outta here," and "Uh-huhs." She turned to one side before stepping out of sight for a second. Seeing her profile explained the voluminous dress. Neva was pregnant.

An arm every bit as large as Tank's appeared from behind the door, a shoe box crammed with mail in its hand. I took the box and tapped her wrist to get her attention. When she stuck her head around the door, annoyance pleating her brow, I held my hands out in front of my midsection, then pointed at her questioningly.

"Gotta go," she said abruptly, and punched the Off button on her phone. "How'd you know?" she demanded in a stage whisper, pulling me inside.

I grinned, unable to suppress it. "That special glow, how else?"

"Glow, my ass! Tell me something, Ms. Warren. How come they call it morning sickness when what it is is morning, noon and night? That must be how that man they found in your apartment got past me. The only time I haven't been watching out like usual has been when I've been back there urping." She grabbed my arm. "Please don't tell nobody about this. Not yet. I ain't even told Cholly."

"Why in the world not?"

"'Cause it means we'll have to move, get a bigger apartment somewhere, and you know how he is about this place. But we can't stay here. Far as I know, ain't nobody in here dyin'—not that I'd wish that on any of our tenants." She stopped, gave that some thought. "Well, maybe one or two of 'em. What I'm sayin' is ain't nobody moving out that I know of. Folks in this building stay put until the hearse takes them away. Cholly's gonna have a fit. So don't say nothing, okay?"

"Scout's honor." I let a two-second beat go by during which I came to a decision, surprised by how right it felt. "If you can make do with a one-bedroom and den, you can have mine. I don't know how long it'll take me to find another apartment, but I'm bound to have found something before the baby arrives."

Neva's eyes went round with disbelief. "You ain't shittin' me, are you, Ms. Warren?"

"Scout's honor," I said again. "I can't stay there, Neva. Not after . . . you know."

She grabbed me in an embrace reminiscent of a grizzly's. "Oh, thank you, Ms. Warren. Thank you. Tell you what. Don't bother looking for nobody to clean it up for you. I'll do it myself. It'll be so spick and span you'll never know . . ." She stepped back, dismay tattooed all over her face. "Maybe I shouldn't have said that. You ain't gonna change your mind after I get it all scrubbed down, are you?"

"No. You have my word. Now, I've got to run. Thanks for keeping my mail."

Neva was definitely glowing now. "Any time. And I'll start on your apartment tomorrow. Lord! Wait'll I tell Cholly!"

I took my leave, thinking I'd give my left arm to be there when she did. At least something good would come out of my bad luck.

Once in the car, I flipped through the pile of envelopes, moving the utility bills to the top. Most of the rest would wind up in the trash—a couple of offers for credit cards, one of those teasers from a magazine distributor telling me I might have won ten million dollars, personalized return address labels from an organization soliciting donations for something or other, a sample of the latest moisturizing deodorant soap, and a couple of auto insurance feelers. If the companies knew how old my car was, they'd stop wasting postage.

Early lunchtime traffic jammed the streets. It took twice as long as usual to get to Duck's, practically assuring that I wouldn't have enough time at the condo to do another thorough search before I'd have to leave to pick up Tyler for the last time. The death knell to my schedule turned out to be a disagreement between a garbage truck and a Diamond cab a block from my destination. They wallowed kitty-corner in the intersection, clumps of reeking souvenirs from the truck's maw strewn across the asphalt, bringing everything on wheels to a halt in all directions. Not a cop in sight. I was well and truly stuck, two cars and one pickup in front of me, a school bus and a limo behind, the only route around the mess the sidewalk, jammed with gawking pedestrians. I sat and fumed, sweltering and suffocating from the stench of the spilled garbage. Getting out to stretch my legs brought temporary relief and an opportunity to determine whether a certain VW bus had gotten caught by this roadblock along with me. Negative. Good. I'd been suspicious for nothing.

By the time I reached Duck's building, all I had on my mind was using his bathroom, after which I'd make a fast search of his storage room, something I hadn't thought to do that first day. The front gate of the garage was up, the repairman working on the gizmo that raised it just leaving as he waved me in with a distracted smile. The gate at the rear was also up. Obviously this was a minimum-security day. I found Duck's slot occupied and slipped into the spot adjacent to it, hoping the tenant for whom it was reserved wouldn't show up before I could get back. These folks took their parking spaces seriously.

I got out and was locking the car when something or someone tried to help me back into it without benefit of opening the door first. I found myself pinned against the side as a hairy white arm snaked around my neck from behind and practically yanked me off my feet.

"Make one sound, lady, and you're dead."

Oh, sure. As if I could scream or do much of anything. The force of the impact against the door had knocked all the air out of me, and the pressure against my windpipe ensured I wouldn't be able to replace it. A hive of bees set up housekeeping in my head. My vision began to blur, and it felt as if my lungs were about to explode.

"Don't gimme no trouble." The voice was a medium-range tenor, the enunciation tinged with a rural flavor, one I couldn't put my finger on. "Where is he and where's the shit he took?"

Oh, terrific. Somebody else looking for Duck. If and when I found him, I didn't care whether he'd gotten to his father or not, I was going to kill him. I fought against the tidal wave of panic pulling me under and forced myself not to struggle. I had to think, no easy task with a brain deprived of much needed oxygen.

"I'm not playin' with you, lady. Where is he?" The pressure across my neck increased. Obviously, the dummy wasn't bright enough to know that if he didn't let up, he'd never get an answer to his question. Frantically I patted the arm, and after a second it loosened its hold enough for me to gasp for breath. I gulped in air, sounding like a tin whistle. I would never take breathing for granted again.

Slowly my brain began to function. I assumed my assailant had no weapon or he'd have let me know it right off the bat. Also on the plus side: my right hand was pinned between my body and the door, but my left was free. It wasn't the best of all possible worlds since I'm right-handed, but my left was better than nothing.

I weighed my options. I've had to hold my own in a fight any number of times, and under ordinary circumstances I'd have jacked up this son of a bitch the first chance I got. I hesitated now because I simply had no confidence in how my knee would hold up in a scuffle. Any doubts I had that I might have made the wrong decision about going out on disability were now put to rest. This was all the proof I needed. If I couldn't even handle myself in a garage, how in hell would I have done on the street?

"Where's who?" I croaked, stalling for time. "Look, you've grabbed the wrong person."

"Don't bullshit me, lady. Give him up. I know he had the shit on him. He's the only one coulda took it, and I've gotta get it back. Where is he?" He yanked me off my feet again, I assume to show me he meant business.

"I swear to you I don't know," I managed when he set me down again. "And I'm tired of people asking. You aren't the only one looking for him, you know."

"What? Who else is? Who, goddammit!" He grabbed a handful of my shirt to turn me around. It was now or never and the devil take the hindmost, whatever that meant. Teeth gritted against anticipated pain, I pivoted on my right leg, leaned against the car for support and slammed my left knee into his crotch as hard as I could. He gasped, turned an interesting shade of puce, and began to fold in two, one hand cradling the family jewels, the other still clutching my shirtfront. I pressed a thumb into the underside of his wrist. He squealed and let go, toppling backward and rolling toward my rear tire. I grabbed him and dragged him free of the car, then flipped him over and planted my knee in his back.

I laced my fingers through shoulder-length mouse brown hair in sore need of a shampoo and pulled his head back. He squirmed, whimpering, but an earthquake couldn't have shaken me off.

"Now," I said, "let's begin again. What's your name?"

It took a couple of brisk yanks before he took me seriously. "Joe, okay?" he gasped. "Come on, lady, I wouldn't have hurt ya. I just want to find the son of a bitch."

"No kidding. So tell me, Joe, when's the last time you saw the son of a bitch in question?"

"The day he went to your place."

"Excuse me?" The last time Duck was in my apartment was in June. "Exactly when was that?"

"Last Tuesday. He came here first," he said, panting. "I saw him coming out. Then went to your place. Didn't know I was after him. Please, lady, I'm gonna be sick."

"Help yourself," I said, realizing that he had an entirely different son of a bitch in mind. "Why were you after him?"

He hesitated, groaning. "I can't breathe."

I reached back, grabbed the seat of his pants and yanked. "Either you tell me what I want to know or you're gonna be a soprano before the day's out."

"Okay, okay. He stole some weed. I followed him all the way from up home to get it back 'fore he sold it. But I kept missin' him. Almost caught him when he went up to your floor, but he had a key and got the door open before I could get to him. I waited and waited, but he never came out."

"With good reason," I said. "He's dead."

"What?" He stiffened. "J.B.'s dead?"

"HEY! HEY!" Footsteps pounded toward us, the sound of big feet and Tank's basso profundo echoing hollowly off the cinder-block walls. "WHAT THE HELL'S GOIN' ON?"

I swore at the interruption, but didn't dare take my eyes off Joe. The sound of Tank's voice, however, and perhaps the prospect of the proportions of the body capable of issuing that much volume must have given my assailant the shot of adrenaline he needed. He bucked hard, throwing me backward. He scrambled to his feet and took off, running hell for leather toward the rear exit.

"Tank, catch him!" I yelled.

"Yes, ma'am," he shouted, and pounded after the only solid lead I had to the link between J. B. Thomas and Dillon Kennedy. First one, then the other vanished, and I levered myself to my feet, limping after them, swearing to exorcise an assortment of pains yelping for acknowledgment. By the time I reached the rear gate there was no sign of Tank and the pursuee. I brushed myself off and limped out to the street, pacing until I saw sunlight skating across a bald pate—Tank approaching from two blocks down. Alone.

He trotted toward me, winded, abashed. "Damn, that white boy can run! Sorry, Leigh. Don't know where he could have gone. One minute he was in my sights, heading between the parked cars down there. Next minute, poof!"

"There's your answer," I said, pointing at the

beat-up Volkswagen bus burning rubber as it pulled away from the curb a block and a half away. "I should have known."

"What'd he do?" Tank asked. "What were you gonna arrest him for?"

"He jumped me back there. Kept asking where J.B. was."

"Who's J.B.?"

"The dude in my kitchen. His name was James Braden Thomas. That guy was tailing him the day he showed up at my place. Evidently J.B. stole his stash."

"So he jacks you up for it? Damn, wish I'd caught him. Guess we'd better find a phone and call the cops."

"I'll do it later," I said quickly. "There's no hurry since we didn't get the license number or anything. Besides, I'd rather tell Tristan about it since he was the senior man on the original call." I watched Tank, hoping he'd accept that lame excuse. I wouldn't report this for the same reason I hadn't come clean about the keys in J. B. Thomas's possession.

"Well," Tank said, "if you need me to be a witness or something, I'm willing. Now what?"

I glanced at my watch. "If I don't get to a bathroom soon . . . And I've got to pick up Duck's niece from day care. I assume you intend to stick with me now that you're here."

He grinned. "Like an anti-theft device on a Georgio Armani suit."

"Where's Tina?"

"Camped out in the lobby. Had a little trouble

with some old ladies up there until we told them we were waiting for you. I been keeping an eye out on the garage in case you went up from here. But we figured you'd show up sooner or later."

Talk about a no-win situation. "Let's move, then."

Between stopping by the lobby to get Tina and being polite to Duck's groupies, I barely made it to the john in time. When I got a good look at myself in the mirror above the sink, I was horrified. My neck sported a wide, ruddy stripe from Joe's choke hold. Terrific. I turned to examine myself in the full-length mirror on the back of the door and winced. No wonder the groupies had gazed at me as if I'd just crawled through a sewer. Buttons missing where Joe had grabbed me by my shirtfront. A pork chop–shaped oil stain on my right hip, which I'd landed on when he'd bucked me off onto my back-side.

Then there were all the negatives I couldn't see: the stinging bruises on the back of my calves from the car door during Monday's attack, the usual angry pain in my knee, the achy hollow in the pit of my stomach as I stared at a future without the job I loved. I was feeling sorry for myself, knew it and felt entitled. I wallowed in it for a moment or two, cleaning myself up and straightening my clothes, then flushed the self-pity with the toilet tissue I'd used to scrub some of the garage floor grime from my hands. I had things to do.

Returning to the living room, I found myself a

witness to a chapter on Positions in an updated
Kama Sutra. Tina hadn't moved, still rooted to the
steno chair in front of Duck's computer, to which
she'd been drawn as soon as I'd unlocked the front
door. She'd asked if she could turn it on, but I hadn't
responded, too close to exploding to explain it
would be a waste of time. Now Tina sat with her
back to the computer with Tank holding her, chair
and all, at waist level, her shapely chocolate legs
wrapped around his backside, their mouths fused in
the kind of kiss that, even watching, made my pulse
race at drumroll speed. Mesmerized, I stood, unable
to look away, with a sudden fierce longing for the
feel of Duck's weight above me, the scent of his
cologne rising in my consciousness until it was
almost real. Unaware that it had happened until
after it had, I moaned, the sound coming from some
place so deep in my interior that until that moment
I hadn't known it existed.

It broke the spell. Tank spun around, still holding
the chair, blinking as he yanked himself back into
the here and now. Gingerly he lowered his burden
to the floor. Tina, probably as close to embarrassed
as she'd ever be, dropped her gaze as she hurried to
tuck in the tail of the T-shirt that had been rolled up
above her bra.

"It's his fault," she said, a mock pout pursing her
lips. "Wouldn't have happened if he hadn't started
chewing on my ear. He knows that drives me crazy."

Tank shrugged and shuffled his feet, a little boy
caught with his hand in the nooky jar. "Sorry, Leigh.
We didn't mean no disrespect. It just sorta hap—"

I jerked up a hand to silence him, a sudden memory levitating behind my eyes. Duck had been trying to demonstrate the intricacies of his new computer setup. I, on the other hand, had been unaccountably horny and far more interested in getting a rise out of him, literally. To hoist his flag, all I had to do was nibble a certain spot at the base of his neck, to which I'd applied myself with vigor and the kind of dedication that consumes a woman when she's determined to get laid. I'd eventually gotten my wish, but I recalled now that he'd been trying to show me how to cancel the password feature.

"Up," I ordered Tina. "Don't say anything. I'm trying to remember something." I replaced her in front of the computer and turned it on, my fingers hovering above the keyboard. What had he told me? A password to erase the necessity for a password. With the Shift key.

It wouldn't surface. I pounded my forehead, furious with myself. Why couldn't I have listened more closely? Why had I been so out of control that night?

Control! That was it, not Shift. The Control key, and . . . I closed my eyes, my face contorted with concentration. A set of numbers as opposed to letters. Not his birthday, or mine. Something I should have no difficulty remembering. Four numbers. The last four digits of his phone number! 4–9–9–3!

I typed them in slowly, praying he hadn't changed this combination. The Windows desktop, cottony clouds against an azure field, appeared, but without the screen full of icons I was used to seeing. Duck had deleted his word processing, database and all the graphics programs. Even if I had time to install them, I'd left his data diskettes at Vanessa's. I hadn't been able to use them on Rich's computer, a Mac. Duck's diskettes had been formatted on a PC. I met the thought of coming back here with them with little enthusiasm. "Damn it," I muttered.

"Whatcha trying to do?" Tina asked.

"Just curious about what Duck was working on before he left. But he's deleted everything." Assuming that was enough of an explanation to satisfy her, I pressed Start again and saw that Duck's browser was still there. He'd deleted the icon from the desktop, but the program itself still resided on the computer.

"Oh, goodie," Tina said, dropping to her knees beside me to watch as I clicked on the name. "The Web and stuff. Was Duck a Webnik?"

It was a term I hadn't heard before, but it fit Dillon Kennedy to a T. "In spades. You know much about computers?"

"That's her major," Tank volunteered, gazing down on her with significant-otherly pride. "Computer science, I mean. If I didn't know better, I'd think she likes computers better than she likes me."

"Got that right," Tina shot back without looking around. "If you're trying to find out the last places he went, there are two or three different places you can look, know what I mean?"

I knew about the address line but had the feeling she might come up with far more information than

I could. I relinquished the chair. "Here, have fun."

This feisty little woman knew what she was doing. Five minutes later, I also knew what Duck had been doing: checking maps of all kinds, including weather. He'd logged onto nineteen or twenty different services, everything from university-sponsored sites to the U.S. Geological Survey. Several had been bookmarked.

"This is boring," Tina said. "Was this a hobby or something?"

"Not to my knowledge." I knelt beside her, peering at the monitor.

"If Duck was lookin' at that many maps, he musta had a reason," Tank, stout defender, said. "Don't know what it was, but it musta been important."

I couldn't imagine why. "Double-click on a few of the bookmarks," I suggested. Tina complied. The more of them she checked, the more elusive Duck's reasons for pulling them up became.

"What part of D.C. is that?" Tank asked, kneeling on the other side. "I don't recognize anything."

"Must be some other part of the country," I said.

"Wait a minute." Tina held up a hand. "All these sites are in his cache—"

Tank poked her in the side. "What's his money got to do with anything?"

She rolled her eyes toward the ceiling and sighed. "Tankie, baby, just hush. I'll explain later. You've heard of computer illiterate?" she asked me in an aside.

"See if you can print them," I suggested.

She clicked appropriate icons and buttons, and

the printer's On-line light began to blink. "You want them all? God, I'd kill for a setup like this. I'm saving, gonna get me one one of these days."

For the next twenty minutes, Tina clicked and printed, clicked and printed. Fretting about the time, I called Kiddy Garden to check on Tyler and explained I'd been delayed but would pick her up within the hour.

Returning to the computer, I found Tina frowning at the monitor. "Why would he have a link from some art gallery in the middle of all these weather maps?"

The image on the screen resembled something done by Jackson Pollack, tiny blobs of intense colors forming nothing in particular. I moved closer, my nose practically against the screen. "That's not art, it's an image from a satellite. The color's been enhanced to distinguish different types of terrain, residential sections, that kind of thing. See this blue blob in the corner? That's water, a lake or something." It held me, tweaking something in a basement corner of my mind.

Tina turned to stare at me. "Why would your man be looking at stuff from a satellite? Looka here, he wasn't into spyin' and shit, was he? I don't want to have nothin' to do with that."

"Now, you wait a minute, Tina! Duck wasn't no goddamn spy!" Tank's volume approached eardrum-bursting decibels.

"Then what's he looking at stuff like this for? And why am I asking you?" Spinning around in the chair, she glared at me. "You're the one I should be asking. What's going on here? Where'd this Duck go?" Her Scotch-brown eyes scanned my face. "You don't know, do you? You don't know anything, why he went, how long he'll be gone, nothing. And my Tankie's supposed to look after you until he gets back? I don't think so. Come on, Tankie. Let's go." Shoving her chair back, she got up.

"No." He folded his arms, and I was reminded of Mr. Clean again. "And don't be bad-mouthin' Duck, either. He's a good dude, the best."

"What?" Clearly, standing up to her was something Tank rarely if ever did. I wondered if I was seeing a first. "You pickin' her over me?"

"No. A man gives his word, he keeps it. If you can't deal with that, I'll call you a cab."

Tina's eyes were the size of a compact disk. Slowly, tears welled into them, hovering on her lower lid before spilling over and streaming down her cheeks. She hiccuped and ran for the bathroom, slamming the door behind her. Tank appeared unmoved.

"Tank," I said, unwilling to precipitate a crisis in their relationship, "Duck wouldn't want to cause this kind of friction between you and Tina. Quite aside from the fact that I don't need a bodyguard, face it: there's no way you can be with me twenty-four hours a day–or twelve, for that matter. I won't allow it and I can take care of myself."

"Oh, yeah? What about the motherfu—, I mean, the little turkey that stole your case? What about what happened down in the garage?" he demanded.

"What about it? Granted, I'd have never caught

up with that kid, but once I came to my senses, I probably wouldn't have wasted the effort, either. The only thing in the overnight bag was a moth-eaten teddy bear. As for today, I had already sub-dued the subject when you came along. If you hadn't interrupted, he'd have told me what I needed to know about J. B. Thomas and how—"

I stopped, mental gears finally beginning to mesh. This wasn't the first time I'd called him J. B. Thomas as opposed to his full name. I'd seen the name before. Where? I closed my eyes, trying to envision it.

"You all right?" Tank asked.

Very small black letters, hand printed, the letter T with a swirly top rather than a straight line.

"Leigh?"

I stood slowly and turned to stare at the blank wall beside Duck's front door where a small matted watercolor had once hung. About the size of a sheet of typing paper. A landscape, impressionistic, remi-niscent of a Monet, dabs and washes of blue and greens, much like the satellite image on the monitor. It had been one of my favorites of the paintings Duck had used to decorate his stark white walls, something he'd picked up at a craft show a couple of years before. I let my fingers trail across the space the painting had occupied, trying to remember what he'd said about it.

"Come on, Leigh, what's going on?"

Tank was a distraction and this was important. There were other clues linked to the absent land-scape, but they, like the painting, were a blur, without focus and, damn it, right under my nose.

"Tank, go see about Tina," I said quietly, trying to retain my contemplative mode, my focus riveted to the wall. I was afraid if I looked away I'd lose my train of thought.

"Aw, she's all right."

"Go anyway. Talk to her. Take your time."

"Yeah, right, so you can skip out on me." He stood wide-legged, arms still folded, a human bulwark.

"I won't do that. You have my word. And mine is as good as yours, okay?"

I sensed his acquiescence. "Okay, Leigh." He backed away a couple of steps, then strode toward the bathroom. The door, however, was locked.

"Tina, open up." Silence. "TINA RAE JONES," he roared, "OPEN THE GODDAMNED DOOR OR I'LL DO IT FOR YOU!"

I whirled, envisioning another batch of kindling scattered all over the floor of Duck's bathroom. Tank, however, anticipating my alarm, was smiling at me. Looking at his watch, he held up the other hand and began counting off on his fingers. Before the fourth one was raised, there was an audible click.

Relieved that I wouldn't need the services of a carpenter for the second time in a week, I relaxed and began concentrating on Duck's explanation as he'd driven the nail on which to hang his newest acquisition, something about stumbling on a display of paintings and sculpture by regional artists at some arts and crafts fair. Duck had been drawn to the little landscape immediately. He'd bought it and, while waiting for it to be wrapped, had been introduced to the artist.

"A kid," Duck had said. "Eighteen, twenty at the most." They'd spent more than an hour together, discussing the painting, the technique, the boy's talent. Duck had been chagrined that he'd stumbled onto the exhibit too late, since he'd lost out on a whole collection of the boy's—J. B. Thomas's, I was sure now—paintings of the same setting from other viewpoints, a lake. Deep Creek Lake. In western Maryland. Was that the blue blob on the satellite photo?

I went back to the computer and stared at the kaleidoscope of colors, squinting at the cerulean in the lower right corner. I was certain this was a body of water, but it could be anywhere. Scooting over to the printer, I retrieved the weather charts and maps Tina had printed. None of the names on the charts were familiar. I needed an atlas.

I darted to Duck's bookcase, noting that things were awfully quiet in the bathroom. I reined in my imagination, refusing to consider what might be happening in there. I scanned the books left on the bottom shelves, where he had kept books relating to travel, along with maps, arranged alphabetically. There weren't as many as I remembered, only a few of Maryland counties, all of them covering the eastern part of the state. None had the names of the towns on the maps Tina had printed.

Frustrated, I turned to the larger books of road maps. Still no names I recognized except Thurmont, near Camp David. And there, farther west, was Deep Creek Lake. Holding the page beside the monitor, I compared the shape on the map with the blob on the screen. They were too similar to dismiss. I added it to the hash spinning around in my mental blender and hoped that whatever was going on in the bathroom would last long enough for me to think this through.

I now had a connection between Duck and J. B. Thomas. Perhaps J.B. had been telling the truth when he'd told Mrs. Luby he'd been sent to pick up something for Duck. There wasn't that much left here, so I couldn't begin to guess what he was supposed to have retrieved.

My own connection with J. B. Thomas had taken on dimensions and nuances I could have never anticipated. I had genuinely liked his landscape, had envied his talent, his vision. Now that vision had been extinguished, the talent wasted, gone because of my toaster. I'd have to deal with it later. I forced myself back to the point of the exercise.

The rap sheet on J. B. Thomas had listed petty stuff in Frederick County, which was east of Garrett County and Deep Creek Lake, but wasn't that far away, either. Then there was Toulouse, assumed procurer of the heroin and the piggy bank. As far as I could recall, Duck's only knowledge of Toulouse had been as a suspect wanted for questioning about a drive-by shooting. But Toulouse's mother had family who lived in western Maryland. Coincidence? I doubted it. Where the elusive Evie Artis fit into the equation . . .

A ping went off in my head, so faint that I almost missed it. I stood very still, eyes closed. I knew something or had heard something, and if I was quiet enough, focused enough, it would come.

I lost track of time, but it was probably less than half a minute before I felt my chin drop. I ran to the telephone table, yanked the white pages from the shelf and ripped a few pages in the process of getting to the Archers. Toulouse's mother was listed using her initials. I dialed, swearing at Duck's model forties phone and how slow it seemed in comparison to the keypad of today.

Malinda answered after two rings. "Yes?" I'd obviously interrupted something.

I identified myself quickly. "Malinda, you said your mother gave your brother money to go up to Sanctuary to stay with your aunt."

"Yeah, Aunt Vangie. So?"

"What's your aunt's full name?"

"Why?" Suspicion coarsened her voice.

"Please, Malinda, you aren't getting her in trouble. You have my word. What's her name?"

"Evangeline Simmons."

That stopped me for a moment. "Was she ever known as Evie Artis?"

"Oh, that. Artis is her middle name. Mine, too. It was the name of her shop before she changed it to The Quilted Cat." She giggled. "She had all this tissue wrapping paper with Evie Artis like—what do you call it? A watermark. It was no good after she changed the name of her shop, so she used it for toilet paper."

"What kind of shop?" The more I knew, the easier time I'd have finding her.

"It's part gallery, part workshop for hand-made quilts. She teaches now, since her eyes have gone bad."

So very simple. Toulouse must have wrapped twists of pot in his aunt's old wrapping paper. "And her gallery's in Sanctuary with—how'd you put it— artsy-fartsy types?"

"Yeah, a whole bunch of them up there. Painters, sculptors, you name it. Now I've got to go."

I felt my lungs expand with a breath so deep it made me light-headed. "Where exactly is Sanctuary?"

"Uh-uh. No way I got time to give you directions to that place. It would take me ten minutes, and my sister'll be here any minute. Ask anybody at Pete's Station and they'll tell you. I got to go." She did.

I didn't care. I wasn't sure how Duck had figured out his Evie Artis was in Sanctuary, but he'd bookmarked a good dozen maps of western Maryland, and that's where Sanctuary was. There were enough pointers, enough links that it felt right. Sanctuary. Yes!

Things were still suspiciously quiet in the bathroom. As I reached for the phone again, I prayed they'd stay that way just a little longer. I must have caught Eddie in the middle of something. "Grimes," he snapped.

"It's Leigh," I said, sensing his impatience. "Just listen, okay? I'm at Duck's. I'm pretty sure he's gone up to western Maryland. Toulouse Archer has an aunt who lives up there in a little town called Sanctuary. Her name is Evangeline Simmons. Evangeline. She's the Evie Duck had fixated on."

I'd expected anything but the silence on the other end of the line. "Eddie?"

"Good work, honey. Damn good work." There was little enthusiasm in his voice, only an undertone of tension. "I couldn't reach you on your cell phone so left a message for you at Vanessa's. The fit has hit the shan."

"What do you mean?"

"Moon got word of how Duck spent the summer buying pot and making nice with dealers. One thing led to another, and somebody tipped him about the goddamned piggy bank. That did it for him."

"Wait a minute," I interrupted. "I know why he kept the bank. It had belonged to his father; it's in that photo I showed you. He's searching for him, Eddie. He's trying to find his dad."

Eddie snorted. "Gimme a break, Leigh. What are the chances the man is still alive? And why would Duck bother if he's supposed to hate him so much?"

This was touchy. "Yes, but you know Duck. He also hates unsolved puzzles. He won't be satisfied until he knows why his father left, where he's been all this time."

Eddie didn't respond. I waited, pulse pounding in my ears. "Well, one way or the other, you've got to find him, and you've only got the weekend to do it."

"What?"

"Moon put us on notice. Either Duck is in his office first thing Monday morning with the bank and the original contents of those baggies or he's toast. An arrest warrant, APB, Internal Affairs, the works. So if you think he's in western Maryland, you'd better get moving. You've got four days to find him, Leigh. Four days."

10

FOUR DAYS TO TRACK DOWN DUCK, THEN do whatever was necessary to bring him back. I had to get out of here and hit the road.

Correction. First I had to dump Tank and Tina, pick up Tyler and drop her off with Vanessa's next-door neighbor, Betty, finish packing, and then hit the road. Pronto.

I leaned an ear toward the bathroom. Silencio. Too bad. If they were hot and heavy into it, Leigh was about to be the cause of nooky interruptus. "Hey, you guys! Y'all fall in?"

I heard a muffled "Shit!" followed by a great deal of foot shuffling. After a couple of minutes, they emerged, Tank wearing a hard-on of such proportions that it was way the other side of obscene. Tina, far more composed, every hair of her short curly cut in place, eyed me with an air of smug triumph. "So. You're in for the night, right?"

My mind was engaged with the list of tasks I had to accomplish before leaving town, which was why it took a second for me to get what she meant. Tina thought I'd be staying the night at Duck's.

Tank cleared his throat, hands clasped in front of his crotch. "You got enough here to eat? You want us to stop by the pizza place and have them deliver something?" Tank's gonads appeared to have caused temporary amnesia. He'd forgotten he'd sworn to go with me to pick up Tyler. Terrific. He could leave feeling he'd fulfilled his obligation for the day. By the time he remembered, I'd be long gone.

"I'll be fine," I assured him. "There's stuff in the freezer. I think I might fill the tub and just relax in it awhile. You guys can run along."

Tank crabwalked toward the door and opened it. "I'll be here first thing in the morning to go with you to the clinic, okay? See ya tomorrow."

"Yeah. See ya." Tina's sidewise glance at me as she followed him out made it clear she intended to put an end to this foolishness by any means necessary. I felt sorry for Tank, caught between his woman and his word.

I slipped out onto the balcony and watched them head for the bus stop, Tina's arm around Tank's waist, her left hand making an occasional foray south to cup his left bun. It must have been too much for him. He waved down the first cab he saw.

I hurried back in, selected the more detailed of the computer printouts, grabbed the atlas, and was almost out of the door when something occurred to me. Duck's clunker of a car drank oil like a camel filling up for a trek across the Sahara. He kept a case of it in his trunk, but the only place he would top off his crankcase would be at a service station so he could dispose of the can properly. He rarely drove more than a hundred miles without stopping to check. If he filled up on gas as well . . . I went back in, picked up the phone and caught bride-to-be Martha Makrow a minute before she was about to duck out for a smoke break.

"Who is it, what do you want and make it fast." I'd seen Marty's nicotine fits. They were genuine.

"Leigh Warren," I said, talking fast. "I need a favor, Marty. I—"

"Where the hell is Duck?" Her voice boomed over the phone. I winced. Everybody had to have heard her. "Do you know what that bastard did? Walked out on Cody and the wedding and—"

"Marty, shut up and listen. I need your help on something. Can I trust you?"

I could practically hear her fuse sizzling. "What kinda question is that?"

"Duck's in trouble, Marty, and I've got to find him. Between us and no further?" I asked, knowing I could count on her to be honest with me.

"Depends. Talk is Duck's gone sour on us, turned rogue." My throat tightened. "I want nothing to do with crooked cops, Leigh. We've got enough trouble what with budget cuts and guys quitting and bad press every damned time somebody hiccups."

I wasn't surprised. The job was Marty's life. She might be marrying Cody Jensen next month, but she'd been married to the Department for almost twenty years.

"Marty, he's got a personal problem, nothing to do with the Department, I give you my word. And I've got to find him as soon as possible. I have a general idea in what direction he headed, but you could narrow it down for me and save me a lot of wasted time."

She was quiet for so long my stomach knotted. Finally, finally: "How can I help?"

I told her what I needed.

"Call me back," she said, and hung up abruptly.

I took one last look around Duck's apartment, empty of all the personal touches that had made it uniquely his. The memories, however, were still there, haunting niches and corners. I'd have to be satisfied with the memories of the love and companionship I'd shared with him here. His frequent cooking marathons when he'd play chef, whipping up dishes I couldn't even begin to emulate. The woodsy aroma of his cologne imbedded in his sheets. The comforting heat of his body as we slept like spoons, butt to belly after lovemaking. The room blurred behind a sheen of tears. No, I could never live here without him and wasn't sure I'd ever come back.

I wish now I'd known how close to the truth that would be.

The clock ticking in my head resonated like the tolling of Big Ben. I deposited Tyler with Betty, hurried across to Vanessa's, packed like a madwoman and, succumbing to a streak of incurable optimism, took only enough to last me four days with an extra pair of panties for good measure. I was on my way out of the door when the phone rang the first time. Tristan.

"Just wanted you to know Crosley called and asked me to tell you he owes you an apology. You're off the hook."

I dropped my suitcase. "How come?"

"Your boy was already dead when the juice—I mean, the current went through him."

"What?" Hooking an ankle around a nearby chair, I pulled it to me and sat down. "What killed him, then?"

"A dicey heart, probably congenital, stressed to the max by pot laced with a derivative of PCP. We'll know more when all the tests come back."

"You mean that stupid s.o.b. dipped his stash in PCP? He could have killed—" I aborted the thought. He had. And I hadn't.

"I doubt he did it himself," Tristan was saying. "Just unlucky enough to buy it. It's not in general circulation; there's just enough around to keep emergency rooms busy on odd weekends. Whoever's concocting this combination hasn't shared it with dealers in surrounding areas, just a few in D.C we haven't been able to pin down. Anyway, it sent the fool's heart into overdrive and killed him. Trash the toaster and forget him. He had no business in there anyway. Just thought you'd like to know."

"Thanks," I said as I tried to digest my reprieve from a lifetime of thinking of myself as a murderer by toaster. I doubt Tristan heard me. He was gone. And not for a second had I considered telling him about the keys and everything else I'd figured out. I didn't particularly like the person I was becoming.

I disconnected, and immediately the phone rang again. Vanessa. The good news: Mrs. Kennedy was much improved and was being moved to intermediate care. But that wasn't what she wanted. "I checked the answering machine a little while ago. Eddie Grimes left a message for you."

"I know. Thanks. I've already talked to him."

"Leigh, what did he mean about Dillon returning the bank by Monday 'or else'? Why should he care?"

This was awkward. I purposely hadn't gone into detail about the contents of the bank. "It was evidence, that's why. Duck should have turned it in and he didn't."

"That accident you mentioned before, it wasn't the one where they found all that cocaine, was it?"

"Heroin," I corrected her. I was surprised she remembered until I recalled that the picture had been in the *Post*, with Duck and Eddie conferring at the rear of the Explorer. Vanessa and her mother would have kept the article.

"Leigh, was there heroin in that bank?" There was a quaver in her voice.

It was not a question I'd anticipated. "No, marijuana. Why do you ask?"

She inhaled so loudly and for so long, I wondered when her lungs would give out. "Then we've lost him," she said softly. "There's nothing you can do, Leigh. If Daddy had anywhere near a reasonable explanation for leaving us, he might have had a chance with Dillon. But if he's hooked again—"

"He who? Duck?"

"No, no! Daddy! He got hooked on painkillers after Vietnam, and one thing led to another. He kicked it, but we lived in terror that . . . Anyhow, we always suspected that's why he left. That's why Dillon's felt so strongly about the drug trade. If Daddy's still got a habit or, God forbid, dealing and Dillon finds him . . ." Her voice thickened and she began to cry. "Lord, this will kill Mama. You might as well not waste your time, Leigh. Go on home." She hung up.

I sat for a moment, the phone in my hand. Go home? I had no home. All I had was an overwhelming desire to recapture the safe and sane world I'd lost because of Duck's insane desire for revenge. Go home? Not on Duck's life. Or mine.

I'd been on the road a couple of hours before it finally hit me: something up there was trying to tell me that if my destination was half an hour from D.C., I should either fly, take a train, bus, cab or stay home because if I drove, sure as shooting something would go wrong. Coming back from Sunrise, a flat and a dead air conditioner in stifling Indian summer heat. This time I'd started out under a bright, clear sky. Temperature upper seventies, humidity not worth mentioning, a minor miracle in a city that could match New Orleans for steamy weather.

Fifteen minutes beyond Frederick, clouds the color of charcoal sidled up from the west, blanketing the mountains in a sepulchral shroud, and suddenly it was monsoon season. A solid wall of water. Visibility the distance between my nose and the windshield and not one inch beyond. It was like driving by braille. The radio spat and crackled, giving no clue as to where I was. I inched along, cursing my luck, the rain, Dillon Kennedy, and all the things that had prevented me from leaving earlier so I might have missed this storm.

Some idiot with suicide in mind ripped past me, sending a North Shore wave cascading across my windshield and slamming me back into the moment. I gripped the steering wheel even harder, wondering how in hell I'd know when I'd reached my exit. And would I be able to see a gas station sign in this downpour?

I'd gotten through to Marty just before I reached New Market. "You were right," she said, speaking softly. "I used the first of August as a starting point and got a couple of hits. He stopped at two stations where he used his credit card. You got something to write with?"

I'd been tempted to pass on Duck's first stop in Frederick, because the second was so much farther west, but if Duck, being one of the few males of my acquaintance who would do it, had asked for directions along with topping off his oil, I might know precisely where'd he'd gone. Fat chance. The attendant had stared blankly at the photo of Duck with no recognition. Considering the location of the second stop, however, outside a town it had taken me five minutes and a magnifying glass to find on the map, there was every possibility he'd be remembered. All I had to do was find it in this deluge.

It was the worst storm I'd ever driven through, bar none. Pulling off on a shoulder of the remote two-lane road until the rain let up wasn't an option. In the first place, I couldn't see the shoulder and in the second, emergency blinkers or no, I might be mistaken for a car driving with them on and get hit from behind. Cursing Duck and praying over every single yard splashing under my tires, I crept along what I hoped was Claybrake Road, straining for a sign, any sign. A motel. A diner. Anything. So when the strange blue and white glow on the right filtered through the wall of water, I was certain my eyes were playing tricks on me. Slowly, I inched toward it, praying I wouldn't misjudge, make the turn too soon, and wind up in a ditch. Barely missing a sandwich board near the door, I parked, cut the engine and sat there until I stopped shaking. I grabbed my bag, dug an umbrella from under the passenger seat, got out, and ran for the entrance. If the place had been closed, I'd have had hysterics on the spot. Before I reached it, however, the door was opened for me.

"Whoo-ee, lady, you must have to be somewhere really bad to be drivin' on a day like this!" A kid, not yet twenty, I was sure, a thatch of unruly straw-colored hair surrounding a blue-eyed, liberally freckled face. "I hate to tell ya, but it's self-service out there. And if you're having car trouble, the mechanic's gone home."

With a desert-dry mouth, I shook my head and stumbled to the soft drink machine. It took two big gulps of canned iced tea before I could speak. "Thanks, but my car's okay. And I don't need gas, just information." I extended Duck's photo. "This man stopped here on August fifteenth. He got a fill-up and used his credit card."

"Yes, ma'am. Checked his oil, too. You're police, aren't ya? Seemed like a nice guy. What'd he do?"

"Nothing," I said, seeing no reason to correct his error. "His mother's in the hospital and I've been trying to find him to let him know. He's into arts and crafts and antiques and was coming up here to—"

"Oh, yeah—I mean, yes, ma'am. He asked Rangley—he's our mechanic—for directions to some place neither one of us had never heard of. Don't remember the name right off, and Rangley won't be back till tomorrow. Drove down to Washington and northern Virginia to get lottery tickets."

"Was it Sanctuary?" I prompted, fingers crossed behind my back.

"No, ma'am, somebody's name. He was looking for a store."

"Evie Artis's?"

His freckles fairly glowed. "Yes, ma'am, that's it. We even checked the phone book but didn't find it. Sorry."

Terrific. Risking another shot in the dark, I asked, "Is there a Pete's Station anywhere nearby?"

He regarded me with a puzzled frown. "Pete's? You mean Peace Station? I wouldn't call it nearby. It's gotta be ten, twelve miles from here." He gave me directions, fairly straightforward ones, all things considered, and peered through the front window after wiping a clear spot in the condensate. "Looks like it's let up some."

There was appreciable difference between his definition of "some" and mine, but it didn't matter.

I had to keep going. I borrowed the key to the ladies', which was fairly clean and had toilet tissue in the stall, but no soap in the dispenser. I could use the soap sample I'd received in the mail. It was still in my bag. New and improved, with aloe vera and moisturizer. Whoopee. I wasn't sure what effect the aloe vera would have, but at bottom I'd be clean and softened.

I ripped open the box, noticing for the first time that it had been sealed with Scotch tape, as if it had been opened previously. Turning it over, I looked at the label. The original one had been covered by a second on which my name and address had been printed by hand, no capitals, all lower case. And stamps covered the bulk rate imprint. What the hell?

Using the mini-scissors on my Swiss army knife, I slit the tape and opened the box. The only thing visible was wax paper. Wax paper? I poked it. It yielded. Whatever this was, it wasn't solid like a bar of soap.

I peered at it with suspicion, my antenna for trouble quivering, testing the air. Briefly, I toyed with the possibility that it might be some sort of explosive device, but that seemed remote. I'm sure I had enemies—what cop didn't—but one who wanted to kill me? I doubted it. Mess me up, sure, but that's about all. Since I'd once received a beautifully wrapped package in the mail that had contained a dog (I assume) turd, I intended to be triply cautious with this thing. I sniffed, but the only aroma I detected was the faint clean smell of soap.

Retracting the tweezer from the other end of the Swiss Army knife, I grabbed the nearest corner of the paper and tugged gingerly. Still no suspicious odor, at least nothing remotely doggy. I maneuvered it carefully onto the metal shelf above the sink. Whoever had wrapped it was an expert; the corners were neat, squared, secured with barely visible tape. I snipped it, lifted the folded ends and saw yet another layer, tissue paper this time. I pulled the outermost wrapper free with the tweezer and spread it flat, being careful not to touch it. This had to be a dynamite medium for fingerprints, and I didn't want to destroy or smudge any that might be there. I was even more diligent with the inner layer. I cut the tape, opened one end.

On the bottom between the two layers of paper, a loose scrap protruded. I wiggled it out. The scrap, a couple of inches square, was more tissue paper with a watermark so faint it was barely detectable, the letters a florid script. Evie Artis Quilt Shop. A note had been printed on the reverse side, the squared-off letters as familiar as my own. FOR E. GRIMES. LAB SPECIMEN.

I stood there, fuming, and taking an oath that whether Duck had killed his father already was immaterial. Because I was going to kill him with my bare hands with malice aforethought, go to jail for it and revel in each and every day I spent behind bars remembering the feel of my hands around his throat as he took his last breath. The sleazy son of a bitch had sent the missing marijuana to me.

11

I TRIED TO DECIPHER THE SMEARED POST-
mark, but at some point it must have gotten wet.
The only letters I could make out were T-A-T-I-O,
the rest of the name and the zip code a blur. It had to
be Peace Station. Had to be. It fell right in line with
everything else pointing to this end of the state.

Take to E. Grimes, huh? I pocketed the note,
rewrapped the package, and with a stray rubber
band from the flotsam in my purse closed the box
and zipped it into my cellular phone case. I unbuck-
led my belt and fed it through the loop on the back
of the case. A box of pot might not be high on the
list of fashionable accessories, but it was the most
practical way to prevent its being crushed. The last
thing I needed was pot strewn all over the bottom of
my purse.

I dialed Eddie's home number on my phone,
wondering what effect the weather would have on
reception. When he picked up with a terse
"Grimes," I had my answer. Static crackled in my
ear like Rice Krispies in freshly poured milk.

"Eddie, it's Leigh. Can you hear me?"

"Barely. What's up?"

"I've got some of the stuff. Not the bank, just what was in it. And not the contents of the baggies; this box is too small for all that. Evidently it came while I was in Sunrise, and the postmark's blurred so I can't tell when—"

"Postmark? You mean he mailed it? He put that shit in the U.S. mail?" Despite the static, his outrage was unmistakable, his voice rising in volume and pitch.

I didn't have time for outrage. "Don't get your knickers in a knot, Eddie, because the only way I'll be able to get it to you in time will be to send it back the same way, unless I can find a Federal Express or UPS place first."

"Jesus." He groaned, probably envisioning himself on the business end of an investigation by the postal inspector. "Okay. Once it's in the warehouse, if anybody asks, I can always say the piggy bank got broken or something."

"Whatever. The question is, should I send it to you at the station or to your home address?"

I'd never heard anyone splutter before. Eddie spluttered, "Not here, for God's sake! No way I'm gonna put my family at risk. Use the post office. Maybe our luck will hold. Send it Priority Mail to the station. It'll be less noticeable than something coming by UPS. Okay, now what?"

"That has to be my concern, not yours," I said. He was already far enough out on a limb. "The less you know the better. I've got to go. I'll be in touch."

I hit the End button, examined my image in the mirror and decided that unless a drug-sniffing dog wandered by, I'd pass as your average law-abiding citizen. But I felt dirty, soiled. There wasn't that much difference between Duck and me. We were both in defiance of the law. He'd withheld evidence and might be a murderer by now. I'd withheld information from Moon and Tristan. I was also now an accessory since I had the evidence Duck had held back, a controlled substance for which I could be arrested at the drop of a hat. I was no better than the thugs I'd been putting behind bars for the last seven years. Because of Duck. The thought made me so angry at him that I went back into the stall, slammed the door closed, and just sat until the red haze faded from behind my eyes. Another ten minutes wasted. Time to get moving.

Outside, the rain had lessened a bit, but that wasn't saying much. It was still a steady, unrelenting downpour, beating against my umbrella with such force that the fabric began to pull away from a couple of ribs. By the time I'd returned the rest room key, had the towhead repeat the directions to Peace Station and had hot-footed it back to the car, the umbrella had disintegrated. But at least visibility was better. Hey, I actually could see past the hood of my car.

It seemed to take a couple of weeks, but I made the trip to Peace Station at twenty miles an hour, Mach speed compared to the previous leg from Frederick. And had it not been for a four-way stop sign, I'd have probably gone straight through the place without realizing I'd arrived. No wonder it hadn't been on any of the maps I'd pored over. Peace Station amounted to one small, white clapboard building with a steeple, four stores, all closed and dark, one shotgun house, its front yard decorated with the rusting corpses of several pickups, a couple of trailers and Port-a-Potties. Beyond it was what appeared to be a big, empty parking lot, probably a Kiss and Ride for commuters.

I pulled into the broad turnaround in front of the steepled building, the only one with an exterior light burning and a car in its parking area. Resigned to getting soaked, I got out and ran to the double doors, squinting to read the small sign taped to the glass. POST OFFICE HOURS M-F, 9 TO 5, SAT 9–12. NOTARY PUBLIC M-F, 9 TO NOON. It was not quite five, so chances were, someone was still around.

Inside, a directory advertised that the building also housed a doctor, a dentist and a lawyer, but there were no signs of life behind the frosted glass doors opening off the dimly lit hallway. Evidently all the professionals had closed up shop and gone home.

The building had a musty smell, like an old house where the windows were never opened. Foot-worn floorboards sloped gently from left to right, making me feel as if I was walking the deck of a listing ship.

As I approached the last door on the right, it opened. A young woman with skin the color of pecans and an intricately braided hairdo backed out, keys in her hand to lock the door. She saw me, and immediately her face froze in an expression I recognized as that of The Not at All Happy to See You Public Servant. "We're closed, miss. Open again nine tomorrow morning." She stuck the key in the top lock, to drive home her point, I suppose.

I didn't appreciate her attitude, but decided to play it cool. I wasn't ready to send off the pot anyway. The soap box couldn't take another trip through the mail. "Thanks, but all I really need is directions to Sanctuary."

She looked at me as if I'd just passed an idiocy exam. "You goin' up there in this weather? I'd wait, if I was you. As bad as it is out there, you'd miss the turnoff. It's hard enough to see in broad daylight. Besides, nobody's sellin' during the week this time of year. Everybody's hustling to get ready for Colorfest. Come back this weekend. Some of the shops will be open then."

This was as good a time as any to test the waters. "Well, I hadn't really planned to do any shopping. I'm going to see Miss Evangeline Simmons."

Her lips widened in a smile, and her posture lost its ramrod stiffness. "You know Miss Vangie? That's different. Tell you what. I'll lead you up to the turnoff. Watch me carefully on Redbank Road, though. The low places are bound to be flooded." She dug out another set of keys from her basket-weave purse. "When we reach the Sanctuary sign," she said, walking to the front doors, "I'll give you my flashers. Turn left there. Stay on that road to the three-way fork—that's easy to miss, too, believe it or not—and take the one at ten o'clock."

"Ten o'clock?" I looked at my watch. "It's that far away?"

Chuckling, she shook her head. "The three forks are at one, eight and ten on a clock. You take the ten. From there it's a straight shot into Sanctuary.

Miss Vangie's in the big house with the black cat sign above the door. Don't you have an umbrella?" she asked, unfurling her own.

"The rain tore it up. I'll manage. It occurs to me, you might be able to help me with something else." I unsnapped the cover of my cell phone case and tried to pry the soap box from its confines. It wasn't as easy as I'd expected, a tight fit. "I imagine you know practically everyone in this vicinity," I said, wedging a finger down along one side.

Her laugh was rich and throaty, echoing against the walls. "It would be kinda hard not to. There's no house-to-house delivery up here. Not enough people to make it worth it. Either you come here for your mail or you don't get it. I'm Lorna Pike, by the way."

"Leigh Warren," I said.

"Leigh Warren," she said, the trace of a puzzled frown appearing as she shook my hand. "That sounds familiar. Should I know you?"

"No," I said, finally freeing the box. "But I received this a while ago. It's postmarked Peace Station. I was wondering if you can tell me who sent it."

The transformation was instantaneous, the relaxed smile and easy manner gone. Lids flickering, she backed away and shook her head. "You must be mistaken. Wasn't mailed from here. And I just remembered, I've got an errand to run." She was babbling, her hands shaking as she struggled to open the umbrella, even though we were still inside. "Two errands, actually, so I won't be able to lead you up. If I were you, I'd come back when the weather's better. Miss Vangie's probably at her son's house anyway. Sorry, I have to go." And she did, in such a hurry to escape that she never succeeded in opening her umbrella. Not that it mattered. Considering how fast she ran to her bright red Escort, I doubted she was hit by more than four or five drops of rain.

Baffled by her reaction, I crammed the box into the case again and stepped outside to watch her, holding my purse above my head. A second later, she got out again and ran back, her gaze straight ahead as if I didn't exist. She locked the door, returned to her car at Olympic track speed, gunned the engine and sped off, water and mud spraying from her tires.

Still puzzled, I trotted back to my car, got in and sat, wondering why my question had caused such an extreme reaction. After seven years in uniform meeting people at their worst, I knew fear when I saw it. Lorna Pike was afraid. Why? Had she known what the box contained and that sending it through the mail was a federal offense? Or was she afraid of the person who'd sent it? That didn't make sense. Why should anyone be afraid of Duck?

The rain offered no answers, so I started the engine, drifted to the four-way stop sign to check for a street name and was rewarded with two boards nailed to a leaning pole. The lower one said Redbank Road with an arrow pointing left. I squinted at the compass mounted on my dashboard. Left would be west. Yes. The radar in my head had begun to ping. He was up here somewhere, I could sense it. I was closing in on him. I just hoped I wasn't too late.

Lorna Pike was right; several low spots on Redbank Road were underwater where creeks had risen high enough to take shortcuts across the tarmac. I prayed my way through them, grateful my car was as heavy as it was. I could call for help on the cell phone if I wound up stranded, but it would be a damned scary wait before it arrived. Daylight had been pushed beyond the mountains, rendering them invisible, the rain drowning out any trace of the early evening sky. The trees grew thick and close on both shoulders, their branches arching across the road, hanging low, weighed down by the water. The effect was claustrophobic, like driving through a tunnel. God, it was so dark, an inky, wet void beyond the windshield, my only navigational aid the cones of faint yellow from my headlights. If there were homes or farms out there somewhere, they were well hidden.

I was also uneasy because Lorna Pike hadn't made any reference to distances. How far was it to the three-tined fork? And once I'd turned onto the "ten o'clock road," how far to Sanctuary? I understood now why she'd urged me to wait for better weather. Intersections—unmarked, no stop signs, no lights—were difficult to see. They might have been private driveways, for all I knew. How anyone found their way around once the sun went down was a mystery.

When I finally got there, the only reason I knew

I'd arrived at the fork was because of a white pickup emerging from the eight o'clock road. He tapped his horn as I angled left and I tapped back, acknowledging our kinship, two idiots out on a night fit only for creatures with webbed feet. I settled down, my raw nerves calming a little. At least I was on the right road and the final leg of this nightmare trip.

I couldn't remember seeing any indication of the speed limit since I'd left the service station, so taking no chances, I kept close watch on the speedometer, staying at twenty-five on the nose. Approaching an unmarked curve at which even twenty would be a ticket to the Great Beyond in this weather, I slowed, which was the only reason why I spotted the ghostly pale glow off to my right. It morphed into what remained of a blouse worn by a girl darting from the trees, arms flailing above her head as she signaled for me to stop. Under ordinary circumstances, it would never occur to me to pick up a hitchhiker, but there was no way I could drive past a woman alone out here on this desolate road, especially one whose top hung in tatters, exposing her bra and midsection.

I finessed the brakes to avoid fishtailing, halting a few yards from where I'd seen her. I unlocked the passenger door before turning to look back through the rear window. She rounded the curve at a run and picked her way along the shoulder. Snatching the door open, she tossed a small denim bag onto the front seat and scrambled in after it. She was so waterlogged, she squished as she sat down.

"Lordy!" she exclaimed, out of breath. "I

thought nobody would ever come by. Ma'am, I can't thank you enough for stoppin'."

"What happened? Car trouble?" I asked, and flipped on the overhead light to get a good look at her.

She gasped, glanced back over her shoulder, then scrunched low in the seat. "Can we go, please?"

I doused the light, her image etched in my mind. Caucasian, twenty to thirty years old, short blond hair plastered to her head, light eyes perhaps gray or blue. Five-five or -six but she was seriously underweight, the arms protruding from the torn sleeves resembling pale twigs. A bruise had begun to blossom along one side of her face, and blood streamed from a dark blotch above her left ear. "Hey, you're hurt."

She shook her head tightly and droplets flew around her, reminding me of a dog ridding itself of bath water. "I'm fine, honest. Please, miss, let's go."

"Seat belt," I said, and waited until hers was engaged. Her breath was rapid and ragged, whistling as she exhaled. Fear enveloped her. I could smell it.

She looked behind us again, then pleadingly at me. "My seat belt's on."

I eased around the curve, gaining speed slowly, adding two and two and not liking the total I was getting. I'd feel like a jackass if she was running from the law. Once again I'd be an accomplice. "Who's after you?" I asked, trying to sound supportive and nonjudgmental.

"No one. I—I fell, that's all." She tried to close

the rip in her blouse. "Sorry I'm such a mess, dirtying up your car and all."

"No problem." I glanced at her jeans and hoped the dark splotch along her left thigh was mud and not blood. That's when I noticed that her feet were bare. "Look, you need help, medical assistance. I'm on my way to Sanctuary, but I don't know the area. Is there a hospital—"

"No!" She pulled in several deep breaths, calming herself. "I'm fine, honest. If you can just—" Suddenly her words became a shriek, then a full-throated scream, her eyes fixed on something ahead.

I followed her gaze in time to see the broad-shouldered, knife-wielding figure step directly and purposefully into the path of the car, as if daring me to hit him. I practically stood on the brakes, cursing as my wheels danced across water standing on the road. The back end slewed right, then left. I knew how to deal with a skid; it had been drummed into us at the academy. But the man in the road changed the scenario, tossed that training out the window. He was too close. Even as slowly as I'd been driving, it was slam on the brakes or turn him into road kill.

The car, its tires fighting for purchase, lost the battle. The front angled right, and nothing I did seemed to stop it. It breached the shoulder and then hurtled down an incline that hadn't been visible before and still wasn't, down, down, down. The trees appeared to be marching toward me, and for one insane moment I was reminded of the brooms barreling down the steps toward Mickey Mouse in his sorcerer's apprentice costume. But these weren't brooms, they were trees. Thick-trunked, old-as-Mother Earth trees directly ahead. There was no way to avoid them, no way. We didn't.

12

SOMEWHERE VOICES SHOUTED, SCREAMED, swore. Hands yanked at me and I fought back, furious at being manhandled. Peace and quiet descended, then the voices began again, pummeling me with questions when all I wanted, needed was to be left alone.

My head throbbed, the pain humming tunelessly, endlessly. I shouted at it to go away. It must have heard me; things quieted to such a hushed whisper that gradually the din was less and less audible, worrisome since I was also becoming less and less aware of not just the pain and the manhandling and the murmuring but of everything. Fatigue began to sap what strength and spirit I had left, and I decided that stewing about it was pointless, that an absence of awareness was to be expected when you're dead. I relaxed, let go, and waited for the light at the end of the tunnel and the warm, welcoming Presence.

So what happens? The humming began again, so softly at first that it seemed an inaudible vibration, like a dog whistle. I'm expecting an angel chorus, and I get a dog whistle. Gradually, though, there was no doubt about it. Something or somebody was humming. No, more like buzzing. And I could hear it clearly. One thing for sure, the dead can't hear. I was still alive—a pleasant surprise, all things considered.

I tried opening my eyes. My lashes, what there are of them, reacted as if they were glued together. After a couple of attempts they separated enough for me to think that perhaps I'd been presumptuous. My face felt very warm, and a blaze of orange seared my vision, blinding me. Either I was dead, after all, which I'd already ruled out, or there was fire close by.

My parents died in a Baltimore tenement fire when I was five. I've had this thing about fire ever since, a gut-deep, mindless fear. And if I didn't get moving this very minute, I would very shortly be charcoal.

Adrenaline jolted through me. All the appropriate mental gears sent the appropriate impulses to the appropriate muscles and I moved as if launched, on my feet instantly and just as instantly flat on my face, the world spinning around me.

"Lord, miss, you can't go jumpin' around like that." Someone tugged at my arm. "Did you hurt yourself?"

I turned over on my back and gazed up into a dark chocolate face that had seen the passing of innumerable decades. Pale brown eyes with the halo of age around them looked down at me with concern. I levered myself to a sitting position, squinting as a lane of bright sunlight lashed across my face. Slowly my head cleared, my surroundings stopped the jerky spin, and I focused on the elderly man bending over me.

A threadbare robe covered faded striped pajamas. He was tall, thin, probably flirting with eighty. Thick white hair grew in tufts above his ears, and a pale five o'clock shadow stippled the right side of his face. The left was clean-shaven; he held a cordless razor in one hand, explaining the sound I'd heard.

Seeing my gaze, he flipped a switch, cut it off and dropped it into a pocket. "Sorry if this woke you up. You was sleepin' so sound, I figured it wouldn't bother you. You feelin' better?"

Than what? I wondered. I took inventory. Headache with more sensitivity on the back right, a singing elbow, pinging knee, a general all-over soreness, as if I'd spent the night in a clothes dryer set on Cotton.

"What happened to me?" I inquired. "Where am I?"

"This is my place. You had yourself an accident a little piece down the road. Me and my boy, Harold, and his wife, we brought you here. My name's Josiah Dawes, Miss Warren."

"Pleased to meet you. Where's 'here'?" I asked, and settled with my back against the bed, unwilling to trust my legs quite yet.

"Reedy's Corner. Doc Williams looked you over. Said you probably have a concussion, but he couldn't say how bad, 'cause there was no way to tell how long you were out."

"Out?"

"Unconscious. Took me 'bout fifteen minutes or so to get my clothes on and rain gear and the like.

Arthritis slows me up, 'specially when it rains. By the time I got to you, you were comin' around, but you conked out again a few minutes later. Doc says he'd be happy to check you over again but you should see your own doctor, let him run some tests. Elsewise, all he found was bumps and bruises, and you've aplenty of those. I woke you up ever' couple of hours like Doc told me, and you seemed all right. You didn't upchuck or anything, and that's a good sign."

He pulled a spindle-backed chair from a corner, sat down and grinned, elbows on his knees. "Even cussed me out a time or two. Tsk, tsk, such language. Where were you going anyway?"

I opened my mouth to respond, then realized I had no answer for him. For me either. "I–I don't know. I can't remember."

"Doc said you might be fuzzy-minded for a spell. You musta took quite a knock. Opened up a place on the back of your head, but he said it wasn't even big enough to need stitches."

I probed the area, felt a knot the size of a pecan under my fingertips, and winced. "An accident," I said, trying to piece the puzzle together. The edges seemed too ragged. Nothing seemed to fit.

"In your car. Ran off the road just past that curve yonder. Folks do it all the time, 'specially when it's raining, and it was raining to beat Jesus last night."

An image flickered. Driving in a downpour, wipers going swish-swish. "Where is it? My car?" I remembered what it looked like well enough. Insipid beige. Parking lot dings in all four doors.

Compass on the dashboard. Service revolver in the . . . No. Not anymore.

"Your car's up at Chunky's. It was his truck came to pull you back onto the road. I don't drive no more, but my boy will take you there. But you oughta eat something first. Long as you slept, you're bound to be hungry."

"What day is it?" I looked at my wrist, which was watch-less. A moment of alarm dissipated when I spotted it on a bedside table, but I was still disoriented, anchorless without a day of the week as a frame of reference to hang things on.

"Friday. It's goin' on two o'clock. We brung you up here, musta been close to seven last night."

I'd slept almost eighteen hours! Trying to pull things into focus, I glanced down. I too was in pajamas, sleeves and pants legs rolled up as if they were far too long. "What happened to my clothes?"

"Right there." He pointed at my jeans and shirt, neatly folded atop an ageless cherry chifforobe, along with my tote bag cum purse. "They were a right mess, soppin' wet, blood stains here and there. My boy's wife, Mary, peeled them off you, 'case you're wondering. She took 'em home and washed them."

"That was very generous of her," I said, cringing at the thought of a stranger handling my Bali briefs. "Give me a few minutes and I'll be up and dressed and out of your hair. I can't thank you enough for taking me in."

"Just doin' my Christian duty. Remember, Doc says you should take it easy until you see your doctor. I hate to put you out, but we're leaving soon. Harold and me'll be going to the airport to pick up my girl and her husband, and then we're all leaving for a family reunion over to Morgantown. I called around to find you someplace to stay until your car is fixed. This is a bad time of year. Practically all the rooms are taken by 'prentices and crafts folks getting ready for Colorfest. Finally found a vacancy over Sanctuary way with Clara Condon."

I squinted, thinking. Was that where I'd been heading? It meant something, but I wasn't sure what.

Mr. Dawes placed his hands just above his knees, and levered himself to his feet. "My boy will take you over after you've had a little something-to-eat. My old woman, rest in peace, would haunt me to my grave if I let you go without a little something-to-eat. Your stomach feel all right?"

A growl rumbled through my middle. "What it feels is empty. I'll be down shortly."

It took me as long to get decent and dressed as it had Mr. Dawes the night before. I was one big ache; moving at all seemed more effort than it was worth. The only comfort I had was the mountains which kept drawing me to the window.

I hadn't been in the mountains of western Maryland before and now regretted it. From the time Nunna had rescued me from distant cousins ill-prepared to take on the care and feeding of another child in addition to the five they already had, I'd lived with her in the shadow of North Carolina mountains. I'd watched innumerable dawns sneak above their peaks from my bedroom window, stippling the treetops with gold and painting a vivid streak across the length of our little town, Sunrise.

I'd witnessed the entire spectrum of green edge its way across the mountains' foliage as a day wore on. I'd sat on the front porch waiting to see the sun snuggle into the valleys between peaks before disappearing for the night. They'd become friends, constant companions. To me they were God's sentries, watching over me. I'd grown to love the mountains and had never understood how people could be born, live and die in their presence and still take them for granted. They gave me strength now, and I finished dressing and went downstairs to find the kitchen and Mr. Dawes's something-to-eat.

It turned out to be the kind of breakfast Nunna used to cook before she began taking saturated fats and cholesterol seriously: fresh-squeezed orange juice, country ham, grits, eggs scrambled with cheese, biscuits as big as salad plates, homemade strawberry preserves, and coffee strong enough to kill. It was delicious. This was a man who loved to cook and loved even more seeing someone enjoy the fruit of his labors. I couldn't even remember when I'd eaten last, and consumed every bit of it, praising him between mouthfuls with as many adjectives as I could think of. When Harold Dawes arrived to drive me into Sanctuary, his father was grinning from ear to ear. I'd made a friend for life.

"That little lady there, she knows how to eat," he advised his son. "Yes, sir. You come back, hear? Now, Harold, you drive real careful. Take

Paintbrush Road goin' over to Sanctuary. Brick Kiln Road got too many ruts. Miss Warren'll be bouncin' all over that front seat of yours, maybe bump her head against the roof. Doc says she got to protect her head for a while. And hurry back. Don't want to keep Bea waiting at the airport."

"Yes, sir, Daddy."

Harold Dawes, Mr. Dawes's "boy," had to be nearly sixty, as shy and quiet as his father was gregarious and yakky, for which I was grateful. I was certain that there was something important I was supposed to do. The younger Dawes's silence on the way would give me time to think. Perhaps by the time we reached my wrecked car, I'd have figured out what I could remember and what I couldn't. He didn't disappoint me. After asking if I was feeling better and whether I was comfortable, he shut his mouth and drove.

I homed in on our destination: Sanctuary. The name wouldn't leave me alone. I was sure I'd heard it before, that it meant something, but precisely what kept dancing out of reach. The scene outside the windshield of Harold Dawes's pickup, however, began to run interference with my train of thought.

The thing I'd missed as a resident of D.C. was the mountains, and I needn't have. Was that why I'd driven up here? To seek solace, to mourn the loss of a career? The loss of a lover and best friend? I didn't think so. I was too mad at him. Then why?

Closing my eyes against the distraction of the mountains, I began to list what I could remember. I started with Nunna's wedding and worked my way forward. The nightmare drive back from Sunrise. And Tank, God, yes, my guardian angel, sent by Duck to keep an eye on me. That much was clear. That had been Monday. I remembered Tuesday, I thought, but Wednesday and Thursday were like groping my way through a drifting fog that lifted every now and then.

I remembered Tyler, picking her up from day care. Working out the reason took a few miles. Mrs. Kennedy was sick and Vanessa had needed someone to baby-sit while she was at the hospital with her mom. Another piece of the puzzle in place.

"You all right, Miss Warren?" Harold's voice interrupted my train of thought.

I opened my eyes, faintly amused at being called Miss by a man old enough to be my father. "I'm fine, thanks. Honestly," I added, seeing his dubious expression.

"Well, okay. Gotta say you sure seem a lot better than I expected, considerin' all the blood you lost."

"Me?" I fingered the bandage just above the nape of my neck and winced. Granted, scalp wounds tended to bleed all out of proportion to what one might expect, but this one hadn't even needed stitches.

"You bled all over your passenger seat. I don't mean to preach, Miss Warren, but you really oughta get in the habit of wearing your seat belt."

I sat up straight. He had to be kidding. "I was a cop, Mr. Dawes. I've seen what can happen to people who think it's not macho to use a seat belt, or didn't buckle up because they were just going around the corner or something. I always wear mine. Always."

He looked thoughtful. "Reckon you musta hit those trees pretty hard, then, to knock yourself over sideways. 'Course, you were half out of the car when Daddy found you."

"I was?"

"Said your door was open like you were trying to get out from under the wheel and passed out. You don't remember?"

"No, not the accident, where I was going, what for, nothing. I missed a curve?"

"Yes, ma'am. Folks do it all the time, rain or shine. Don't even mention snow and sleet. Problem is, it's practically a U-turn. Most just slide down the embankment a little ways. You went a lot farther, right down into the biggest tree you could find. Musta had a right smart of speed to do that."

For some inexplicable reason, the strains of the "Sorcerer's Apprentice" began to play in my ears. I clicked it off, trying to imagine the scenario he described. It didn't compute. I rarely exceeded the speed limit if I could help it, and I certainly wouldn't have in the rain and on unfamiliar roads.

"That doesn't sound like me," I said. "Perhaps a tire blew. I'm afraid to ask what condition my car's in."

One side of his mouth twitched. "I wouldn't count on driving it any time soon, was I you. Chunky—he's the one pulled you out—said it might could be fixed, but it's gonna take time and probably won't ever run as good. Said as old as it is, you'd be better off taking a total loss, pick up a good used car with the insurance money."

I decided not to take offense. They had no way of knowing the loving care my engine had always received, how well tuned it was, despite its exterior dings and dents. There was no way I could afford to replace it, especially on disability. I frowned, remembering being concerned about being able to pay for something else. Duck's condominium! He'd withheld evidence, disappeared and had left me his condo. With a sudden sense of impending doom, I remembered his note. *I never dishonored my badge.* But he no longer wore a badge! I remembered that, too, and why. And I was supposed to find him. Up here in the mountains?

"Is there some place I can rent a car where we're going?" I asked. I'd have my own ferried to my favorite mechanic to see what he thought. The tow charge was bound to bankrupt me, but if anyone could repair the damage, Phil Taliafero was the one who could do it.

My question about securing a rental struck Harold Dawes's funny bone. He had a hearty laugh. "Sorry, Miss Warren. I was just trying to imagine a rental agency in Sanctuary. No, ma'am, nothing like that there. And I've never known Chunky to let anybody use his truck. Somebody'll loan you a car for running around the area. That's the way folks are around these parts. You got any family or a friend who could come get you?"

I scanned a mental list, rejecting names as they came up, unsettled at how few there were. "No." I wouldn't have considered Duck, even if he'd been available. With the shape his car was in, I doubted he'd have made it past . . . I felt my frown deepen. A gas station with a redheaded attendant. I'd stopped there recently, used the rest room. Something had happened in that rest room. Damn it, how long would my memory remain hit-and-miss?

"Don't you worry none," Harold was saying. "Chunky will figure out something, knowing him."

"I certainly hope so. I've got to be back in D.C. by Monday."

"Back to the job, huh?" he asked. "Well, maybe things will work out by then. They could be worse."

I didn't say so, but I didn't agree with him and suspected things were even worse than I knew, if only I could remember exactly what that was.

We made the remainder of the trip in blessed silence, during which I tried to settle my backside in a more comfortable position. The seat was hard and unyielding. By the time we turned onto Sanctuary's main street, it was a contest which end hurt more, head or tail. One good look at Sanctuary, however, and I forgot my aches and pains and yelped, "Holy sh—, uh, cats!"

"Yes, ma'am," Harold said, grinning.

It was the craziest-looking place I'd ever seen. The description *artsy-fartsy types* seemed more than apt. It wasn't one I'd have normally used, but someone had and just recently, I was sure.

A good many of the houses were log cabins or small clapboard, but no two were alike. A few were two-story, and almost all had what appeared to be a large extra room tacked onto a side or the back. On the first one we passed, the individual logs had been painted to look like paintbrushes, the bristles of each brush a different color. A giant paintbrush was suspended from the roof of the front porch and beneath that, a sign: WILBUR CATES, WATERCOLORS. The next cabin resembled a gingerbread house. A hand-lettered placard in a front window announced DELILAH'S DOLLS. Each and every abode I could see left no doubt as to the artistic calling of its owner.

The house of one of the potters looked like a scoop of butterscotch pudding plopped on a plate, a big, beige mound. Only when we passed it did I realize what it represented: a giant kiln. There were jewelry makers, woodworkers, quilters, stained-glass makers, scupltors, glass blowers, basket makers. You name it, Sanctuary had it.

There were few people afoot, a man unloading a shopping cart stacked with blank canvases of assorted sizes, another pushing an empty wheelbarrow, his jeans and shirt mottled with paint splatters, a woman with a basket balanced atop her head striding with regal carriage along the side of the road.

A middle-aged couple jogged with dogged determination toward us, the woman's bleached blond hair in stark contrast to her dark skin. Another picture flashed across my retinas: a woman running toward me, her fair hair a ghostly white against the night. I'd picked her up. Or had I dreamt it? I must have. I didn't pick up hitchhikers. The dream dissolved, and I realized that everyone I'd seen here so far was some shade of brown.

"Sanctuary's a black community?" I asked.

"No'm. Used to be, but now they got all kinds and colors. The first settlers here were freed slaves makin' their way to a place like this in West Virginia when one of those rain storms like last night flooded out the road they were taking. This is as far as they got, and they never left."

"How many of them were there?"

"Several families is all I know. Word got back to other crafts people, and it did like Topsy, just growed. There aren't that many permanent residents now, just a few hundred maybe. The others come and go, show up for a while or sign on as apprentices, then move on."

"Where do they live?"

"The apprentices stay with whoever they signed up with if there's room. Some come in campers and RVs and live in them. A few pitch tents. Otherwise, there are a few rooming houses here and there, and back home in Reedy's Corner."

"No hotels or motels?"

"No, ma'am. Helps keep the traffic down. Most Sanctuary folks travel to big arts and crafts fairs, sell for themselves. And they open up to the public here once a month. That's what the add-ons are on a lot of the houses. It's their weekend selling space. Here we are."

We'd pulled over in front of an old three-story clapboard house that, judging from similar ones back in Sunrise, probably predated the first World War. It was the first normal-looking edifice I'd seen. It was a sore thumb among all the others, but it was also relieving to the eyes. I hoped I wouldn't have to impose on the owner's generosity too long, but at least I wouldn't be staying in a house that looked like a artist's palette or a weaver's loom.

"Landlady's name is Condon. Clara Condon. I'd go in to introduce you proper, but Miss Clara's a talker and I need to get on back and pick up Daddy. It was nice meetin' you."

I took the hint and got out. "Please tell your wife how much I appreciate her washing my clothes. You and your family have been absolutely terrific."

"Glad we could help."

"Uh, one last thing," I said as he yanked the truck into first gear. He jiggled it back into neutral.

"Ma'am?"

"I—I was alone when your father found me? I mean, there was no one else in the car?"

His eyes gave him away. He thought I'd lost it. "You sure you're feeling all right, Miss Warren? I can run you back over to Doc Williams's clinic in the Corner, if you want."

I patted his arm. "I'm fine. You go on, or you and your father will miss your sister's plane. And thanks again."

"You take care, hear?" He yanked the truck into gear again, made a neat three-point U-turn, and rumbled back toward Reedy's Corner.

I climbed the steps and stood on the porch until he disappeared from sight, wondering whether I'd made a mistake not taking him up on his offer to check in with the doctor. Memory-wise, my head felt as if it was full of scrambled eggs. There were bits missing, nibbled away by the concussion, I assumed, other bits floating around searching for wherever they belonged. I still harbored a certainty that there was something of vital importance I was supposed to do. It was the same anxiety I'd experienced on the job, racing to the scene of a major accident or some other life-threatening situation. Someone somewhere was in grave danger. But who? And why?

13

IT WAS TIME TO SHUT DOWN AND LEAVE
the subject alone for a while. Once Miss Condon
showed me to the room, I'd take a few minutes to
breathe, down a couple of aspirin and then go find this
Chunky person and my car. I took one last look at the
mountains, gleaning strength and serenity from them,
then knocked on the door. Footsteps thudded and a
roly-poly figure silhouetted by light from the end of a
hall which ran the length of the house appeared from
the right rear and waddled toward me.

"Ms. Condon?" I peered at her through the
screen.

"Miss." She moved toward me on feet far too
small for someone carrying as much weight as she
was. Stepping outside, she closed the screen door
behind her and stood, blocking it. I found her
expression curiously unwelcoming; the dark brown
eyes, blinking rapidly, appeared to look everywhere
except at me. "I'm sorry, Miss Warren, but the
room's no longer available."

"Excuse me?"

Somewhere inside, a phone rang. She jumped, as
if startled, but ignored it. "Well, see, when I talked
to Josiah, I thought the roomer I'd promised it to

wasn't coming." Her gaze darted from the porch post on the left to the one on the right, then at a point just above my head. "Well, he just called and said he was on the way. Car trouble or something. And since I'd already promised the room to him— that was last week, Tuesday it was, and he's stayed here before—I can't rightly rent it out from under him. So I'm sorry as I can be, but you'll have to find some place else." Inside, the phone stopped.

I managed to keep my mouth shut, wondering what the hell was going on. It wasn't just that Miss Condon was such a lousy liar; she was also extremely nervous. Inside, footsteps hurried toward us, and a stocky young man with an oriental cast to his eyes and bone-straight shoulder-length black hair appeared at the door.

"Excuse me, Miss Condon. The phone—"

"Thank you, Len." She groped behind her for the door handle, anxious to go. "Ask whoever it is to hold on. I'll be right there. I'm so sorry, Miss—"

"Take your time," Len said. "The lady hung up. She said she was your niece, Lorna, and you should call her back after, I quote, 'you know what.' Hi." He grinned at me. "You the new roomer?"

"Apparently not," I said. Lorna. I knew a Lorna. Didn't I?

"The room's rented." Miss Condon managed to get the screen door open far enough to wedge her girth through sideways, as if she opened it any wider, I might slip in after her. She jammed the hook into the eye, locking the screen, then closed the inside door. A dead bolt shot home. Point taken. All the windows were open, however, and Len's voice carried clearly as they moved into one of the rooms on the front.

"That wasn't the lady you said would be taking it?" He sounded confused. "The one that had the accident? Why didn't you let her have it? She looked okay to me. I thought you were so worried about that room staying empty all season."

"I can't talk to you right now," Miss Condon said, her voice fading as she apparently moved toward the rear of the house.

I stood there, stumped, and like Len, tried to ferret out her reason for refusing me. She obviously had little experience with or liking for telling lies. Why had it been necessary in the first place? And what was I going to do now? Mr. Dawes the elder had said he'd called several places before Miss Condon's and hadn't had any luck. He hadn't, however, mentioned whether they were all in Sanctuary. Since I was here, and well and truly stuck for the time being, I'd have to check out possibilities myself.

I tapped on the door gently. Miss Condon stepped into the hallway, a phone in her hand, and just as quickly disappeared again. It was Len who answered the door.

"Hi again," he said, coming out onto the porch. "Sorry about the mix-up. You need something?"

"You bet. A room. I was hoping Miss Condon would direct me to other places in town that might have a vacancy."

He scratched an ear. "She's on the phone. And I haven't been here that long, so all I know about is this place and the one a couple of houses from here. Wait a sec, though. Be right back." He darted into the house and took the stairs to the second floor two at a time.

I sat down on the top step, rubbing my forehead. I felt lost and didn't like it. I'd managed to be in control of things, at least most of my adult life. I'd been focused, a self-starter, goal-oriented and determined, not necessarily to be the best, but to do my best. But from the time Duck and I had split up, nothing had gone right, from my wrecked knee to my apartment, no longer mine because of the body in my kitchen. And Mr. Dawes claimed things could be worse.

"Here you are." Len sat down beside me. I'd been so engrossed in that gruesome memory that I'd forgotten about him.

He handed me a sheet of paper that looked as if it was a photocopy of a photocopy of a photocopy. "They sent me a list of places I could stay when my apprenticeship was accepted. Don't know how many are left this late in the season, but you may get lucky."

"That would be a nice change. Thanks. I really appreciate this."

"No problem. A few of those addresses are on this street, so they should be easy to find."

"What about Chunky's garage?" I asked. "He's got my car."

"Yours and everyone else's in Sanctuary. No auto traffic allowed except for deliveries. End of this block, make a right. It's about half a mile away."

"End of the block, then right. Thanks."

"I have to warn you, though. Chunk won't be there until tomorrow. He makes these really wild sculptures out of car parts, and Friday is his day to hit junkyards."

"I may not need him at all," I said, "if there's someone else there who can tow my car to D.C."

"Forget it." He shook his head. "Chunk takes the roll-back on these scouting trips, so you'd better count on being here at least overnight. If you can get his attention, the kid who works for him can give you more information. Take it easy. Maybe I'll see you around." He winked at me and went back into the house. I left and started walking.

Overnight. That might not be so bad. Push came to shove, I could spend the night in my car, which at this point was almost a comforting idea. Better get on to Chunky's, see how much damage I'd done and pay for my poor car to be towed to D.C. tomorrow. I might even be able to ride back in the tow truck.

But there was still my conviction that I'd come up here for a reason, something to do with Duck. I hated not knowing the right thing to do. I also hated feeling that it might not be my choice to make, that Fate was playing this hand without me and I could like it or lump it.

Forty minutes later, I'd begun to think I needed to find the listing for camping equipment in the yellow pages. So far I'd stopped at five addresses on the way to Chunky's and had been turned away five times. At all of them I'd detected the same level of discomfort and nervousness that Miss Condon had exhibited. I had the distinct impression that The Word Was Out: there's no room in Sanctuary for Leigh Ann Warren.

It didn't make sense. I doubted I was being refused because of my color. My appearance perhaps? Granted, I didn't look my best; a few of my bumps and bruises showed, and I wore a Band-Aid just above the nape of my neck. But my clothes were clean, pressed even. Hey, it was the first time I'd ever worn jeans with a crease down the front.

Yet four boardinghouse owners had claimed to have no vacancy. I really would have been inclined to believe them, except that I'd gotten the impression they'd known I'd be coming. My experience at the fifth house confirmed it. The elderly woman sweeping the porch saw me approaching and scurried inside, slamming the door behind her. "No rooms!" she shrieked from behind the curtained glass. "Go away! No rooms!"

I stared up at her in astonishment. Then I got mad. This wasn't fair. I marched up the steps and banged on the door.

"Go away!" the voice called out. "I already told you, we got no rooms! Now you're trespassing! If you don't get off my porch, I'm going to call the police!"

"You do that," I said, deciding that this was where I would draw the line. Out of respect for her age, I tried for a reasonable tone. She seemed frightened enough already. "I'm fresh off a police force myself, so perhaps I'll be treated with more courtesy by your officers than I've received in Sanctuary so far."

Silence. Finally the door opened a couple of inches, and a medium brown eye peered through the crack. "You were with the police somewheres?"

"Yes, ma'am," I said, reverting to my Southern-ingrained manners. "Washington, D.C. If I hadn't been injured on the job, I'd be with them yet. Now, I'll accept your word that you're full up, but would you mind telling me what's going on here?"

"I–I don't know what you mean."

"I had an accident last night and my car's at Chunky's. I'm on my way there to see about it, but I'm told I'll be stuck here overnight. Yet everywhere I've checked so far, I've been told there's no room, and I'm almost certain that in a couple of instances, that wasn't true. As a cop, I learned to trust my instincts, and my instincts say something fishy's going on. Why is everyone turning me away? You have my word it'll go no further."

The eye regarded me with indecision for a moment. "I–I got a call," she said, just above a whisper. "I don't know who it was. Couldn't even tell whether it was a man or a woman, but they said if you came asking for a room, I was to tell you no or there'd be nothing left but ashes for me to rent."

"What?"

"I'm sorry, but this place is all I've got. It's my livelihood and if I lose it—"

"Say no more." I turned away, as if the door hadn't been answered. "Believe me, I understand," I said quietly over my shoulder. "Thank you for being honest with me."

"I'm sorry, I really am." She closed the door gently.

I descended the steps slowly, dazed. What kind of town was this? Threaten to burn down an old woman's house if she gave me a room? Why? How could I be a danger to anyone? This was my first time here, and the only people I'd spoken to so far were landladies. I knew nothing about Sanctuary, knew no one here, at least as far as I remembered. Discouraged and unsettled, I made tracks for Chunky's, feeling suddenly conspicuous, as if eyes were peeking through curtains everywhere I passed.

I should have expected it, but Chunky's place of business looked more like a sculpture garden than a garage. The works of art Len had mentioned rose like two- and three-story totem poles in front of what had probably been the major part of an eighteen-wheeler, its sides decorated by hundreds of hubcaps painted graduating hues of the rainbow. They glowed in the mid-afternoon sun, the effect mesmerizing.

The totem poles consisted of an incredibly arranged assortment of auto parts stacked one on top of the other—steering wheels, fenders, bumpers, grilles, running boards, batteries, carburetors, crankcases, components I didn't even recognize. They jutted out at odd angles, some cantilevered above the others, spray-painted in metallic colors. A series of billboards positioned behind the trailer ineffectually masked three gasoline tanks bearing the logo of a brand I'd never heard of, and beyond that a giant parking lot jammed with cars, minivans, RVs, converted buses, and motorbikes of all sizes and horsepower. Since there were no price tags on any of them, I assumed this was the parking lot for the town's vehicles.

There were no wrecks waiting for surgery, including mine. In fact, if there was an area for repairing cars, I didn't see it. Perhaps that was located elsewhere, along with wherever he assembled his fantastic sculptures.

The door of the trailer was so well camouflaged by the hubcaps that it was a moment before I noticed it. I tapped. Someone yelled, "Come on in! It's unlocked."

The knob was the hub of a bicycle wheel. I stuck my head in and decided it was time I stopped being surprised at anything in this town. The interior of the trailer had been separated into several rooms. I could see a sofa and a lounge chair through an open doorway on my left.

The immediate space was an office with a dynamite computer setup complete with Zip drive, printer, fax, scanner, and copier. Carousels of CDs and diskettes filled a shelf above the computer. A giant glass-fronted key cabinet sat beside the door and next to it one of those lateral file cabinets I was determined to buy someday. There wasn't a sheet of paper in sight. It was the neatest office I'd ever seen.

"Come on in." A kid, probably still in high school, looked back over his shoulder at me. "Help ya?"

I gaped at him, then realized it and shut my mouth with such force that it hurt my teeth. He was gorgeous. Skin the color of coffee laced with cream and cinnamon, sleek jet brows and short, curly hair, lashes so long I was willing to bet he had to trim them on a regular basis, even white teeth. Whoever his parents were, they'd mixed up one dynamite set of genes and chromosomes and whatever.

"Hi," I said, stepping in. "I'm Leigh Warren. Chunky brought my car here last night. I was wondering if it could be towed to my mechanic's place in D.C. I'll gladly—" I stopped, brought up short by his expression, one of out-and-out incredulity.

"You're the beige four-door went off the road over Reedy's Corner?"

"Uh, yes. Something wrong?"

His effort to assume an air of diffidence failed. "I don't think Chunky was expecting you. In fact, nobody was. We thought you'd be in a hospital somewhere, at least at Doc Williams's."

I winced. "My car's that bad?"

"Chunky thinks it's fixable, but that isn't what I meant. I just didn't know you could lose that much blood and be walking around the next day. Made me feel queasy just looking at it."

"That's scalp wounds for you," I said. "Bleed like crazy. Can I see it?"

"Your car?"

I began a reassessment of the kid's mental capacity. "Yes, my car. I'd like to see it."

"Oh." The tip of a pink tongue slid across his lips. "Well, it's not here."

That was unexpected. "Where is it?"

He shrugged uncomfortably. "I don't know. All I know is, it's not here."

I started to count to ten, made it to six. My temples began to throb again. "When's the last time you saw it?"

"Right after Chunky brought it in last night."

"Did he say where he would take it? Some other garage or body shop?"

"No, ma'am. I didn't talk to him. He didn't even know I was here. I'm usually not, not that late, anyhow, but I was working on a graphics project on the computer. I'd just closed up and checked the parking lot to make sure all the gates were locked. When I came around the front again, the roll-back was here. No Chunky but he must have been around somewhere because he'd left the motor running."

"And my car was on the flatbed."

"Yes, ma'am."

"Where did he put it when he took it off?"

"The roll-back, you mean?" He looked blank. "Why would he do that?"

I made it as far as seven this time. "If he didn't roll it off, how'd you manage to see the blood?"

"Oh. I climbed up to look in. See, at first I thought Chunk had found himself a junker to use on the sculpture he's working on because he'd brought it back here instead of taking it to Mr. Minor's in Reedy's Corner." My blood pressure began a slow climb. "I wanted to get a closer look, check out the interior, see what he thought he could use. But when I saw the front seat . . ." He swallowed and turned faintly green. "Oh, say, here's your stuff."

He opened a closet door I hadn't noticed, probably because it was tucked in a corner. There was my battered blue Samsonite. I'd forgotten I'd had it. That meant I'd left D.C. planning to stay. I wouldn't know for how long until I checked to see how many pairs of panties I'd packed.

"Thanks. Now, about my car," I said, trying with difficulty not to cop an attitude. "There's no possibility my car's going to wind up on a totem pole out front, is there? I mean, since it's not here, I've got to wonder what happened to it, know what I mean?"

"Oh, no. No." He shook his head so fast and so hard, his brain probably rattled. "I mean, Chunky wouldn't do something like that, not unless you were dead." He blinked, having caught up with what he'd said. "Even then he'd do it legal. That's just the way he is. He should be back by six at the latest. I'll tell him you were here and want to talk to him."

It was the best I could expect, under the circumstances. I left, my head roaring with questions and feeling a hell of a lot more empathy for the bag ladies of the world. For the first time I could fully appreciate what life must be like for them. And I didn't like it, not one damned bit.

14

WHERE TO GO? WOULD A TOWN THIS SIZE have a library? Or a diner? Someplace I could park my rear and my baggage with no time limit so I could start knitting all these varicolored skeins together? As difficult as it was knowing I had no place to go, the realization that parts of my brain were out to lunch and might or might not return to work any time soon was downright scary. Casting a jaundiced eye at Chunky's sculptures, I turned my back on them and started walking.

The whimsical exteriors of the homes I passed didn't seem quite as charming anymore. Just for the hell of it, I stopped at two more addresses on Len's list, with the expected results. I was persona non grata. I'd turned the corner on the main street again when I saw the big white house with the black cat above the door. I'd missed it before because it sat on a long, narrow lot, positioned so that the side of the house faced the road. That side was painted to look like a patchwork quilt, but the rest was a pure white with black shutters at the windows. Above the entrance was an angle iron and hanging from it was a cat, curled up nose to tail, snuggled under a patchwork quilt. Below the cat a board dangled: THE QUILTED CAT.

I checked Len's list. This address wasn't on it, but something wouldn't let me leave. Racking my brain, I stood there staring at it, as if I'd grown roots. Evie. Evangeline Simmons. The name popped into my head as if someone had opened the lid of a jack-in-the-box. Just as suddenly the whole phone conversation with . . . who? Malinda. At the moment I couldn't work out who Malinda was or where I'd met her, but I remembered clearly looking up a phone number, calling her. Evangeline Simmons was Malinda's aunt.

Evangeline! Evie. Artis? If Duck's Evie Artis and Malinda Whatever's aunt were one and the same, logic dictated that this was my reason for being here. This was the person I'd been coming to see!

Painted rocks and the remnants of summer blossoms lined the walkway. It was an old house, two floors, and I could see now that the end facing the street had been a late addition, its bay window sparkling in the afternoon sun. I rang the bell. It didn't ring. It meowed. Inside I could hear softer echoes of it nearby.

"Whatcha ringing for?" someone yelled. "Door's unlocked like always. Come on in."

I opened the door to be greeted by a trio of felines—one black and white, one calico, one Siamese mixed with alley, from the size of it. The black and white and the semi-Siamese examined me warily; the calico took off, skidding on the highly buffed hardwood floors as it tore out of the room.

Cats and I have an unspoken bargain. I respect them as individuals, as well as a unique species, and do not expect them to act like dogs, for whom human companionship and approval matters a great deal. Most cats couldn't give less of a damn, and I liked them for that. Don't get me wrong, I can be as much of a fool about dogs and cats as the next pet lover, but I knew better than to let cats know it. So I ignored them and called, "Mrs. Simmons?"

She stepped into the doorway at the rear of the room, and I managed to mask my surprise. There was something familiar about her, but aside from that she was the biggest woman I'd ever met, every bit as tall as Janeece with the heft to go with it. She was also pretty and must have been downright stunning fifty years ago. Her hair, a snowy white, framed a dark chocolate face with skin as clear and smooth as a baby's rear. I couldn't see her eyes, concealed behind glasses with triple-thick lenses. She moved into the room like an ebony Amazon queen, her steps sure, unhesitating. "Well, now, who might you be?"

The cats sat down and watched the exchange at full attention.

"My name is Leigh Warren."

"Pleased to make your acquaintance, Miss Warren. What can I do for you?"

I hadn't been certain how I should proceed and decided to be honest. It was simpler. "I'm guessing I'm here to find out if—"

"Wait a minute, Leigh Warren." Her expression was puzzled. "You're guessing? You don't know?"

"Not with certainty. I had an accident last night and—"

"Oh, you're the one. I'm glad you're all right. Why don't you have a seat? You look a little peckish. Would you like a cup of tea? Or maybe cider? Come on back to the kitchen."

"Cider would be terrific." I glanced around for some place out of the way to stash my suitcase. There were more than a few spots to choose from. This was a sizable house, the space along the front one big room, the right half furnished with a sofa, two plump love seats and several easy chairs arranged before a fireplace high and deep enough to stand in.

The left half of the room was the equivalent of an art gallery, the walls lined with incredibly beautiful quilts of all sizes. Some seemed more utilitarian than others, constructed of sturdy fabric scraps, while others were more fanciful and purely decorative, made of lacy squares and triangles, velvet, satin.

The annex nearest the street was a workroom, containing two large quilting frames ringed with hard-back chairs. A half-finished quilt was spread on one of the frames; three women of different generations but obviously related were stitching along one side. They smiled, their expressions curious but welcoming. The quilt on the second frame looked complete.

Evidently, my invitation to go beyond the front rooms amounted to a "she's okay" for the cats. One led the way, the other followed me into a combination kitchen and dining room that spanned the rear of the house. The dining table was set. A quick count revealed places for twelve.

"Are you expecting company?" I asked. If so, she was well prepared. This was the kitchen of a serious cook; there were two of everything—two refrigerators and gas ranges, two built-in ovens, only one microwave but a pair of sinks of different sizes and depths, one in an island dead center of the space. Calphalon pots, pans and assorted utensils, some of which I'd never seen before, hung from a rack above the island. I experienced a moment of nostalgia, as Duck's Calphalon set drifted through my consciousness.

"Company?" Mrs. Simmons asked, pouring cider from a gallon jug. Her face cleared. "Oh, you mean the table. I came from a big family, and keeping it set that way sorta reminds me of the old days. Plus my quilters are in and out of here sunrise to sunset, and they're all welcome to anything I have fixed. Come sit over here." She waved toward a smaller cherrywood table tucked into an alcove at the far end of the kitchen. I swallowed. There was no comparison, but it reminded me of mine. And Nunna's. This was a homey room, the kind you could sit in all day, just hanging around and chewing the fat.

I took a seat, and my hostess placed a coaster on the table, then a tall glass filled to the brim with genuine full-bodied cider, not the see-through watery stuff you get from the grocery stores. I took a sip and practically purred with pleasure. This was good stuff. The cats must have thought I was talking to them. They stropped my legs, each trying to nudge the other out of the way, then reached a compromise by settling down across my feet. Fortunately, I had two of them. If the calico came back, there'd be trouble.

"This is wonderful," I said.

She slid into a chair opposite. "It's not bad. Next month's will be better. Now, Miss Warren, let's start over. Why did you come?"

"When I saw the cat above your door, I remembered that I'd talked to your niece, Malinda, I'm not sure when. I think I was on my way to see you when I had the accident. Mrs. Simmons, do you know a man named Dillon Kennedy? His nickname is Duck."

There was no hesitation in her response. "No, ma'am, I don't. I would remember somebody named Kennedy. And I've known some turkeys in my life, but can't say I've ever known a Duck. Is that all you wanted to find out?"

"I . . . I don't know. Are you sure?" I dug out the photo of Duck, then realized there was a distinct possibility she wouldn't be able to see it clearly.

"What's that? A picture of him? Give it here." She reached into a capacious pocket on the front of her apron and pulled out a large magnifying glass. After examining the snapshot, she shook her head. "Can't say I've ever seen him before. But except for family members, regular Sanctuary folk and quilters, my circle is fairly small. There's a heck of a lot of people in Sanctuary I wouldn't normally see— apprentices, weekend visitors. So he could have been in town, for all I know. Is that all you wanted to find out?"

"I guess," I said with a shrug. "My memory's so hit-and-miss that if there was more, it's dropped into a black hole somewhere."

"Poor child." She patted my hand. "Tell you what. Don't worry about it. I'm not going anywhere and, God willing, it'll come back to you. When it does, the door's unlocked. You're welcome any time. So you know Malinda."

"I guess I must, but I can't picture her."

"I can fix that." She got up and left the room. The cats watched her but stayed put.

"You guys comfortable?" I asked. They yawned in unison and dropped their heads onto their front paws.

Mrs. Simmons was back in a moment, a five-by-eight studio portrait in her hand. "Here's Malinda and her twin, Jimmy. Does that help?"

I took the photo, at first charmed by the attractive brown faces, clearly proud to be wearing their caps and gowns. It wasn't until I focused on each individual face that my head seemed to explode with a series of disjointed images, like a slide show in fast-forward with the images out of sequence. The girl's face was very familiar, and I knew I'd seen it recently. She'd been angry and upset about something, shouting at someone. Me? Her brother's features were also familiar for a couple of reasons. "Toulouse," I blurted. "This is Toulouse Archer."

"My nephew, rest his stupid soul. Little James. You knew him?"

"No, I didn't." I flailed around for the right question to ask. "Did—did you see him often?"

"No. Hadn't laid eyes, bad as they are, on that child since we went down for the twins' graduation from high school. That's going on five or six years ago. Then my sister calls, says he's on his way up to see us."

"Us?" I interrupted.

"Like I told you, we're a big family. Lots of cousins, second and third removed. Anyhow, Lord, that boy had talent. He hated his nickname because he wasn't all that short, but he had a way with a paintbrush. My sister called, said she was sending him to keep him out of trouble. Wilbur Cates agreed to take him on, see how he worked out as an apprentice. Next thing I know, Malinda calls saying Jimmy got himself killed in a traffic accident. So I guess it wasn't supposed to be. It was Jimmy's time and that's that."

I kept my mouth shut, the graduation photo in my hand. Looking at Toulouse, I made another connection. He resembled the kid in Chunky's office trailer. I described him and asked if he was one of the cousins she'd mentioned.

"Oh, yes. That was Paulie, my sister's grandchild. Computer smart but not a lick of sense otherwise."

Belatedly I saw the resemblance with my hostess as well. They were a handsome family, but so far I hadn't learned anything that would help me find Duck. An idea occurred to me that probably wouldn't pan out but there was no harm in trying.

"I saw a lovely watercolor by a young black man

who may live in this area. James Braden Thomas."

"J.B.?" she asked. "Another wing of the family. Thomas, Braden, Simmons, and Cates, that's us. Haven't seen J.B. for a while, but I'll see he gets the message he has a fan."

Learning that J.B. had a family and people who cared about him launched another guilt trip, this time that I knew J.B. was beyond receiving messages. She didn't and I wouldn't be the one to tell her, either. I closed my eyes, rubbed my temples. Up to this point I'd had sufficient distractions to keep my mind off the assorted aches, especially from the neck up. All at once it seemed they were yelping in unison.

"You all right, baby? Look, let me get Paulie over here to walk you to wherever you're staying. He's got sense enough to do that. I'll give Doc Williams a call, ask him to stop by to see you."

I'd have shaken my head but didn't dare. "Thanks, but I haven't found a room. Apparently everyone's full up, or say they are."

My skepticism must have shown. "What do you mean, they say they are?"

I described my seven attempts to find a room, tactfully omitting the explanation of the elderly woman who'd dredged up the nerve to tell me why she had to refuse me.

"That don't sound like Sanctuary folks," Mrs. Simmons said, mangling the rules of grammar. "I've known them to let apprentices sleep in their bathtubs a night or two. Well, this isn't a rooming house, but there's one thing I got plenty of, it's space.

Mama and Papa raised ten young'uns under this roof, so you've got your pick of bedrooms."

I hadn't anticipated this, and as grateful as I was, I was also concerned. I couldn't put her at risk. Without revealing where it had happened, I told her about the threat made against the owner of the fifth house.

"What? What?" She rose, an avenging goddess. The cats, sensing her anger, sat up and watched her with anxious eyes. Shoving her chair out of the way, she slammed her hand onto the tabletop. The cats jumped with alarm and were gone, streaks of color as they disappeared from the kitchen. "What the hell is going on in this town?" Mrs. Simmons demanded.

One of the ladies from the quilting annex appeared in the doorway. "Something wrong, Vangie?"

Mrs. Simmons turned to her, then glanced back at me. "No, honey. Everything's fine. How's it going out there?"

"Coming right along. Crystal's learning real fast. Well, if you're sure, I'll get on back." She nodded at me, her expression not quite as friendly this time, and left.

Mrs. Simmons slumped into her seat again. "Sorry. Didn't mean to blow up like that. But what's happening to my people?"

"I don't know, but everyone I talked to about renting a room seemed afraid, so I assume all of them had received the same orders: get rid of me or suffer the consequences."

My hostess drummed her fingers on the tabletop. "I've been sensing something's not right here recently, but I thought it was just my imagination. Can't half see so I figured my ears were playing tricks on me. There have been other signs, too, little things, but I . . ." She shook her head. "I've gotta think about this. Come on, child. You're looking punier by the minute. I'll take you upstairs and call Doc, ask him to stop in. You stretch out and relax. Take a nap. I'll wake you when he gets here."

I didn't have the will to resist. Following her to a pleasantly feminine room at the top of the stairs, I took her advice and stretched out on the white wrought iron daybed. I was probably asleep before she made it back to the first floor.

The sun had gone down, but it was actually the silence that woke me, probably because it was just that: silent. I pushed the light button on my watch. Eight-ten. I couldn't for the moment figure out where I was; I just knew it wasn't home. Face it, if you live in the city, and in an apartment to boot, there's no such animal as complete silence and you become accustomed to that. There was no intermittent grumble of a refrigerator, or crackle and pop of parquet tiles settling. The hum of traffic was also missing, no honk of horns or voices of night people on the street.

I sat up, my eyes gradually adjusting to the darkness of the room and the minimal illumination supplied by a night light out in the hall. Daybed. A six-foot chifforobe. Rocking chair in the corner.

Fluffy sheers at the window. I sniffed. Cornbread? This wasn't Nunna's, that was certain. I'd known people to come to blows over who would get the last of her biscuits, but for some reason, more often than not, her cornbread resembled cement blocks.

The second aroma I detected, that of hot, spiced cider, nudged things into place. This was one of the upstairs bedrooms of Mrs. Evangeline Simmons. Evie Artis Simmons. Suddenly, despite the headache, which seemed to have lessened a good bit, it was as if I'd groped my way out of a blinding fog into the sun. My memory might be wearing a few Band-Aids, but for the most part I was fairly sure it was back. Except for the accident, which still eluded me, I thought I had recaptured most of the previous day. The rest would come, I was sure of it.

This house was empty, I was sure of that, too. I wondered where Mrs. Simmons had gone and why the doctor hadn't come. Not that I needed him all that much. I felt better, rested. I was getting used to the headache, and the soreness at the back had begun to itch, a good sign. If I could find a bathroom, I'd clean the spot to make sure and change the dressing. But not just yet. I'd been chafing for solitude since I'd gotten back from Sunrise. Now that I had it, I'd better make good use of it.

Moving to the rocker, I sat by the window, the night so dark here that there was no delineation between sky and ground, the glow from nearby homes resembling low-hanging stars. Evidently the residents felt no need for exterior security lights, even though it was clear that a snake was slithering through this bit of paradise. How could my presence here represent such a danger that someone would resort to the threat of arson to see that I had no place to stay? Was it something they thought I knew? For that matter, just what did I know? Only that Toulouse, Mrs. Simmons, J. B. Thomas and dirty-haired Joe were tied to Sanctuary. Toulouse and J. B. Thomas were dead. Mrs. Simmons claimed not to have met Duck, but even if he was here somewhere, I couldn't believe he'd threaten every landlady in town so I'd have to leave. That left Joe, who I could link to J.B. and a cache of missing marijuana. Bingo. Joe would definitely not want me around. Tough. I wasn't leaving. Couldn't if I wanted to.

It was past time for me to see if Chunky had returned. I didn't have a number for him, but Information would. I groped around in my bag for the phone, hoping I wouldn't have to turn on a light. Even though this was a big house, the darkness whittled it down to a more intimate size, made me feel as if I'd snuggled up with a baby-soft blanket around me. I found the phone, but was puzzled that it wasn't in its case. Things might have been tossed around during the accident, but there was no reason for the cell phone to have fallen out of a case that snapped closed. Or had I failed to put it back in the last time I'd used it? An admitted creature of habit, I almost always did, to protect the phone and because I liked the case. It was the only Coach product I had, and Duck had given it to me.

Rather than turning on the lamp on the night-stand, I opened the door wider to let the hall light spill into the room, then dumped the contents of my bag on the bed. It was amazing—and embarrassing—to see everything I routinely carried spread out across the chenille. Wallet, checkbook, lipstick, comb, brush, a few letters to be mailed once I'd bought stamps. The mail caused a hiccup in the back of my mind, but I couldn't figure out why and kept taking inventory. Appointment/address book, Tootsie Rolls, travel-sized hand lotion, toothbrush and bottle of mouthwash, an assortment of pens and pencils, notepad—a holdover from the job— tissues, paperback novel, maps, pepper spray, cologne, a tiny Tonka truck Tyler had given me, Swiss Army knife, sewing kit, corn plasters. And that was just from the main compartment. But that's where I kept the phone, and the case was not there.

Shoving it all back in, I checked the outer pocket of the bag. Lots of stuff but no case. There was always the possibility that it had fallen out in the car, but that still failed to explain the separation of phone and case. When was the last time I'd used it?

I'd called Marty from a truck stop, and I clearly remembered securing the phone. I punched the Power button and hit Recall. The number on the digital display was not Marty's. This was Eddie Grimes's home number. Why would I have called him after I'd left town?

I activated Redial. No answer. I tried his pager number. Not turned on? A cop with his pager turned off? Then I remembered. Eddie had to be at choir rehearsal. He and Marilyn sang in a gospel choir, and during rehearsal and church services he routinely disabled his pager, maintaining that for two hours a week, he was on God's clock. And I couldn't for the life of me remember which church he attended. The only consolation was that I couldn't blame it on the accident.

I turned off the phone and moved back to the rocker. Where was Duck? In Sanctuary or some hamlet nearby? I knew he'd headed in this direction because he'd used his gas card at the service station. I felt the muscles of my face go slack. The service station. I'd stopped there, too. That's where I'd talked to the carrot-topped attendant and— And what? I'd shown him Duck's photo and he'd remembered him! And he'd given me directions to . . . to Peace Station! Then what? Why the nagging conviction that something further had happened there? Dismayed, I rubbed my temples. I thought I'd regained most of the day before, but I seemed to be two or three hours short. I might or might not ever recall the accident itself, but it seemed more and more important that I recapture the period preceding it.

I relived the drive, heard the drumming of the rain against the roof of the car, felt again the pain in my hands from gripping the steering wheel so tightly. I walked myself through the scene in the service station. Then—

The rest room. I'd used the rest room. *That's* when I'd called Eddie because I could see myself using the phone. But why had I called him? The answer would have to wait until tomorrow when I could reach him. But I could reach Chunky tonight.

He was supposed to be back by six. Forget calling him. I wanted to talk to him in person. I wanted to hear his description of the scene of the accident.

I was halfway down the steps when the front door opened. Mrs. Simmons strode in, saying to a figure behind her, "She's probably still in bed. Don't you go waking her up if she is."

"You dragged me over here from Reedy's Corner this time of night to watch her sleep?" The man who stepped in wore an expression that was one part exasperation, two parts fatigue. "Fix me a cup of coffee so I can stay awake going back." The voice was grumpy, familiar, one of those I'd heard amidst the chaos and confusion of the night before. This had to be Dr. Williams. Graying, with a full slate-colored beard to match, he was medium height but slightly stooped, and took up a lot of room from side to side. "And just where might you be going?" he asked, scowling up at me.

"What?" Mrs. Simmons, on her way to the kitchen, turned and looked back at him, then up at me. "Leigh? You must be feeling a lot better."

"I am, thanks. Dr. Williams, I'm so sorry you had to come out so late. It really wasn't necessary."

"Well, I'm here," he said gruffly, "and let me tell you, young lady, I didn't come all this way for nothing. March yourself back upstairs, please, ma'am, so I can look you over."

I hated to delay seeing Chunky any longer, but the glint in the doctor's gray eyes made me suspect he might be a couple of degrees more stubborn than I was. I conceded and returned to the room, the steps behind me creaking under his weight as he followed me up.

He wasted no time, his examination thorough, his questions probing but to the point. Up close, I could see traces in his gray hair of the redhead he'd once been, with the kind of fair skin that the sun would burn in very short order. I waited with more than a little anxiety as he pulled the bandage from the back of my head, but his touch was so gentle, I barely felt it.

"How's it look?" I asked.

"Not bad at all. Swelling's down, wound's good and clean. You could probably go without a dressing, but let's be cautious and put another one on. You can take it off, say, tomorrow night. Just avoid using any kind of hair product back there until your doctor says it's safe."

"I'll do that." It was now my turn for questions. "Dr. Williams, did you see my car after the accident?"

"Yes," he said, packing medical paraphernalia back into his bag. "Josiah called me when he'd reached you, and I joined him there. Why?"

"I haven't seen it yet. And I was a D.C. cop. I'm just trying to get a picture of the scene. Call it a holdover of an occupational hazard. I take it I was sprawled across the passenger seat?"

His brows flipped upward a notch. "No. The door on your side was open and you were half in, half out when Josiah called. I was concerned about him moving you before I got there, but that was lessened when you rolled out onto the ground under your own steam and stood up."

There was something a bit surreal about hearing something in which I'd been involved but couldn't remember.

"Of course, you passed out again when you ran into the woods. Josiah said he had the devil's own time trying to get you back into the car."

"I ran into the woods? Where the heck was I going?"

"Off to see the Wizard, for all I know. You were undoubtedly disoriented, in pain and not thinking straight. Josiah said you headed through the trees, mumbling that you had to help. Fortunately, you passed out before you'd gone very far, or Lord knows when we'd have found you. I see you rescued your belongings from Chunky's place. Anything damaged?"

"No. All I had was a few clothes. And I'm missing the case my phone was in, but I assume it's still in the car."

He shook his head. "No, ma'am. Josiah and I got everything out of the car and put them in Chunky's truck. Why? Did we miss something?"

"I . . . don't know." It was now time to tackle the question that had been dogging me since this morning. "Dr. Williams, Mr. Dawes mentioned the amount of blood on the passenger seat. I know that scalp wounds can bleed like crazy, but would you have expected mine to have bled that profusely?"

"Well, now I have to admit I was a little surprised, once I got a good look at your wound. You must have hit your head against something pretty hard, but what and how I don't know. Your headrest's pretty soft, and there was no blood on it or your seat, for that matter. Of course, the skin's hardly broken. But you certainly showed no signs of someone who'd lost that much blood."

I took a deep breath and voiced the concern that had been haunting me. "I'm almost certain it wasn't mine."

He blinked. "Pardon me?"

"My blood, I mean. I'm pretty sure I wasn't alone in the car. There was a young woman with me."

"Oh?" His scrutiny of me became more intense, as if revising his earlier diagnosis.

"My memory's still spotty, but I think I picked her up last night. I have this image of her running toward me from the trees, but that's all it is, a momentary picture that comes and goes. I think she was with me when I wrecked the car, and it's her blood on the passenger seat."

Dr. Williams's gaze turned inward, a frown creasing his forehead. "I'd be inclined to believe that possibility except no one could have walked away, not with the amount of blood she lost. And you were definitely alone when Josiah got there. Do you remember what she looked like?"

"White, thirty at the outside, light eyes, blue or gray." As I talked about her, her features seemed to become clearer. "Shoulder-length blond hair, very thin. Her arms were like sticks. Oh, her blouse was torn, and she was carrying a purse that looked like it had been made out of a pair of jeans."

"You're certain it might not have happened some other time?"

"Positive. I have never picked up a hitchhiker before. But the weather was so bad last night. That's the only circumstance under which I can imagine stopping for anyone. And a woman alone? I couldn't have passed her by."

I was encouraged that he hadn't dismissed the possibility out of hand. "Well," he said after a moment of thought, "I guess I'd better report this to Major."

"Who's that?"

"Major Hamilton. He's the law, such as it is, in Reedy's Corner. He came out last night, too. I've got to go deliver a baby," he said, getting to his feet, "but I'll see he gets a message about this and let him know you're here at Vangie's. Now, I'd advise you to take it easy the rest of the evening."

I was still intent on getting to Chunky's, despite the hour, and said so. He shook his head as he folded his stethoscope back into his bag.

"No point. His trailer was dark when I passed. Nothing he could do for you anyhow, not this late."

"The question is what he did with my car last night. It's not here and I need to find out where he took it."

"Oh, I wouldn't worry about that. The only place he'd take it would be to Minor's."

"Where's that?"

"In Reedy's Corner. In fact . . ." He paused, the seams in his face settling into a puzzled expression. "I wonder why he didn't come instead of Chunky. I can't imagine Josiah calling Chunky to pull you out. Look, I have to get moving, but maybe I can help ease your mind about your car. Vangie, I've got to use your phone," he yelled down the stairs.

"Since when do you ask permission?" she yelled back.

He grinned, went out to the hallway to a telephone on a small table that looked as if it were made of tongue depressors or popsicle sticks, and dialed. "Minor? Doc Williams. I'm at Vangie Simmons's with the lady who went off the road over by Josiah's last night. She's worried about her car, and I told her Chunky would have dropped it off at your place. Have you got a few minutes to talk to her? Her name is—"

He stopped, frowned, listening for so long I went and sat down on the top step to wait. "Hmmm. All right. Thanks, anyway. I'm sure there's a very simple answer. You take care." He hung up and looked back at me. "Seems we have us a little puzzle. Your car isn't there. Major stopped by the garage last night to tell Minor to expect it, but Chunky never showed up. And according to Major, Josiah didn't call Chunky to come pull you out. Chunky drove up with his roll-back before Josiah had a chance to call anyone, even me."

"You mean, he just happened by?" I asked.

Doc fingered his beard. "There's some question about that. Major asked him the same thing and never got what he considered a satisfactory answer. He let it slide last night, thinking he'd follow up on it today. Only nobody's seen him since. Chunky and your car seem to have disappeared."

15

DESPITE THE DOCTOR'S CHARACTER REFerences and assurances that Chunky was honest to a fault, even he couldn't come up with a logical reason for the man's defection. He left to deliver a baby and Mrs. Simmons, determined to find out more, sent for Paulie, who, mystified by his boss's absence, seemed further out to lunch than usual.

"I don't know where he coulda gone," Paulie said, looking completely lost. "I mean, he didn't call or anything today. Like I told Mr. Major, I haven't seen him since he left to go get Miss Warren's car."

"How'd he find out about the accident?" I asked. "As I understand it, Mr. Dawes didn't call him."

"Well, somebody did, but I don't know who. All I know is, he didn't want to go." He scrunched up his face and scratched an eyebrow. "Well, it wasn't that he didn't want to go exactly. He's always willing to help out if Mr. Minor's busy or something."

"Major and Minor Hamilton," Mrs. Simmons explained. "Brothers. Major's a justice of the peace, and Minor owns a filling station. So if Chunky didn't mind going, what was the problem?"

"I'm not really sure, Aunt Vangie. See, at first he

said sure, he'd start right out and he was about to hang up. Then whoever he was talking to musta said something else and Chunky, he says, 'Do what?' real loud and sits down again and says, 'No way, get somebody else.'"

"Not 'get Minor'?" I interrupted, feeling that the wording might be important.

"No, ma'am. 'Get somebody else' was what he said. Then he listens for a while and then he says 'You wouldn't,' and then he says, 'You'd better have a good reason for this,' and hangs up. I asked him was something wrong because he looked kinda sick, but he said he was fine, that he was going over to Reedy's Corner to get a car that had run off the road and to close up for him."

"And you didn't see him when he came back," I prompted.

"No, ma'am, just the roll-back parked out front, like I told you. Haven't seen it since, either."

Mrs. Simmons sent him home with a vat of chicken salad and half a chocolate cake for his trouble. I'd guess he'd taken ten steps outside when he popped in the door again.

"Miss Warren, I forgot to tell you, when I gave you your suitcase, I didn't see your other bag because—"

"What other bag?"

"The one made out of a pair of jeans. It was sorta tucked down in a corner. It's kind of messy with blood and all, but I can bring it by tomorrow or—"

"Don't bother," I cut him off, immensely relieved to have proof that my memory had not been faulty.

"I'll be there first thing in the morning to pick it up."

He left again, and Mrs. Simmons leaned over the table to pat my hand. "I don't know that we need to worry about Chunky quite yet. I mean, he might have gotten held up getting parts for a sculpture he's working on. You wait. Bet he'll be back tomorrow."

I kept my thoughts to myself. If Chunky was indeed as honest as had been touted by Paulie and the doctor, then something was dreadfully wrong and I was more than a little concerned about the sculptor, especially considering the mysterious call he'd received. I was more concerned about him than I was my car.

Needless to say, I didn't get much sleep that night.

And in the chilly light of Saturday morning, the anxiety fluttering in the pit of my stomach was as much a reminder of the status quo as the annoying sensitivity at the back of my head was. I managed to stay horizontal until almost eight, then showered and dressed. I was threading my belt through the loops of the khaki cargo pants I'd exchanged for my jeans when my fingers froze on the buckle, a picture flashing behind my eyes with the clarity of a just-developed photograph.

Pale green walls. Old-fashioned black and white tile floor. Two stalls behind me. A basin and grainy mirror with a shelf below it, an empty soap dispenser on its left. And me, Leigh Warren, squeezing a small, rectangular box crammed with marijuana into my cell phone case, then threading it onto my belt.

My legs became flaccid and I slumped onto the bed, staring into yesterday, remembering the whole incident—calling Eddie, slamming into the stall to sit until I'd wrestled my anger with Duck to a level I could handle. Now the phone case was gone and there was no way for me to find out if Mr. Dawes had noticed it on my belt because he was in Morgantown somewhere at a family reunion. I doubted seriously that Major Hamilton had found it or I'd be in jail by now. Call Eddie again? No. There was nothing he could do to help.

I scrambled to my feet and finished dressing, spurred on by a growing list of feats to be accomplished. Get over to Chunky's to see if he'd shown up. Determine the status of my car. Retrieve the denim tote bag my passenger had left. See if there was anything in it that might help me identify her. Check the woods beyond the scene of the accident to see if I'd somehow lost the cell phone case when I'd run into the trees on foot. Continue my search for Duck by finding out what I could about the late J. B. Thomas. The smell of coffee wafted up the stairs, and I hot-footed down to the kitchen to find my hostess up to her elbows in biscuit dough.

"Mornin,'" she said, clearly enjoying herself. "Breakfast will be ready in two shakes. There's bacon and scrambled eggs and biscuits in the warmer and coffee's on the stove. This batch is for later. I don't open early like I used to, but I still try to feed folks who drop in."

As tempting as everything smelled, a trucker's breakfast two mornings in a row was more than I could handle. I opted for coffee and a couple of biscuits while I pumped Mrs. Simmons for information. Duck might not have gotten around to talking to her, but at some point he had definitely linked up with J.B.

"J.B.," she said, and shook her head. "He's turned out to be the most trifling member of the family. Lived here for a while when he was going to middle school. Painted landscapes on any kind of paper he could find. Even toilet tissue," she said with a bemused smile. "So talented, but went off the tracks somehow. Hasn't picked up a brush this year, according to Wilbur."

"Cates?" I asked, remembering his unusual log cabin.

"Sort of the local watercolor guru. J.B. had been living and working with him until recently. Got himself kicked out, is what I hear."

"Where'd he go?"

"Who knows? Bunked with a friend, probably. Or squatted in one of the old abandoned farmhouses around here. The county's condemned them, but kids break into them, and apprentices will use them if there's no more rooms available. Why are you interested in J.B.?"

I saw no reason not to tell her. "I think he and my friend Duck met at a Colorfest. Duck bought one of his paintings and said if he ever had a chance, he'd like to buy more of them. He was coming to this part of the world, so he might have tried to find J.B." I downed the rest of my coffee quickly, gathered my things and left before I might have to start improvising.

The Sanctuary beyond the Simmons house bore little resemblance to the quiet little town I'd ridden into yesterday. The streets teemed with people, scurrying from one artist's abode to the next. This was Sanctuary Saturday, a sales day. If Duck was still here, I'd never find him in this mob.

Chunky's appeared to be the only place not doing business. A computer-generated sign on the door of the trailer said CLOSED. I knocked anyway, then a second time, and after a moment Paulie opened the door. Behind him, the computer's monitor fairly shimmied with blobs and streaks of color. There was a three-dimensional effect about them. If this was the form Paulie's talent took, I was impressed.

"Oh, hey, Miss Warren. Come on in." He seemed relieved that it wasn't a customer, but I thought I detected a level of discomfort he hadn't exhibited before. "Chunky's not here, but he must have stopped by last night, maybe, and left in a big hurry. The door was unlocked when I got here. If I'd done that, he'd have kicked my butt."

"Did he leave a message or anything?"

"No, ma'am."

I couldn't decide whether to be pissed or perturbed and settled for a fifty-fifty mix. "Well, I'll take the denim bag and check back later to see if he's returned."

Paulie scrutinized the toes of his shoes, shifting from one foot to the other. "Er, it's not here, Miss Warren."

"Excuse me?"

He lifted his gaze to look at me, his expression pained. "It's gone. I guess Chunky must have taken it, because I swear it was here when I left last night. If I'd known you were at Aunt Vangie's, I'd have dropped it off right after I closed up. It was right there." He pointed at the niche from which he'd removed my suitcase. "See? There's even some"—he paused, swallowed—"some brown stuff that came off it, dried mud maybe. Or dried blood."

There were indeed dark-colored grains on the floor. Why would Chunky remove it? Did he know to whom it belonged? Was his intent to return it to her? Or hide the fact that it existed? Would honest-as-the-day-is-long Chunky Whatever-his-last-name-was do something like that? Willingly? I added, remembering the implied threat Paulie had related. What the hell was going on here?

"Okay. Don't worry about it, Paulie," I said, to let him off the hook. "I'm sure Chunky must have good reasons for everything. I'll give you a call later. What's the number here?"

I crossed to the phone and saw that not only was it a multi-line with a data port, it was one of the newer models with caller-ID. "How many calls have you received since Chunky left night before last?" I asked.

He looked blank. "Calls? Uh, let's see. Miss Ruth, that's Chunky's mama. Both Mr. Major and Mr. Minor called wanting to know when he was gonna bring your car. That's all."

"Would you recognize their numbers if you saw them?"

"Ma'am?" From the expression on his face, I'd asked a challenging question.

"Come here." My patience with this computer whiz was rapidly diminishing. "Look at these numbers. Whose is this?" I pushed the button to list incoming numbers in reverse.

"Uh . . . uh, that's a Reedy's Corner exchange, so that musta been Mr. Major. And that one would be Mr. Minor. That's Miss Ruth's." He frowned at the next number. "I don't know whose that is. Sure is a funny exchange."

I wrote it down after checking to be certain there weren't other numbers to be considered. I suspected that Paulie's funny exchange was probably a cellular phone. With Marty's help, I might be able to confirm that. The problem would be tracking her down on a weekend this close to her wedding day. She was probably out shopping or arranging something or other.

"Look, Paulie," I said, sitting him down to make sure I had his full attention. "I have a lot of running around to do, and need some means of transportation. Do you have any ideas?"

This was obviously a difficult question for Paulie. He gave it considerable thought, so much so that I began to wonder if he'd fallen asleep with his eyes open.

"Can you drive a stick shift?" he asked finally. "'Cause if you can, you can borrow my Uncle Bunk's Civic. He's selling today, so he won't be needing it."

I assured him I could drive anything on wheels

and would be happy to pay his uncle for the use of his car. Paulie ventured that filling the gas tank would be enough, since half the time his uncle forgot to do it. Evidently a vacuum between the ears ran in the family.

Paulie used the phone and after a surprisingly brief conversation with his uncle hung up. "He says you're welcome to it if you don't mind coming to get the keys. It's parked out back of here, but I can't go for them, either. With Chunky gone, I'm in charge of security."

I allowed as how I'd be more than willing to go for the keys myself, jotted down directions to his uncle's house, and let Paulie return to the intricate patterns streaking across the monitor of the computer.

Paulie's Uncle Bunk lived on the main street almost smack up against the town limits, so I'd have quite a distance to go before I'd have the keys to the Civic. The streets reminded me of a beehive, with more and more of the little buggers arriving by the minute. In spite of the numbers, the crowd was orderly, using the walkways even though there was no vehicular traffic on the roads. In fact, there was a festive air about the day, people smiling, total strangers stopping to show one another their purchases. They were having fun.

I found myself envious of their carefree attitudes and becoming more hostile with each step. After I'd almost snarled at someone who'd bumped into me, I moved off the walkway to put myself through an attitude adjustment. Granted, I was angry and anxious, but these shoppers were not responsible for my problems. Dillon Upshur Kennedy was. I needed to use my anger to find him. And the list I'd made last night of all the ceramicists and potters in Sanctuary's twenty-one-page telephone book was as good a place to start as any. Duck would not have been able to leave this town without stopping in to see the techniques other potters were using. He might also have dropped by the studio of Wilbur Cates while J.B. was still there. Looking at the addresses, I saw that I'd pass four ceramacists' studios on my way to Uncle Bunk's, and Wilbur Cates lived a couple of doors beyond my destination. I had to be fast, but it was worth a try.

By the time I reached the first shop, I had the routine I'd use down pat. Snag the potter or an apprentice at a slack moment, say my husband and I had lost one another in the crowds, show the photo of Duck and ask if they remembered seeing him.

My first, second and third stops, nothing. Quick shakes of the head, absolutely no hints of recognition. Frustration mounting, I had just left the third studio crammed to the hilt with hand-thrown bowls, vases and lamp bases when I stopped short, consumed with a certainty that I'd missed something.

Retracing my steps, I went back in, mystified. Glancing around, I saw no familiar faces and no reason to explain what I'd felt. On my way out again, I had to wriggle around a diminutive shopper on tiptoe as she tried to maneuver a hefty-sized lamp base to the edge of an upper shelf near the door. Foreseeing a catastrophe in the making, I stepped in behind her and offered to help.

She smiled at me over her shoulder. "I'd sure appreciate it. It's times like these I absolutely hate being vertically challenged. Here, I'll get out of the way." She stepped aside and I took her place. I considered myself average height but still had to stretch a bit to reach the lamp base. I'd managed to move it and get it securely in both hands when I saw the row of flower pots and bud vases on the narrower shelf just above. I froze in shock, my fingers slipping, the lamp base tilting dangerously toward my head. Fortuitously, another pair of hands appeared from behind me and grabbed the base, lifting it off for me. One of the young apprentices, identified as such by a plastic badge, had saved me from purchasing a bag full of shattered pottery because the signs were prominently displayed: YOU BREAK IT, YOU'VE BOUGHT IT. Whatever the price, it would have been worth it. On the shelf above the rescued lamp base was a bud vase perhaps six inches tall, its shape, the indented side, the thumbprint in the indentation identical to the one Duck had been so dissatisfied with, the only ceramic article he'd left in his abandoned condo. The only difference was the glaze. This one was a pale green with a mother of pearl sheen to it.

I thanked the apprentice and, terrified that I might drop it if I tried to reach it myself, asked him if he'd take down the bud vase for me. My hands trembled as I caressed its smooth finish. With a lump the size of Texas in my throat, I upended it to look at the bottom. Dillon Upshur Kennedy rarely signed his work with his initials; instead he would etch a tiny duck in the unfired clay and add the year. The bottom of this bud vase was unsigned. There were no initials, no tiny duck. But I knew without a shadow of a doubt whose hands had shaped this piece.

"Is this for sale?" I asked the apprentice.

"Yes, ma'am. Pay Mr. Cleveland." He turned away to rescue another lamp base from disintegration.

I followed him and waited until he'd finished. "Excuse me, is there any way to find out who made this? It's unsigned."

He gazed at it, then shrugged. "Not really. You could ask Mr. Cleveland. He might know." He nodded toward the stocky hawk-faced man near the cash box engaged in animated conversation with the woman buying the lamp base I'd almost purchased by default.

I took my place in line behind her, about to explode with impatience as they debated the wisdom of exchanging the lighting hardware for a fixture that would require a halogen bulb. When the debate had finally ended and the purchase had been paid for and boxed, I moved forward and extended the vase. "How much is this?" I asked. It seemed an appropriate opening gambit, especially since there was no price on it.

Mr. Cleveland pursed his lips. "Well, I'd say ten dollars would be fair."

I hesitated, eyeing it with pretended indecision. "I don't know. Would you take eight?"

It was his turn to pretend. He kept me waiting for a full fifteen heartbeats. "All right. Eight it is."

I went for my wallet and peeled off a five and three singles. "I do love the glaze. It's an unusual mixture. I'd like to talk to the person who made it, ask him—or her—how it was done."

"You're a potter, too?" he asked, wrapping it in newspaper.

There was no way I could fake any knowledge of throwing on a wheel. "The only experience I've had has been with commercial greenware and stains. But I've always wanted to learn to use a wheel and mix my own glazes. Who made this?"

He unwrapped the vase and examined it. "I think this was done by a guy in a master class last month. Don't remember his name. I'm not good with names."

"Any chance that this is the one?" I extended the photo of Duck again.

Frowning, he looked at me more closely. "Isn't this the same picture you showed me a few minutes ago?"

I plastered a sheepish smile across my face. "Yes. I suspect my husband made it. He's always saying I should take more interest in his hobby, and I'd like to prove to him I can recognize his work when I see it. His name is Dillon Kennedy, nicknamed Duck, and he's a glaze-mixing fool. He's messed up more than one load firing mixtures that exploded all over one another in the kiln."

Mr. Cleveland grinned. "Can't tell you how easy that is to do, especially with reds. Let me see." He reached for a pair of glasses and examined the photo. "It might have been him. No mustache, though, and his hair wasn't this short. That's the best I can do." He handed it back. "I'm not good with faces, either, just hands. And I was only there the first day of the class. Miller took over for the other three. This is his studio. He'd remember, but he's in New York for a gallery opening."

I'd have to be satisfied with Mr. Cleveland's "maybe." "How long ago was the class?"

"Three weeks ago. We hold one once every quarter if you're interested. Sign up early, though. Only have places for twelve and they fill up fast."

Accepting my bud vase, I told him I'd certainly think about it and took my leave. Outside, I parked under a sycamore tree to think. Three weeks ago. Was Duck still in the vicinity or had he moved on in search of his father? I wished now I'd had time to ask someone in the Department to digitize the photo of Duck Senior and add twenty-five years to his face. Someone here might have recognized him, in which case I could be fairly certain that Duck wouldn't be far behind.

But it was too late for that. And J. B. Thomas had showed up at my apartment roughly twelve days ago, so I could assume that Duck hadn't left after the master class. If he'd stayed around, others had to have seen him. If nothing else, he'd have had to find somewhere to hang his hat.

And that raised a possibility. According to Mrs. Simmons, practically everyone in town had heard about my accident on the same night it happened. If

Duck was here, he'd have probably heard, too. I added the checking of boardinghouses to my list of things to do, despairing of how little time I had left, and got moving again.

By the time I held the keys of the Civic in my hand, I had struck out at the studio of the fourth potter and with Wilbur Cates, who looked at the photo, shook his head and, in response to a question about J.B., told me that he hadn't seen him in a month and would throw him out again if he showed up. As diplomatically and ingenuously as I tried to find out what J.B. had done, there was no penetrating the force field of his anger on the subject. I thanked him and got out of there before he could calm down enough to wonder how I came to know J.B. in the first place.

I rushed back to Chunky's as fast as I could, my knee beginning to protest about halfway there. Still no word from the sculptor. Paulie's description of the location of the Civic in the lot jammed with a hundred-plus vehicles convinced me to let him play parking attendant and retrieve it for me. Waiting out front for him to bring it around, I cast a jaundiced eye at Chunky's totem poles and promised myself if he'd removed so much as a hub cap from my baby, he'd find a vital part of his anatomy as a prominent feature of a totem pole of my own construction.

Paulie arrived in what looked like a brand-new car. "It was practically down to fumes, so I put in five dollars worth at the pump."

I took the hint and forked over the money, then

got behind the wheel, reveling in the new car smell. "How long has your uncle had this?" I asked, listening to the purr of the engine.

"A couple of months maybe. Somebody stole the last one of his. It was better for driving off-road to collect wood for his artwork."

"It wouldn't have happened to be an Explorer?" I asked, playing an unlikely hunch.

Paulie shot me down in flames, saying, "No, ma'am, an Outback. Somebody took the one before that, too, so Uncle Bunk decided he'd stick to something basic. Four-wheel-drive vehicles don't last too long around here anymore."

"Why not?"

"Well, Chunky's tried to keep it quiet, but five of 'em have walked off our lot in the last six months. That's another reason I've got to stick around, to keep an eye on the security panel. Oh, and you'll have to take the back road to get out of town. No vehicular traffic allowed on the streets, especially on sales days."

Which nudged another question to the fore. "Then where do all the shoppers park?"

"Over to Reedy's Corner and Peace Station. There are big public lots over there. Folks leave their cars there, and the Pike boys ferry them over here on buses that leave every half hour."

"How do they get back to their cars?" I asked.

"Same way. Bus picks them up behind the town hall all day long. I'd better get back inside. You need directions or anything? Where are you going anyway?"

"To Reedy's Corner, where I wrecked my car, for one, then to Major Hamilton's to talk to him."

"He's probably directing traffic at the public lot. Okay, here's how you go."

They were the kind of directions you write down or forget the whole thing. Few road names, just landmarks: a couple of windmills; a red barn with a cow face painted on the side; a big oak with a trunk split by lightning; a mailbox that looked like a miniature church. As disconcerting as that was, I arrived at my destination with no trouble and understood immediately why I hadn't been the first to fail to negotiate the curve.

Even approaching it from the opposite direction in broad daylight put a strain on my driving skills. It was practically a U-turn, a switchback of sorts. I drove beyond it perhaps a quarter of a mile before I found a niche safe enough to leave the spanking new car I'd borrowed, and walked back.

"It's a mother," Paulie had volunteered, speaking of the curve. He was right. I wondered how I'd survived it. On one side there was no shoulder to speak of, and the adjacent terrain soared upward at practically a ninety-degree angle. In other words, a minor cliff. On the opposite side, the shoulder was perhaps half the width of a midsize car, its cant away from the tarmac. From there the slope continued in a perilous descent through underbrush to the point where the trees began, tall, ageless, sturdy, unmovable. An open wound in the trunk of a stately old evergreen marked the point of impact of my poor Old Faithful. I'd walked away from it only because there were no substantial limbs near the lower section of the tree.

Something as small as my cellular phone case would be difficult to see from the road. The only problem was, once I got down there I wasn't sure I'd be able to get back up again. The incline was too steep. There had to be a way. Even though my memory hadn't cleared enough for me to recall precisely where I'd seen the hitchhiker coming out of the trees, I had a feeling that it hadn't been that far from here. I might have to walk a ways back to find it, but if she'd managed to make her way to my car, an easier climb had to be back there somewhere.

Looping the strap of my purse over my head, I approached the edge of the shoulder and started down. Before long, I'd lost my footing and gravity took over. Underbrush ripping at my clothes, I slid the rest of the way on my behind, winding up a couple of yards away from the injured tree.

On my feet again, I took inventory and determined that aside from a few scratches on my arms and a coat of damp dirt on my backside, I'd live. I was on familiar ground now, in that I'd spent many a day scanning terrain inch by inch for evidence after a crime. I began a methodical search of the area and moved a good distance into the trees, probably farther than I'd managed the night of the accident, but I was taking no chances. The result? Shards of my headlights, a couple of pieces of my grille, one windshield wiper, the remains of a balloon (not mine), a hubcap (not mine), and a fine-tooth comb (also not mine). So the phone case had not come off as I'd stumbled around in delirium going for help. And Doc Williams seemed sure there'd been nothing left in the car. So what had happened to it?

Giving up, I started back toward the Civic, picking my way along the edge of the forest. I'd gone no more than a dozen or so steps when I noticed a pair of parallel grooves running along ahead of me. They were visible only on softer ground where weeds and fallen leaves weren't as thick underfoot. They were too irregular and not deep enough to have been made by bike riders. Had something, or someone, been dragged this way? It had to have been fairly recently while the ground was still wet. It had yet to dry out, to which, thanks to my slide down the hill, my damp rear end could attest.

I followed the grooves for some distance, losing them to ground cover occasionally but persisting until I could pick them up again. I suffered a moment of indecision when they veered off into the trees. The woods were dense here, enough so that not only did I have some doubt about being able to see well enough to continue trailing the indentations, there was a distinct possibility once I passed the point that I could see this area, I might not be able to find my way back to it. I had a fairly good sense of direction, but given how closely the trees grew to one another and the heavy foliage overhead, I had little faith that my mental compass would be able to keep track of which way was north. And Hansel and Gretel I wasn't. I had nothing with which to mark my path. I did, however, have a high-powered penlight.

Assuring myself that God looks out for fools and babies, I forged ahead, stepping from the bright, late morning sunlight into a dusk-in-February gloom. Six feet into the forest and it was damned near night. I hesitated but not for long. With the beam of the penlight glued to the ground, I plodded on, refusing to look anywhere else but down. Creatures I couldn't see scurried away in panic, and birds I wouldn't have been able to see even if I'd looked up screeched their indignation at my invasion of their territory. It was unnerving, but I'd asked for it and now I was stuck with it.

The drag ruts weren't as easy to follow now because the terrain had become an unending carpet of moldy leaves and needles, twigs and pine cones. I scuffed a path through them to help me backtrack if the ruts finally succumbed to the forest's litter. That happened sooner than I'd thought it would and I stopped, sweeping the penlight's high-focus beam from side to side in a wider arc than before. That's when I saw that I'd been so locked onto the ruts that I hadn't realized this was actually a clearly defined path through the trees. It hadn't been at the point I'd entered the woods, but somewhere along the way the ruts had begun to follow it.

Immensely relieved, I kept going. A path had to lead somewhere, didn't it? Wherever it ended, it felt as if it would take forever to get there. In actuality, I'd scuffed along for only a few minutes when I began to detect that I could see my surroundings more clearly. It was getting brighter. The trees were thinning.

I slowed and proceeded with even more caution. Which was just as well, on two counts. On the first, with another few steps I'd have been completely out of the woods. They stopped abruptly, beyond them a field of chest-high weeds and in the distance a shack listing dangerously to one side, as if a giant had leaned against it. On the second count, there was the sudden explosion of bark from the tree to my right. I hit the ground like a boulder and flattened my gut against the ground. It hadn't happened often, just enough for me to recognize it when I heard it. Someone had shot at me. I was the bull's-eye in somebody's target. For the first time in my life, I missed my bulletproof vest.

I took stock of my situation. The woods offered limited protection. Most were evergreens of some sort, shaped like Christmas trees with branches so low on the trunk I would have difficulty working my way under them. The others nearest me, while thick enough through the trunk, were too far apart to do me any good. If I managed to get behind one, I'd be stuck there.

My only salvation was the field of weeds. I crawled forward off the path and slithered into the forest of feathery gold stalks faster than a cockroach across a counter with a rolled-up newspaper descending on it. I'd fought my way through a good couple of yards when a vice gripped my ankle. My heart jolted. Whipping my free knee to my chest, I flipped over on my back, prepared to kick the shit out of whoever had grabbed me. I never got the chance.

"Goddamn it, Leigh! What the hell are you doing here?" Dillon Upshur Kennedy. Duck.

16

I HAD ABSOLUTELY NO CONTROL OVER what happened next. I hit him. Not an open-hand slap, either; it was your balled-up fist across the chops kind of blow. Fueled by the gut-clenching fear that had gripped me when the bark had gone flying, and the gut-churning fury I'd lived with since Monday, I held nothing back. I got him good and by God, it felt good. Stunned him, too. Knocked him silly. He lost his grip on my ankle and slumped to one side, blinking as if a flashbulb had gone off in his face.

"You hit me!" he croaked.

"Damned straight."

"Why? I missed you, didn't I?"

I sat up. "That was you shooting at me?" He rolled over onto his stomach so I could see the pea shooter .22 tucked in his belt at the small of his back. I hadn't thought I could get any angrier. I was wrong. I closed my fist to belt him again.

He saw it coming, sat up, and in one swift movement reached over and grabbed my wrist. "One's all you get," he said, then released me, a grimace contorting his features. Turning his head awkwardly, he peered down at his left shoulder, where a widening blossom of blood had begun to seep through his T-shirt. He muttered, "Shit."

"I didn't do it," I exclaimed, sounding like a five-year-old who had indeed done it.

"I know it. And keep your voice down. We've got to get away from here. Now listen. We're gonna be heading for that shack. Get behind me and follow me precisely, not one foot to the side in either direction, understand?"

"If I remember correctly, my IQ's as high as yours," I said snippily. "That place doesn't look safe. Why are we going there?"

"So what happened to me won't happen to you. You ready?"

"Just wait a minute." After the mental anguish I'd gone through this week, I was in no mood for a game of follow the leader. "I am not ready. What the hell is going on? Why are you out here in the middle of nowhere? How'd you get hurt? And have you found your father yet, or am I too late?"

Something flared behind his eyes before they lost all expression. He gazed back at me, stone-faced. "So you found out about that."

"No thanks to you. We've got a lot to talk about, buster. I want some answers and I want them *now*!"

"Really?" he asked. "Right now, this very minute, when there's every possibility we're in the crosshairs of the son of a bitch up there in that forest ranger's tower?"

I dropped to my stomach and looked around, craning to see the tower. If he hadn't mentioned it, I could have walked right under it without realizing it, camouflaged as it was by trees that had grown up around it. "Well, maybe not this very minute," I capitulated. "But I've got a car back out there on the road, and I scuffed a path through the woods so I could find my way out again. Let's give it a try."

"Uh-uh. If that guy's up there, we'll be clearly visible as soon as we leave the field until we're several yards deep into the woods. He's good enough to pop us both in that time. Our best bet is to keep low and use these weeds for cover. It's lucky you're wearing khaki. You'll blend right in. And the shack is sturdier than it looks. Now, are you ready or not?"

Two minutes with him and he was already bossing me around. "All right. Let's go."

He rose up high enough to get his bearings, then set off at a trot, bent low. I lasted an embarrassing twenty or so steps before I cried uncle. "Duck, wait up."

He looked back over his shoulder. "What?"

"My knee can't take this. I could probably do it standing straight up, but not practically squatting."

He looked at me with dismay. "Sorry. I forgot. I don't know what we're gonna do, because with this shoulder I can't carry you, babe. And it's too far to go on hands and knees. Let me think." He sat down, let his head drop to his chest. For the first time there was time to get a good look at him. What I saw made my heart clench with anxiety.

Mr. Cleveland's memory was more accurate than he thought. Not only was Duck thinner than he'd been in June, his well-muscled arms were smaller, his mustache was gone and his hair, which he'd always worn on the short side, was longer than I'd ever seen it. His color, normally a deep, rich mahogany, seemed faded, as if it hadn't seen the sun in a long time. It was also surprising the difference being clean-shaven made to his appearance. He looked younger, more vulnerable. And there was no animation, no joy in his face or eyes, none of the aura of loving life that had always drawn others to him. Is this what hatred did to you?

"Think you can stand being topless for a few minutes?" he asked. "I need your shirt. Camouflage."

I had no idea what he had in mind, but seven years of experience with him were enough that I didn't waste time asking questions. I peeled it off and handed it to him.

"New bra," he commented, then draped my shirt over his head. "If I'm not back in fifteen minutes, take your chances and work your way back to your car."

"Where are you going?"

"To check out the tower. It may be empty. It isn't manned on any particular schedule, as far as I can tell, just hit-and-miss."

"But why would a forest ranger shoot at us anyway?" I asked.

"That's no forest ranger, believe me. The tower's been abandoned for some time, from the looks of it, and a couple of particularly unsavory characters have taken up periodic residence. Look, I don't have time to explain. It's important you stay put for another fifteen minutes. This field is booby-trapped and you can get hurt. Time me, okay?"

I glanced at my watch, and when I looked up again, he was gone, the only indication of his progress the swish of weeds as he pushed his way through them. As exposed as I felt with no top on, he'd been right to use my shirt. Running with it over his head, he was practically invisible until he reached the tower a football field length away.

He circled around it, staying as close to the base as he could before starting to scale the ladder. It appeared to be an awkward climb, and I realized his shoulder wound was making it more difficult for him. It seemed to take him an awfully long time to get to the top. He was immobile for a moment, either resting or listening for sounds of life in the enclosure. Then I lost sight of him, but only for a second. Very shortly he appeared in the opening on my side, waved, and I began breathing again.

For some reason, five minutes elapsed before he climbed down. He made the descent with considerably more ease, returned to my side in no time and handed me my shirt. "The coast is clear for the time being, so you should be able to get back to your car okay."

"I take that to mean you aren't coming with me?"

"Can't. It's complicated, and I don't know how long it'll be before somebody shows up in that tower. So scram, okay? I'll be in touch."

"You bet your butt you'll be in touch, because I'm not going anywhere without you. I came here to stop you from doing something stupid if I could and to take you back with me whether you've killed your father or not."

"Killed my father?" He tried to fake astonishment but could see from my expression that it was a wasted effort. "Okay, okay. I admit if I'd found him, I might have done just that. The operative word is *might*. I may still have to, and the operative words are *may have to*. Right now I've got other priorities, which means I stay here. Now, will you get going, please?"

"No. We've got to talk, and I'm not letting you out of my sight until we've done it. Makes me no never mind whether we do it in the car, in the shack, or right here in the middle of all these damned weeds with bugs and snakes crawling through them. You choose. It's up to you."

The bit about the snakes was a cheap shot. Duck hated snakes. It worked.

"The shack," he said tightly. "I can get you back to your car another way. Come on. Stay right behind me." He stood, and with an occasional glance over his shoulder, strode toward the left-leaning outbuilding.

The closer we got, the worse the shack looked. It was larger than I'd thought, and it wasn't until we were actually in it that I realized what it really was. "Duck, you dummy," I said, "this isn't a shack. It's a barn. A small one, but still a barn."

"Barn, shack, what's the difference? It kept me dry the night it rained like blazes."

I gaped at him. "You were here that night? I wrecked my car right over there, going to Sanctuary to look for you."

He turned. "Is that what all the activity was about? I'm sorry, babe. Glad you're okay. If I'd known . . ." He closed the door behind us and didn't move for a moment, waiting for our eyes to adjust to the lower light level. The interior proved how deceiving the exterior was. It was both larger and longer than it appeared from outside, and only one end of it leaned. Otherwise, it seemed fairly sturdy and weatherproof. It had the close, moldy smell of a building that hadn't been used in a long time, but it wasn't unpleasant. There were several stalls directly opposite us, and rusting farm implements littered the side on which we'd entered.

"Think you can make that climb?" Duck asked, tilting his head toward the loft at the far end.

"If you can, I can."

He smiled at me in the gloom and, without warning, pulled me to him. Before I could react, I was being thoroughly and passionately kissed. His hands moved from my waist to cradle my face, and my response was automatic. I melted against him, my arms circling his torso as I tried to glue myself to every inch of him I could. He took a moment to nuzzle the hollow of my neck, the tip of his tongue igniting circles of fire under my skin, before he got back to the business at hand, or rather lip. My toes curled in ecstasy. Backward. Lord, I'd missed him. I almost forgot how mad I was at him. Almost.

I pushed him away. "Don't think you can seduce me into changing my mind about taking you back to D.C."

"To tell you the truth," he said with a wicked

smile, "what I had in mind was seducing you out of your pants. It's been a long time, babe."

"Don't call me babe," I snapped. "And we're going up to the loft to talk, nothing else. You've got a lot of explaining to do."

He sobered. "Yeah, I guess I have. Come on." Taking my hand, which I snatched away for effect, he led me to the ladder. "After you."

I hesitated. The ladder felt sturdy, but from the bottom the loft looked a long way up, and once I was up there, the floor looked a long way down. With little head for heights, I backed away from the edge. Watching Duck make the climb wouldn't help him one way or the other.

To my relief, the floor up here seemed clean, with bales of hay stacked at one end, loose straw piled at the other. A rake leaned against the wall beside a wide double door. Perhaps because of the low light level, I hadn't noticed that a walkway of sorts spanned the length of the barn along the side above the door we'd entered, leading to a much more shallow loft at the end that listed toward the left. Shutters shielded a window there.

I crossed to the double doors, one of which was slighty ajar, peeked out and wished I had a camera. It was postcard or calendar material. Now I could appreciate singing about "amber waves of grain," even though I doubted this was grain. Whatever it was, acres of it, far more picturesque from a distance, undulated in the breeze, a maize-colored surf crashing against an old, ramshackle two-story house snuggled in a hollow that seemed a lot farther from the barn than I would have thought a barn should be. Not that I was all that familiar with the layout of farms, except for the few on the outskirts of Sunrise, but this house was at least a half mile away. Perhaps it was on different property.

Duck had moved in behind me. "Pretty, isn't it? Don't be fooled. This place is dangerous. You got anything in that steamer trunk you carry I can use as a pressure bandage?"

I like big purses. They hold lots of stuff. It was something he'd always teased me about, but I had regained my pique and was in no mood for dissing of any kind. Still, he was bleeding.

"Nothing that'll do much good. We'll have to improvise. What exactly happened to you?" I asked, removing the wrapper from my last pack of Kleenex. With a finger I pulled the neck of his T-shirt out to get a better look at the wound. All I saw was a skimpy gauze square becoming more saturated by the minute.

I pressed the wad of tissues against the gauze. "Hold this a minute." I unbuttoned my shirt and took it off again, removed my bra, then quickly put my shirt back on. Duck watched, a slight smile playing around his lips. I draped the bra over his shoulder and tied it under his armpit, securing the tissues in place. "You haven't answered my question. How did this happen?"

"Got shot with a jerry-rigged zip gun," he said tersely, "which was what I was trying to prevent happening to you."

"By taking a potshot at me yourself?"

"I saw you coming from the window at the other end. Without knowing whether there was anyone in the tower, I couldn't yell at you, so I did the only thing I could think of. Unfortunately, I was too far away to be sure I'd hit anything. Probably aggravated the shoulder scrambling down and getting out there in time to catch you."

"In other words, this is my fault, right?"

"That's not what I meant. Better that I shoot at you than that maniac in the tower. Like I said, there's dangerous stuff going on back here, worth trying to kill anyone in the vicinity."

"Did it ever occur to you it might be because they don't like trespassers?" I asked, my mood not improving.

"It's more than that. The whole area's full of all sorts of nasty tricks, the kind that maim and kill."

"Well, then someone's probably got a marijuana crop they're trying to protect. What are you doing back here anyway? Poaching?"

Adjusting the knot under his armpit, he scowled. "What's that supposed to mean?"

"Considering your recently developed fondness for cannabis, it's a logical question."

"My what?" He seemed genuinely puzzled, and not a little indignant.

"Word around the Sixth, which has gotten to Cap Moon by the way, is that you've become a pothead."

He looked outraged. "Me? A pothead?"

"Well, what else were they supposed to think after you kept that damned piggy bank, exchanged the pot in the baggies with oregano and spent the summer making purchases from known dealers?"

"If anybody switched the contents of those baggies, it was Wilkies, not me. Yes, I kept the bank. As for everything else I've done, I was trying to track down the source of the pot, for Christ's sake! That shit was killing people! I had to find out where it was coming from!"

"And you thought your father had something to do with it, right? You left D.C. fully intending to find him and kill him. Otherwise, why would you sell your beloved kiln, give Mrs. Luby your Negro League collection and sign your condo over to me? You figured you'd be spending the rest of your natural life in jail, right?"

I could see his pressure rising. Tough. I wanted an explanation any way I could get it.

"Okay, okay," he said finally, wriggling back into his shirt. He sat down and slumped against the wall. "I admit I flipped, blew a gasket. When I saw that piggy bank—"

"I know all about the history of the bank and your dad leaving and Christopher's death, everything. So you can skip that part. You can also skip that stupid ultimatum you issued me and turning in your badge. Start at the point you decided to hit the road."

"Jesus, is there anything you don't know already?"

"You bet. Everything else. Let's hear it."

"All right." He took a deep breath, shifted his shoulder awkwardly. "Look, finding the bank really threw me. I mean, after all these years, out of the blue my father's good-luck piece shows up. I wasn't sure what to think. What were the chances he was still alive? Mom is seventy-two. Dad was four years older. Statistics say the odds were against it."

As much as I hated to interrupt him, I felt obligated to. "There's something you should know. Your mother had a heart attack at Vanessa's Sunday night. She's doing okay," I said hurriedly, to stave off the panic in his eyes. "She had a rough couple of days, but when I left to come looking for you day before yesterday, she had rallied and was out of the woods."

"Where is she?" he asked, his voice hoarse.

"University of Maryland Medical Center. That's another reason you have to go back. She's been asking for you."

"Oh, God." He lowered his head again, then got up and began to pace. "I don't know what I'm going to do. I'm so close now, so close."

"To what?" I demanded. I'd hoped that the news of his mother's illness might be enough to finish this once and for all.

"To nailing the bastards who've been distributing the shit that's been killing people, that's what. I was just about to turn in the damned bank and forget the whole business about my old man when I noticed the color of the weed in it. There was an odd cast to it, sort of a metallic glint. On the q.t. I had a lab do an analysis, and it turns out the pot had been saturated with something they couldn't identify. It's in the PCP family but a form my buddy in the lab hadn't seen before. All he could say was that its effect on the body could be disastrous. You've seen how manic PCP can make you. Pete said this stuff might be half again as bad and, depending on the health of the smoker, could very well kill him."

I groaned. The role as bearer of bad news was beginning to wear on me. "Duck, it killed J. B. Thomas."

He jerked to a stop mid-step. "What?"

"I found his body in my kitchen—"

"Your kitchen? What the hell was he doing in your kitchen? I sent him to my place to get Pete's address and phone number. I'd left it in the back of the case my diskettes are in. He was supposed to knock in case you had moved in and use the key only if you didn't answer. He was to take the pot he'd bought off one of those bastards who's been manning the tower to Pete's lab for analysis."

"According to Mrs. Luby, he couldn't get in. She very obligingly gave him my name and address so he could leave a message, since she knew I was now the owner. He evidently lucked out when he tried the other key at my place. When I got back from Sunrise on Monday, there he was. He'd made himself at home, had settled down at the table and lit a roach. He had a heart defect. The way it was put to me, his heart sort of exploded." I saw no point in bringing up the toaster, since in the end, it had had nothing to do with J.B.'s death.

Duck turned and clenched a fist to pound against the wall, then thought better of it. "That fool! Why would he do that? He knew that stuff might be poison! And he swore to me he'd cleaned up his act!" He circled the floor, seething with frustration. "It's my fault. I should have known—once a pothead, always a pothead. Now the supply I sent is gone." He paused, look down at me. "Well, maybe not. Did you get the box I sent you?"

Uh-oh. More bad news. "I got it, but it's gone."

He blinked. "Gone where? I put a note in it telling you to give it to Eddie so he could have it analyzed. What did you do with it?"

"I didn't open it until I was on my way here. I thought it was a free soap sample."

"My God, you didn't toss it, did you?"

"No, once I saw what it was, I stashed it in the cellular phone case you gave me and put it on my belt. When I came to after the accident, it was gone. That's what I was doing today, searching the woods for it. I couldn't find it. But while I was looking, I spotted drag marks that started in the vicinity of where my car wound up."

"Drag marks?" Duck squatted, his scrutiny of me intent.

"Yes. I picked up a hitchhiker in the rain, a blond girl. She was with me when I skidded off the road and hit the tree, but she wasn't in the car when the man who heard the impact got to me. The doctor who came to the scene said the passenger seat was so saturated with blood that it was doubtful whoever had lost it could have walked away under their own steam. The drag marks may explain what happened. I followed them until I lost them in the woods, just about where the trees start thinning."

Duck kept his counsel for several long, empty minutes. "Things are worse than I thought. I'm pretty sure your hitchhiker's dead."

I think I'd always suspected that, but the impact of hearing it still raised goose bumps down my arms. "Why?"

"Because I was down there in the field when this big, burly white dude came out of the trees just about where you did. He had someone over his shoulder in a fireman's carry, but it was so dark and raining so hard there was only so much I could see clearly. I thought he was carrying a fair-haired woman, but half the white guys here have long hair and a lot of them are blonde so it could have been a male or female. He took her toward the tower. I started back here, and that's when I accidentally triggered one of the booby-traps and got myself shot. I lost them after that, but from the looks of that tower, your hitchhiker lost the rest of whatever blood she had left up there. And your cellular phone case is up there. Take my word for it, you don't want it anymore."

So they'd gotten to me before Mr. Dawes showed up. If they thought they were stealing a phone, they'd been disappointed. On second thought, they'd probably been pleasantly surprised. I felt sick and vaguely responsible, even though I'd had no part in what had happened to my passenger. In picking her up, I'd done as much as I could to help. "Is her body still there?" I asked.

"No. I don't know when it was removed. Do me a favor. If there's anything else I should know, tell me now and get it over with, okay?"

So I did, starting from my arrival back in D.C., including Tank, Tina, my conversations with Eddie and Toulouse's mother and sister, the confrontation in his garage, the Monday deadline, the absent Chunky and my missing car.

"Holy shit," Duck said. "No wonder you hit me." His lapses into profanity were testament to how long it had been since he'd seen Tyler. His discovery of what a parrot she could be, even on occasions when he thought she wasn't in hearing distance, had convinced him to watch his mouth. He gave me a wan smile. "And for the record, I didn't mean that Tank was supposed to practically move in with you. All I said was something like 'check on her now and then.' Don't know why he took it to such extremes. Now, give me a minute, okay? I need to think."

As far as I was concerned, he could take as long as he liked. I planned to wait him out. I crawled to the door again and peeked through the crack. Except for one difference, the scene hadn't changed, the weeds shifting to the whims of the wind, still resembling crashing waves in an ocean of gold. The difference was the unexpected appearance of the roof of a vehicle bouncing through a distant field toward the dilapidated house.

"Duck, does someone live there?" I asked.

"In the house?" I could tell he was still in a contemplative mode, and regretted having to disturb him. "No. I've been in it and it's vacant. Looks like there have been squatters, though—footprints in the dust, food wrappers, a pile of clothes, some of them a woman's. They look too fresh to have been around very long. Why?"

"There's a car out there." I knelt so he'd have a clear view above my head. The vehicle left the field. Once out of the weeds, it proved to be a black Jeep Cherokee. It skidded to a halt on the far side of the front porch. I longed for binoculars. Without them, all I could tell was that the person who exited the Jeep and entered the house was male, probably white, and on the heavy side. Despite the distance, there was something familiar about him.

"That may be the dude I saw carrying the girl," Duck said. "I know him."

We watched for what seemed a long time. Finally, Duck couldn't stand it. "I'm going down there," he said, testing the security of the pressure bandage.

"Then I'm going with you." I stood up.

"Not on your life. Look, babe—sorry, I mean, Leigh—I'm here because on Memorial Day weekend a skinny twelve-year-old kid went soaring out a sixth-floor window after he'd completely destroyed the apartment he lived in. He knocked holes in walls, ripped doors off their hinges, overturned the refrigerator."

"I remember that."

"Good." He went back to check on any activity outside, watching as he spoke. "That kid had been smoking weed tainted with whatever that stuff is. A twelve-year-old! I had to do something. I could have asked for a transfer to Narcotics, but that wouldn't have been enough. I'd still have to stick to the book, and in my case the book would be a straitjacket, preventing me from doing what needed to be done."

"Because of the remote possibility of your father's involvement? Duck, you couldn't be sure he was still alive."

"Regardless, once the relationship surfaced, which it would have eventually—"

"Only if you told them," I said.

"I'd have to. Them's the rules. And they'd have kicked me off the case—that's if I'd managed to get assigned to it to begin with. Personal involvement, possible conflict of interest—"

"And they'd be right," I added.

"Maybe so, but I couldn't risk it. If my dad had anything to do with this, I wanted to get to him first."

"To punish him for it or for walking out on you twenty-five years ago?"

"Twenty-six," he snapped, looking at me for the first time. "And I don't know." He turned back to the opening in the door. "I had to find out, one, whether he was alive and, two, if he was, where he fitted into the picture. No matter which way it turned out, I had to find the scum responsible for that poison. Since I couldn't be sure what I might have to do once I found the perpetrators or if I'd survive the encounter, I put my affairs in order."

"Yeah. Thanks a lot," I grumbled.

He smiled over at me. "Ungrateful wench."

"Sticks and stones. Have you found your father?"

"No. But I do know that Toulouse was here. Never even stopped to see his family. Went to ground for a few days, then stole the Explorer from the public lot and you know the rest. Where he got the hard stuff he was carrying, I don't know and don't care. I'm after the marijuana. It's taken me over a month, but I've located a dealer in Sanctuary. Had to make a couple of buys before he trusted me enough to promise a more potent batch. Then for some reason he started putting me off."

"How'd you hook J.B. into it?" I asked, then wished I'd worded the question differently.

"He volunteered. I ran into him my first week here, and he remembered me. We became bullshit-tin' buddies, and by that time I'd found out he was persona non grata because he'd started smoking pot and fouling up big-time. I let him know I'd made a couple of buys but that there was a more potent pot around somewhere. He said he'd sworn off it because when he was smoking he didn't care whether he painted or not and his art was his life. He said he could get the stronger stuff for me."

"Which he did," I said, remembering the roach in my saucer.

"Which he did, but when he gave it to me, I sensed something was bugging him. He tells me that the guy he got it from was high and running off at the mouth about how they were testing the new crop, trying to perfect the right amount of the addi-tive. They've been using Sanctuary's kids and a few apprentices as guinea pigs, throwing pot parties, then gradually introducing them to the stronger stuff. Then they blackmailed them to get them to steal cars and ferry the laced product to D.C."

"What was to prevent them from smoking it all themselves or selling it and not coming back?"

"A threat to burn out their families. That was enough to keep them in line. What did it for J.B. was finding out they'd hooked his younger sister. He was trying to figure out what he could do to stop them. He was upset enough that I thought I could trust him with the truth. He went to D.C. for me."

"Didn't you wonder when he didn't come back?" I asked.

He nodded. "I gave him enough money to stay in a motel until he had the lab results, but I knew he should have been back before now. So I tailed one of the scum suckers I'd bought the first batch from. I lost him in this vicinity, so I've been here ever since scoping out these two tracts of land. There's no sign of a crop, nothing except for that jackass manning the tower—which I'd better check again before I go over to that house. You've held me up long enough, babe. And you're staying here."

"How do you figure on stopping me?" I asked. "I may have a bum knee, but I don't have an open wound that's bleeding. I decked you once. I can and will do it again if I have to." It was a gutsy move because I was pretty sure he could still take me if he really wanted to, and there were several coils of rope in the vacant stalls down below he could use to hogtie me. I crossed my fingers behind my back and glared a dare at him. He bit.

"Damn it, you are one hardheaded woman. All right, but the rules are the same. I've mapped out all booby-traps, so stay behind me and don't veer from my route by one single step. Clear?"

I agreed, and after checking to see if his wound had stopped bleeding, we climbed down and crept toward the tower, moving in fits and starts with one ear listening for any sign that the man in the Jeep was leaving. All we heard was the wind through the weeds and trees. I remained below while Duck climbed the tower. It was vacant.

Relieved, we practically ran to the house, approaching it from the back before circling to peer in the windows. It was a small house—living room, dining room and large kitchen on the first floor, probably no more than four rooms and bath on the second. Deep front and back porches. No visible sign of a cellar.

Innumerable coats of paint had flaked off layer by layer, so the clapboard siding was now completely bare. Several windows were broken, and shutters dangled from rusting hinges. Generations of termites had held banquets where the siding met the brick foundation, and as far as I was concerned, the floor of the porch was also suspect.

We edged around to the front. The door was open, exposing a central hall and stairs to the second floor. Most of the treads were missing, and boards had been nailed across the bottom to block access.

The Cherokee was still there, parked on the far side of the porch, wires dangling under the dashboard. It was empty. And so was the house.

17

THE ONLY PERIOD THE HOUSE HAD BEEN out of our sight had been less than a minute, the length of time it had taken us to leave the loft and the barn. That's not to say the person we saw couldn't have left within that minute, but where could he have gone? There was nothing else around, no outbuildings of any kind. The house sat in a hollow, with a steep hill rising at its rear, the incline such that it would take a climber several minutes to scale it. So in spite of the fact that every room on the first floor was empty, we were positive that the man was still on the premises.

We retreated to the rear yard to reconnoiter, positioned so we were out of sight of the tower but could still see if anyone got in the Cherokee.

"We agree we would have seen him if he'd left, right?" Duck asked. "And only a monkey could climb the banister to get to the second floor. So there's obviously more to that house than is visible, some sort of trapdoor to a cellar."

"Why would anyone dig a cellar with no access to the outside?" I asked.

"There's got to be one. All we've got to do is find it."

I stood watch while Duck scoured the area around the house. All he found was a cache of beer bottles and the handle of what we supposed had been an ax. He returned and collapsed to the ground beside me, his face expressionless. There was something he wasn't telling me.

"Nothing?" I asked.

"No luck. The only way must be in the house. One thing's sure. I can't do any poking around in there until that dude's gone."

"I? As in you, singular?" It was fighting time again. This was getting old. "Not alone, Duck. You have no idea what you'll be walking into, and all you have is that wimpy twenty-two. You're going to need backup. You have solid grounds for what you suspect is down there. I say we report this to Major Hamilton. He serves as the law in Reedy's Corner and—"

He grinned, and I saw a shadow of the Duck I knew. "Let me guess. You haven't met the honorable Major Hamilton, have you? He's sixty if he's a day and makes Eddie look overweight. I'm more than willing to alert the county police, but nobody's going to give anybody a search warrant based on mere suspicion. They have to have something concrete. It's up to me to get it for them. Alone."

We argued about it until it was obvious someone would have to compromise and it would not be me. Duck knew me well enough to recognize that.

"Okay, okay. You're backup. Make yourself comfortable. No telling how long we'll have to wait."

Two hours elapsed, during which no one emerged from the house, but every winged insect in the vicinity became aware of our presence and began a picnic on any exposed flesh they could find. I threw in the towel when a gnat flew into my eye. There's nothing like it, unless you've had the misfortune to have a hot poker stuck in your eye.

"That's it," I said, once my tears had washed out the gnat. "I can't stand this any longer, and I've got to return that car." Duck nodded. He didn't look good at all. It wasn't hot, yet a mustache of perspiration beaded his top lip. "And you need to see a doctor. Come back with me to Mrs. Simmons's and—"

"No," he cut me off, blotting his face on his shirttail. "I need to stay out of Sanctuary. Ever since J.B. left, I've had the feeling I've been made. You know what I mean, that prickle at the back of my neck, like someone was trailing me. And Joe, my supplier, cut me off. All of a sudden he says he's gone out of business, even though he smells like a reefer in tennis shoes. I figured it was time to split and found a room over here in Reedy's Corner."

"That works out fine. Doc Williams lives around here somewhere. This Joe of yours, describe him."

He lapsed into police lingo. "White male, thirty to thirty-five, five-ten, about one-fifty, light brown and blue. Oh, and yellow teeth."

"Say no more," I stopped him. "That fits the character who jumped me in your garage. Drives an old Volkswagen bus?"

"That's him." Alarm flared behind his eyes.

"Remember, I said he told me he followed J.B. because J.B. had taken some pot and he had to get it back."

"You're saying he swiped it instead of buying it?" Duck looked sick.

"Sounds like it. He almost caught J.B. at your place and then followed him to mine. If he had sense enough to check my mailbox, he saw my name." I stopped, convinced now that Joe had been the mysterious caller threatening the landladies with arson. If he had heard I was the one who'd had the accident, he would have done what he could to see that I didn't stay in Sanctuary.

Duck was looking at me curiously, so I continued. "Sorry, just a stray thought," I said. "Anyhow, at some point Joe went back to your building because he ran into Mrs. Luby and company. They probably told him everything he'd ever want to know and then some, including the fact that you're a cop. Have you used your own name here?"

"Of course," he said with spirit. "If my old man was here, I wanted him to know his son had arrived. I also figured it would make him easier to find. Somebody might recognize the name and comment on it."

"Well, we'd better assume you're right and they think you're still a cop. And I'd better start back before they send Major Hamilton looking for me. How'd you get here?" I stood up and massaged my legs awake.

"Walked. I'm only about a half hour's walk west of here."

From the looks of him, I had serious doubts that he was any shape to make it back under his own steam. I suggested the only thing that made sense.

"Look, show me that other way back to the car and ride with me. We can stop anyone and ask where Doc lives, so he can take a look at your shoulder."

"No way. He'd have to report it, and I don't need that."

"But—"

"The bullet went straight through, but there's no mistaking the fact that it's a gunshot wound, which ties his hands. All I need is more disinfectant and bandages. And aspirin."

I could see that this was one I wouldn't win. "All right. After I've returned the car and checked to see if Chunky's resurfaced, I'll find a drugstore. There's bound to be one somewhere in Sanctuary. I can take one of the Pike boys' buses back here. Where's your car?"

"At the rooming house."

"Good. We can use your car to get back here, and camp out in the barn as long as we need to. How's that sound?"

His smile was wry. For the time being, I'd taken charge and he knew it. "Fine, babe. Let's take a look at the tower—"

"Again?" There was no way he'd be able to climb that ladder.

"If there's anyone in it, we'll be able to see him from here. The only time you can't is when you're close to it."

That was a relief. We listened for sounds of life from the house and heard absolutely nothing. And if there was anyone in the tower, he wasn't visible. Duck led me to the edge of the field behind the house and along the perimeter where an irrigation ditch ran toward the woods. It was treacherous footing because of the mud, but the combination of the depth of the ditch and the height of the weeds hid us from anyone watching from the direction of the house and, for the most part, the tower.

There was yet another path through the woods, not quite as clearly defined but manageable. When we reached the road, I saw the Civic not two car lengths away.

We cleaned off as much mud and weed debris as we could, and with Duck navigating, I drove him to his boardinghouse, a rancher of fairly recent vintage. Grimacing with pain, he untied my bra, stripped his T-shirt off and draped it over his shoulder, effectively hiding his wound.

"When you come back, use the side entrance," he directed. "That's the door for roomers. How long do you think you'll be?"

"With luck, a couple of hours, minimum. What's the phone number here?"

He rattled it off, and I wrote down it and the address. He opened the door and put one leg out. "Leigh." His eyes were sad. "I'm sorry about all this, about everything. I never meant to hurt you, you know that, don't you?"

A lump filled my throat and I nodded. "Scram," I said. "I'll be back as soon as I can."

He stepped out, and came around to my side. "I love you, Leigh. Always have, always will." His fingers traced the line of my cheek. Then he turned and walked away.

Back in Sanctuary, the news was both good and bad, and once again poor Paulie was stuck with delivering both. "This is the phone number where your car is," he said, shoving a slip of paper at me nervously. "It's at a service station up in Fellows Ridge."

"Where's that?"

"Up near the Pennsylvania line. The man who called sounded real mad. He said he'd found a front seat to replace yours, but he said the money some-body named Joe gave him—"

"Joe?" My stomach bolted. This was not good.

"Yes, ma'am, that's who he said. He said it wasn't near enough money for the seat and the labor, plus the trip to the car-parts place that had the seat. He wants more cash before he goes to pick it up. I asked him was he sure it wasn't Chunky brought your car in and he said, no, it was a Joe driving Chunky's roll-back with our phone number on the doors. That's how he tracked us down. He said he called the number Joe gave him all day yesterday and today and nobody answered, so he called here. He wants the extra money or he says he's not touching your car."

"Fine with me," I said. He wouldn't be getting anything from me, but at least I knew where it was. "Still no word from Chunky?"

"No, ma'am. I called Mr. Minor and asked him to get a message about everything to his brother. I'm real scared, Miss Warren. Chunky never loans his truck, never! If this Joe had it, either he stole it or forced Chunky to give it to him, like a carjacking or something. Something bad must have happened to him or he'd have called."

There was little I could say to ease his mind, but I murmured words of comfort anyway, hoping they sounded more reassuring to him than they did to me. He accepted the keys to the Civic, promising to return them to his uncle at close of business. I asked and was given the location of the one and only drugstore, and with a blatant lie about meeting a friend who'd be arriving on a bus from Peace Station, I got directions to the bus pickup.

I hurried to the drugstore and left fifty dollars poorer with a first-aid kit, enough bandages to wrap a mummy, a sling, an ample supply of aspirin and four bottles of water. I had turned onto the walkway to Mrs. Simmons's front door when it opened and a petite figure stepped out and turned to speak to someone still in the house. I stopped so short, I almost tripped over my feet. Tina Rae Jones? How the hell had she tracked me here? And was Tank with her?

Dumb question. "I'll be right back, Tankie," she said. "I want to hit that basket place we saw. Be sure and let her see the lining of my vest. And save me a biscuit, okay?"

I've never moved so fast in my life, executing an about-face and sprinting across the yard in front of the annex to duck around the rear of the house, causing more than a few raised brows by passersby.

I was so muddled I couldn't remember whether the basketry studio was to the right or left. The screened-in back porch was a few feet away and the only thing that saved me. I ran up the steps, praying the screen door was unlocked. That prayer was answered. The one that followed, however, was not.

Inside, Tank was crossing to the kitchen table, where a platter was piled high with bicuits the size of dessert plates. My mouth watered as he slathered on a deep red concoction and devoured half of it in the first bite. Almost immediately three women burst in, two holding and admiring a colorful quilted vest similar to the one he'd worn the day we'd met.

"What kind of stitch is this?" one asked.

Tank's basso profundo carried easily as he launched into the kind of detailed explanation that revealed he'd made the vests himself. Was that the job he hadn't wanted to tell me about?

"Come on, I'll show you," he said, cramming the rest of the biscuit into his mouth. "It's real easy." Brushing crumbs from his hands, he left, his fan club trailing in his wake, except one who was obviously more interested in the contents of the platter. She pulled out a chair and sat, reaching for a plate. I waited out her slow and deliberate demolition of the first biscuit. That took five minutes. When she placed a second and third on her plate, I knew it was risky to hang around any longer. I tiptoed off the porch and headed for the end of the house farthest from the street.

It took me twice as long to get to the bus pickup

because of the route I used to avoid running into
Tina. There I found a line of people waiting. Two
buses—the old yellow school bus variety—came
and left before I could get on. Then, arriving in
Reedy's Corner, I discovered I had no idea where I'd
wound up in relation to Duck's rooming house.
Armed with directions from a local, I had my second and third unpleasant surprises. Reedy's Corner
was larger than I'd thought and there were no cabs.
It appeared I had at least a four-mile walk ahead of
me, and the sun had already begun to drop toward
the mountaintops. Duck would have to pick me up.
I rooted out my phone and called the number he had
given me. Eight rings later, an unfamiliar voice
responded. "Yes?"

I asked for Dillon Kennedy.

"Sorry, he's not here."

I'd begun to suspect as much and asked how long
he'd been gone.

"Can't say. I've been here the last couple of
hours, and he was gone when I got here."

In other words, he'd left not long after I'd
dropped him off. And I knew without a doubt
where he'd gone.

18

FOR THE FIRST TIME IN MY LIFE I WAS forced to hitchhike and, like Blanche DuBois, "rely on the kindness of strangers." Assuming this was a town where everyone knew everyone else, I played the only card I had. I offered to pay a lady who was coming out of the grocery store across the street from the bus dropoff to give me a ride to the home of Mr. Dawes. I explained that he'd come to my rescue after an accident, which she knew about, of course. She readily agreed even though she eyed my disreputable slacks with consternation. Mr. Dawes, she said, was a deacon in her church. I was just happy she didn't know Mr. Dawes and son had left town.

She dropped me off at his door just as the sun oozed beyond the horizon, and hurried on her way. Purse slung over one shoulder and shopping bag of drugstore paraphernalia over the other, I ran back out to the road and trotted toward the treacherous curve, remembering to proceed facing oncoming traffic. I had to find the point where Duck and I had come out of the woods before it got too dark to see. I had my flashlight, but if I used it, I might as well run through the trees with a bullhorn announcing,

"Hey, y'all, here I come!" Fortunately, the Duckmobile was parked in the same place I'd left the Civic earlier, and that simplified the problem.

I found the field only because I knew the general direction to go. When I reached it, I was momentarily stunned by its beauty. The setting sun had set the amber weeds aflame with a color I couldn't begin to describe accurately, a deep reddish gold, the tips brushed with mauve. Whether my khaki shirt and pants would still be an effective camouflage was open to question. It was a chance I'd have to take.

I was farther west of the first path I'd taken. Posted behind a tree, I squinted at the tower. If someone was up there, I couldn't see them. I moved toward it slowly along the tree line to find the route I had taken with Duck to get to the barn. I hoped he was still there, that he was waiting for darkness to fall. Watching closely for a lane of broken stalks as I walked, I made it to the barn without setting off any booby-traps, but it was a nerve-wracking trip.

It was almost pitch-black in the barn, and I had no choice but to use the flashlight. I closed the door and called, "Duck?"

Tiny feet scurried off to my right. Otherwise, silence. I called again. Something with a tail zipped through the beam of the flashlight. I shut it off and backed out, jaw clenched to keep from screaming. If Duck was still in there and playing possum, hoping I'd go away, he was in luck because I was going. Once I'd regained my composure, however, I also regained my common sense. Duck had gone to the house without me.

Now I had another problem. We'd crossed to the house from the tower, not the barn. To play it safe, I needed to retrace my steps to the woods, then angle right along the tree line until I reached the irrigation ditch. I swore, apologized to the gods in case I'd irritated them and, with my heart thudding like a bass drum, backtracked. I was so apprehensive that I was pushing my luck making this trek a third time in one day that when I reached the edge of the field, I had to sit down and wait until my legs stopped trembling. The creeping darkness finally got me going again.

The ditch was farther away than I remembered, and I welcomed the soft sod underfoot when I finally reached it. In a number of spots its bottom narrowed to inches, so treading carefully, I moved along placing one foot directly in front of the other. I could barely see my white shoes, and the house and barn were rapidly fading into invisibility. I'd forgotten how fast it got dark in the mountains once the sun dropped behind them.

I was congratulating myself for having made it down the ditch to the point directly opposite the rear of the house when I tripped on something. I threw out a hand to catch myself against the hill, and as I went down, felt something with a sharp edge scrape across my left ankle. I pushed myself upright, then sat down. The ankle was on fire. Terrified that a snake had bitten me, I said to hell with it, used the flashlight to take a look and found a horizontal rip in my sock, the skin under it seeping blood along a scratch a couple of inches wide. Not a snake bite, then. I might have to get a tetanus shot, but I'd live. What had gotten me?

Shielding the beam, I played it along the far side of the ditch. At first I saw nothing, not even the root or whatever had caused the fall to begin with. I swept the light from side to side and finally spotted it. A board, its end in splinters, projected from the soil, as if it had been buried parallel to the slope of the hill. On closer examination, I saw that it was not alone. There was a row of them. The light, as the saying goes, dawned. No wonder we hadn't seen it this afternoon. The door to the cellar was hidden under a thin layer of sod.

I found the board farthest right and, using my Swiss Army knife, dug upward along the outer edge of the board. When I reached the top of the door, I backtracked to what I hoped was the midpoint and scratched and scraped in search of a knob or handle. Nothing. There had to be a way to open the thing from the outside.

Finally, I stuck two fingers under the edge of the door and tugged. It came open so smoothly and quietly that, unprepared, I almost lost my grip. I placed a stout twig against the jamb and lowered the door onto it, unnerved by the complete absence of light down there. This needed thinking about. I pocketed the knife and sat down again, pried open the first-aid kit and pasted a bandage on my ankle—a delaying tactic, pure and simple.

Under ordinary circumstances, I bear no resemblance to the heroine in the Gothic novel who climbs the stairs to the attic or sneaks into the basement when no one in their right mind would do such a thing. The very thought of breaching the black hole beyond that door made my knees wobble like gelatin sans fruit, and I wasn't even standing up. But Duck was probably down there and might need help.

All right, I might shortly have to be stupid and go down there, but making certain I wasn't being stupid for nothing seemed an attractive idea. Duck might well be in the house instead. Checking to be certain of that would also put off my foray into the cellar, an idea that appealed to me even more. Parking my purse and the fifty dollars of drugstore supplies beside the closed door, I moved to the rear of the house. In daylight, the planking of the back porch had looked worse than the front, so avoiding it, I began to circle the house counterclockwise, looking in windows.

No sign of anyone in the kitchen or the room on the side. The interior was so dark it was only fit for bats, yet another disconcerting possibility. I rounded the end of the front porch and froze. An unfamiliar shape, huge and ebony against a night sky, loomed at the other end of the porch. I remained immobile, blinking blindly until I could make out what it was. The cab of a truck. Closing in on it, I realized that because my first view of it had been head-on, I couldn't see the rear, a flatbed—Chunky's roll-back, with a load covered by a tarp. I longed to look under it, but I'd have to use the penlight, which required more nerve than I possessed at the moment. But the presence of the missing truck gave me a legitimate reason to alert the authorities. I checked to make sure the cab was empty before continuing my circle around the house at a trot. There was no sign of life on the first floor, but that didn't matter any longer. I wouldn't have to invade the cellar alone.

Back at the irrigation ditch, I rescued my phone from the litter at the bottom of my purse, found the paper with Major Hamilton's number and dialed. The last thing I expected to get was an answering machine. I left a message that I'd found Chunky's truck, and was describing the location when a beep interrupted me, followed immediately by a dial tone. Seething, I tried again, waited out Mr. Hamilton's dry recitation of office hours for justice of the peace, opened my mouth to finish the first message and was cut off by a series of beeps and a dial tone. The answering machine was full. What now? His brother?

I dialed. Busy signal. Terrific. It was time to call the professionals. I punched 911. There was a ring on the other end, then "We're sorry, your call cannot be completed as dialed. Please—" Crazed with frustration, I punched End. In desperation, I called Mrs. Simmons.

"Leigh," she exclaimed. "Child, where are you? We've been so worried."

"In Reedy's Corner. I've found Chunky's truck and I need—"

Suddenly another voice interrupted. "Leigh Warren, goddamn it, where are you?" Tank. Why was he still there?

"You wouldn't know if I told you," I hissed. "Get

off the phone and let me speak to Mrs. Simmons! This is important!"

"What is it?" he demanded. "Have you found Duck?"

From somewhere behind me, I heard a rhythmic knocking.

"Hold on a minute," I said into the phone, flattening myself against the ground. I turned my head toward the house, trying to detect the source. It stopped for a moment, then began again. Bump-bump-bump, pause, bump-bump. A second time, same pattern. Three followed by two. I had no idea whether this was Morse code for SOS, but I was certain of one thing: it was coming from the house, to my astonishment from the second floor.

Tank was swearing into the phone, trying to get my attention. "For God's sake, shut up and listen!" I said softly, but with enough emphasis to break into his tirade. "Tell Mrs. Simmons to call the Hamiltons, the authorities or somebody. Chunky's truck is next to an abandoned farmhouse in Reedy's Corner, a couple of hundred yards north of the curve where I wrecked my car. There's an old forest ranger tower nearby and a small barn. Tell whoever she calls to be careful; the fields east and south of the house are booby-trapped. Got that?"

"Hamilton, Reedy's Corner, farmhouse north of curve. Ranger tower, small barn, booby-traps."

"Right," I said, relieved that he'd managed to retain the important points. "There's someone in the house. It may be Duck, and if he's where I think he is, he's trapped. Gotta go."

"Leigh, wait!"

I punched the End button, cutting him off, and dropped the phone in the cargo pocket on my left leg. Grabbing the first-aid kit, I crammed it into the one on my right. It was bulky but didn't hamper movement. I stood still, listening. Bump-bump-bump. Pause. Bump-bump. I was not mistaken. It was coming from a room with a broken window, upper left. How the hell had he gotten up there? No one could have climbed those stairs.

I whacked the heel of my hand against my forehead. I should have realized the answer immediately. This house was the same vintage as Mrs. Simmons's and a few I'd known growing up in Sunrise, all of which had stairs to the upper floor from the kitchen as well. There was no way to tell how clearly Duck could see me, but I waved anyway, to indicate I'd heard.

As wary as I was of the floor of the back porch, I climbed the steps and gingerly approached the rear door. Locked. I'd have to risk the front. Flattened against the siding, I inched to the front porch again and listened. No sounds from the truck and dead silence in the house now.

I crossed the porch to the front entrance, grimacing as a board protested under my weight. As earlier, the door stood wide open and I had no choice. The flashlight was an absolute necessity. I tiptoed through the living room and went directly to the kitchen. There were two doors side to side. The first opened onto a pantry. The second wore a cheap lock, the sliding bolt kind, the only purpose of which was to keep it closed. I eased the bolt back, prayed the hinges wouldn't shriek, and opened the door. A closed stairwell, musty but sturdy and whole.

Shutting the door behind me, I started up in my hated, toddler-on-the-steps gait, testing each tread for give and groan. At the second-floor landing, I checked for any problem areas underfoot. The hardwood planking looked secure, but I moved slowly and with caution, knowing termite damage wasn't always visible and would be even harder to detect in the dark.

I made it along the hallway without incident and found myself facing a pair of doors at the rear. A small silver padlock dangled from the hasp of the one on the right. I yanked on it; it didn't yield. On a whim I stood on tiptoe and felt along the molding above the door. Bingo. I used the tiny key, opened the lock, then the door and dropped the lock into one of my cargo pockets. They wouldn't be holding anyone else prisoner up here.

Pulse throbbing with anxiety, I swept the beam of the flashlight around the room until it captured the bound and gagged figure huddled near the window, the eyes above the fabric covering his mouth wide with fear. My throat closed as if clutched in an invisible hand. No Duck. It was a man, perhaps forty, medium brown complexion, and I'd never seen him before in my life.

After a second my brain engaged. I hurried to him and pried the gag from his mouth. He swallowed, wetting his lips, running his tongue over his teeth.

"Chunky, I presume," I said, groping for my Swiss Army knife to cut him free.

"Yes, ma'am," he croaked. "Can't thank you enough. Who're you?"

"Leigh Warren. You picked up my car Thursday night. How long have you been here?"

"Don't know. What's today? I've lost track."

"Saturday."

"Just Saturday? Since Thursday night, then. Feels more like a week."

But if he'd been here since the night of the accident, he couldn't have removed the denim bag from the trailer.

"Careful with that pig-sticker, please, ma'am," he said, watching me saw through the rope around his wrists. "I need to stay healthy. I gotta kill me somebody."

I managed to hide my smile. His nickname was obviously someone's idea of a joke. This was my week to deal with men who weighed less than I did. Chunky looked to be of average height, but I doubted he could remain upright in a good stiff wind.

"Why would anyone do this to you?" I asked.

"Bunch of damn crooks, pardon my French. Got me to come out here in the first place by threatening to vandalize my artwork, so I went. Then they wanted me to take your car to some shop I never heard of to replace your passenger seat, and I wasn't gonna do that without your permission. Lanky white boy got mad and decked me. Next thing I know, here I am, like a pig waiting for slaughter."

The rope finally gave way, and he rubbed his wrists and ankles, wiggled his feet. "I'm too old for this kind of thing, but I'm gonna kill me somebody."

"Get in line," I said. "Think you can walk now? We've got to get out of here." I helped him up. He tried his legs, and nodded.

We started down the steps, the beam of my penlight guiding the way. At the bottom, I extinguished the beam and paused before opening the door, listening just in case. It was a smart decision.

"No more," a man's voice exclaimed angrily. "This is the last move we're making. Shouldn't have left the barn to begin with."

"The barn didn't have a fuse box and meter. You figure the damn plants were gonna grow in the dark?"

I recognized the second speaker, unlikely to forget Joe's nasal twang any time soon. The first voice was familiar, too, but I couldn't place where I'd heard it.

"Well, this next place is it for me. And no more of your designer shit, either. If a buyer wants pot, he gets pot. If he wants PCP or smack, there's plenty other places he can get it, but not from me."

Evidently there'd been a falling-out among thieves. They were getting louder, with little concern about being overheard.

"You're cuttin' off your nose to spite your upper lip, old man." Joe. "The market's there for the juiced-up mary jane. That little bit we put on the streets in Washington and Baltimore proved that."

"I've been doing fine with just pot for years. You

want to branch out, you're on your own. There are too many people trying to find out where that designer crap of yours is coming from. Hurry up. We've got a lot to do before we leave."

The voices seemed alarmingly close. Footsteps approached the door and I hefted the flashlight above my head, ready to knock hell out of whoever opened it. To my surprise and relief, they opened the pantry, on the other side of this stairwell wall with a door that matched this one. I'd seen nothing on the shelves or the floor, but I could swear they were walking into it. Hinges squeaked. Footsteps pounded on stairs. So that's where it was!

Gradually their voices faded. I nudged Chunky and eased the door open, relieved that they hadn't noticed it had been unlocked. We tiptoed past the pantry and had our suspicions confirmed. The rear wall stood open, and steps descended to a landing where a bulb glowed dimly from the ceiling. I sensed rather than saw Chunky move into the small room and grabbed the back of his shirt. He glared at me. I put on my cop face and stared him down. He blinked first and backed out. We tiptoed from the house, and I breathed easier for the first time in ten minutes.

The Cherokee was back. It held no interest for my companion.

"The Chunker!" he exclaimed, and I shushed him. "I knew I heard my engine." Before I could stop him, he'd opened the cab door. He grabbed a flashlight from under the seat and began an inspection, stooping to check the tires and the hoisting mechanism.

I used the opportunity to investigate the Cherokee. The rear was jammed with bags of potting soil, empty plant and seed-growing containers. The door on the driver's side was ajar and the keys in the ignition. I pulled them out, nudged the door as it had been left and went to hurry Chunky along. Passing the cab, I stopped and looked in. Chunky hadn't noticed the keys were in his ignition, too. I thanked heaven for dumb crooks, eased the door open and removed the keys. "Got a present for you," I said as he scuttled from beneath the flatbed. "Here." I dangled the keys and his grin lit up the night.

Secure that neither vehicle would be going anywhere, I had an easier time convincing him to leave his beloved and retreat to the rear of the house.

"What were you doing back here?" Chunky asked.

"Trying to find a way to the cellar from out here. A friend and I searched for it earlier today with no luck. I found it tonight by accident." I patted the sod. "Looks like it hasn't been opened in years."

"Might look that way, but it has. Young fellow went down there late this afternoon. Only reason I didn't knock when I saw him was because I wasn't sure whether he belonged to the bunch that locked me up. By the time you came, I figured I didn't have anything to lose. You got any aspirin or the like? I almost beat my brains out rapping my head against the windowsill."

"As luck would have it," I said, and gave him the supply in the shopping bag. "There's bottled water, too. The man who went to the basement today. What did he look like?"

"Black guy, around my color, my height. Round face, kinda boyish-looking, maybe because he didn't have a mustache."

Duck, damn it. He had found the door this afternoon. "Did you see him come out?"

"No, ma'am, never did. So I reckon he's one of the bad guys." He tossed several aspirin in his mouth and swallowed them dry.

"He may have left through the pantry," I suggested.

"If he did, he left with his buddies," he said, and sat on the hillside to tie a shoelace. "They've been tramping back and forth today, and I could hear anytime somebody drove up. The car doors would slam, and in a few minutes those screechy hinges in the pantry would sound off. I could tell every time they went down and came back up. And I never heard anyone leave any other time."

Duck would have waited until there were no vehicles around, but they might have returned and stumbled onto him. The resulting possibilities sent a chill along my backbone. They could have forced him to leave with them, but where would they take him? If they'd found him, it made more sense that they'd truss him up as they had Chunky. Another possibility was that they hadn't found him and he was trapped, hiding. I wanted to strangle him. Why couldn't he have waited for me? I only hoped reinforcements would arrive soon.

Chunky, his shoelace tied, lifted his head and

sniffed. "Gasoline. Where's it coming from?" He hopped up and sprinted toward his truck, but stopped halfway and came back. "I don't smell it over there." Nose to the wind, he hopped the ditch and dropped to all fours. "Here somewhere."

I hadn't detected the odor, but we both realized where it was coming from at the same time. I felt for the twig I'd wedged against the jamb and slowly lifted the door several inches.

"Uh-oh." Chunky's eyes stretched wide. "That's it, all right. What the Sam Hill are they doing?"

I knew without a doubt. "They're going to torch the place. Chunky, Duck may be trapped down there!"

"Who?"

"The one you saw go down. I've called for help, but if those bastards have arson in mind, I can't wait. I've got to check to see if he's there."

Chunky's slender form was barely visible against the night sky. "Well," he said dryly, "you can't tell me they didn't plan to barbecue me with everything else, so reckon I owe you. But if we're going, let's do it before I lose my nerve."

I could have hugged him. "Thank you."

We wasted no more time on words. Chunky helped me open the door all the way. The black hole below yawned, and for a second I relived the fear of darkness which I'd suffered as a child. Determined to overcome it before it did me in, I descended the stairs using the dirt wall on the left for support as I patted a foot on each tread to detect when I'd reached the bottom. My unlit flashlight was in my right hand, gripped so tightly my knuckles ached. Twelve steps. On solid ground, I waited for Chunky. He stepped down behind me, breath whistling through his teeth, and groped for my hand. I gave it to him.

The tunnel under the yard seemed to extend for miles, the only relief a faint glimmer of light at the far end. Chunky squeezed my hand and, hugging the wall, we began our walk toward the unknown, the smell of gasoline becoming more intense with each step.

Storage alcoves had been gouged along the walls of the tunnel, the first with shelving still intact, the second and third bare except for broken gallon jugs on the floor.

"Moonshine," Chunky whispered in my ear.

A fascinating tidbit of local lore, but I was more interested in the fact that the alcoves were deep enough to offer a place to hide, if Joe and the other man passed in front of the entrance to the tunnel. No sooner had the thought occurred to me than Joe did precisely that. I two-stepped into the next alcove on my right, yanking Chunky along with me. Eyes closed tight, I stopped breathing. We couldn't be seen unless one of them actually went past us, but I still felt exposed, like a deer caught in a pair of head-lights.

I could tell that Joe had moved away, and I stepped into the corridor again. Chunky jerked me back.

"What?" I mouthed.

Eyes popping, he nodded toward the alcove

opposite. There were two shelves near the top, a pile of rags on the ground beneath them.

"What?" I mouthed again, nerves fraying.

He released my hand and jerked a thumb at the alcove, more specifically at the pile of rags. His vision was clearly better than mine. He'd discerned what I hadn't. Protruding from the pile of rags was one pale, dirty bare foot, the heel clotted with mud. They'd allowed my passenger to bleed to death in the tower, had discarded her like a toy no longer cherished, and were now about to oversee her cremation. I felt the sting of tears and wiped them away before they could spill over. We had to make sure Duck wasn't cremated along with her. If he was here. That question was answered sooner than I could have hoped.

"Don't think I've forgotten you've still got Kennedy's gun," the hauntingly familiar voice said. "Leave it here. Guns are nothing but trouble. Drop it down his shirt or something."

I clapped my hand over my mouth. They had him!

Joe giggled. "Hey, Cleve, I know what I'm gonna do: tuck it in his damned crotch. If the fire doesn't get him first, the bullets will explode and blow his nuts off. Damned pig. Soon to be a roasted pig, him and Debbie and Chunky."

I'd identified the other voice. Cleveland, of the master class in ceramics. And I'd shown him Duck's photo!

"Stop drooling," Cleveland snapped. "Killing is not funny; it's a necessity again. You think I enjoyed knifing Debbie? I did it because I had to. She was running to turn us in. Too bad about Chunky. He's a talented man. If he'd gone along with us getting rid of any evidence Debbie had been in that car, he wouldn't have to die. And it's your fault the Warren woman's still alive. You were supposed to hit her hard enough to break her neck, remember?"

"She moved and I missed." Joe sounded sulky. I broke out in a sweat.

"You missed because you could hardly wait to get your hands on that pot she was carrying."

"It was mine, ours!" Joe protested. "I could see that metallic glint soon's I opened the car door and the light came on. Seems to me you'd be glad the shit was spilling out of the case. She might have been able to trace it back to us."

"Back to you, you mean," Cleveland corrected him. "And she still may, if we don't take care of her soon. First things first. Let's get this last crate into the Cherokee, and do the deed. You got enough matches?"

Joe snorted. "Don't need but one. It's your turn to back up the steps this time."

There ensued a lot of huffing, puffing and grunting. Their voices receded. Chunky and I hurried toward the end of the tunnel.

The cellar was empty, cavernous, littered with debris and reeked of gasoline. The fumes were nauseating. Two naked bulbs hung from the rafters, casting a yellow circle of light on the dirt floor under each. The corners were in deep shadow, which is why under other circumstances, we'd have missed him. Duck sat against a rough-hewn floor support, head lolling, arms extended behind him, hands tied on the back side of the post. He'd changed his shirt, and the whole of the left shoulder was dark with blood.

I handed the Swiss Army knife to Chunky and pressed my fingers into the hollow of Duck's neck. His pulse was barely detectable. His skin was cold, clammy. Panic washed through me. He was in shock.

Chunky sawed through the last strands of the rope. "I'll take his head, you take his feet." Grabbing him under the arms, he lifted Duck's torso. I felt for the .22, but Joe had shoved it too far down the front of Duck's pants for me to retrieve it quickly. I hoped the safety was on and hoisted his feet. Duck may have looked thinner, but as we hurried out of the cellar into the tunnel with him, his dead weight felt like a ton.

We were panting past poor Debbie when the inevitable happened. My knee began to speak in tongues. Translation: WHATEVER YOU'RE CARRYING, IT'S TOO HEAVY. PUT IT DOWN OR ELSE!!! I couldn't. The aforementioned IT was Duck. His life depended on our getting above ground, away from Joe and Cleveland, and to a hospital a.s.a.p. So it was grin and bear it.

Grimace and bear it was closer to the truth. So far twenty pounds of groceries had been the limit of my tolerance. Duck's feet and legs exceeded that several fold. With each step I could feel the stress on the ligaments around my rebuilt patella, the grind of bone against bone where cartilege had disintegrated. Stress became strain, strain became agony. I bit down on my lip. Perspiration streamed from my temples, ran rivulets between my breasts and down my spine as the pain-o-meter ratcheted up, notch by notch. Walking backward, I couldn't see how far we had left to go. Doesn't matter, I told myself. I had to keep going.

Chunky wasn't even breathing hard, and it occurred to me that for anyone who could lift hunks of car and stack them on top of each other, Dillon Kennedy was a piece of cake.

"Okay?" he asked softly. I couldn't respond, couldn't even expend the energy to nod. "Almost there," he prompted. "Hurry. Think I hear them coming back. Maybe eight steps to go. C'mon, you can make it. Six, five, four more. Three. Two. One. Terrific." I bumped into the rear wall and sagged. "Stay right there," he said. "I'll swing around and back up the steps."

He pivoted, practically folding Duck in half in order to make the turn. There wasn't much room between the bottom step and the dead-end wall I was braced against. But once in front of the steps we couldn't be seen from the cellar.

Bent practically double, Chunky stepped backward onto the first tread. "Not bad at all. How many altogether, you think?"

I didn't think, I knew. Twelve.

Cleveland's voice rang clearly from the house. "Will you please stop farting around, douse the steps and light the match?"

Joe's response was muffled. Some part of my brain figured he was probably in the pantry. Our luck was holding. If he was going to start the fire there, he wouldn't realize Duck was no longer in the cellar. He'd go back through the house to get out. Once they found the keys gone from both vehicles, they'd have to blow some time hot-wiring them or, if we were lucky, just take off through the woods on foot. So for the time being, unless I passed out first, we were out of danger. Right. Suddenly from very nearby a shrill sound shattered the night.

"What was that?" Chunky whispered.

Cleveland, somewhere in the house, yelled, "What the hell was that?"

"I don't know. I heard it, too." Joe.

It came again, a nerve-jangling, teeth-grating chirp. I wanted to die. And just might. My damned cell phone was ringing.

19

I DROPPED DUCK'S FEET AND CRAMMED A hand into my pocket to silence the thing.

"Find out where that came from!" Cleveland yelled.

"Fuck it! I'm getting out of here!"

Even from where I stood, I could hear the slosh and splash of liquid being spilled, presumably down the steps from the pantry. Suddenly an eerie orange-red glow suffused the air at the far end of the tunnel. Tongues of flames trailed across the opening, and then *whoosh!* The cellar, what little I could see of it, erupted in a blaze of light. I watched, paralyzed with pure, animal fear as it billowed into the mouth of the tunnel and raced toward me.

"Jesus!" Chunky yelled. "Get his feet, Miss Warren! Hurry!"

It took every bit of fortitude I had to push myself away from that wall. I groped for Duck's ankles and lifted them. Chunky managed the next step up, then the next one, hauling Duck far enough so I was in position to take my first toward safety. Up with my good leg, the left. No problem there. I raised my right, put my weight on it and almost passed out as a pain as white-hot as the heat racing toward us sliced through my knee. Sobbing, I collapsed onto Duck's legs.

"Get up, get up!" Chunky screamed.

I tried. I really tried, pushing myself onto all threes. That's as far as I could get.

"Can't, Chunky," was the most I could manage. "Go."

He tugged, took another step backward. As strong as he was, he'd never get Duck out in time. The fire wouldn't stop at the wall, it would fill this stairwell, feasting on fresh night air. And that would be that. It had all been for nothing.

Suddenly a huge figure filled the open area at the top of the stairs, blocking my view of the starry night sky. "Let him down easy, then come on out, sir." Tank. Tank? Was I hallucinating? No. The conflagration in the tunnel supplied ample light now. Black smoke billowed toward us, marching ahead of the fire.

Chunky lowered Duck's head and shoulders and ran up the stairs as I felt Duck's body being pulled from under me. Tank lifted him as easily as he would a two-year-old, was up and out in three long-legged strides. Duck was safe. So was Chunky. Two lives saved, I thought as smoke wafted into the end of the tunnel, then a blast of incredible heat. Two out of three wasn't bad. Nunna would be proud of me. It was a comforting thought with which to die and the last thing I remember.

I wasn't unconscious that long, but might as well have been for all the sense I could make of what was happening outside the ancient ambulance in which I found myself imprisoned for what seemed an awfully long time. There was a lot of swearing and screaming out there, lots of sirens and racing engines. Overlying it all was the roar of flames as it consumed the house and spread to the surrounding fields.

Then Tina climbed into the back of the ambulance with me, yelled, "Hit it, guys!" and slammed the door. She wore the most intricately patterned quilted vest I'd ever seen, so attractive that it distracted me for a moment.

"You aren't hearing any of this," she said to the attendant on the jump seat near my head. She sat next to him and glared at me as the vehicle lurched to a start. "Something tells me you're going to come out of this smelling like a summer rose," she said, "and that's a shame, because if it was up to me, Leigh Warren, your ass would wind up in the slammer for the next ten years."

I blinked the tears out of my eyes and stared at her. It wasn't so much what she said as her delivery that got my attention. Gone was the D.C. street cadence and the soft semi-Southern accent typical of Washington locals. She hadn't sounded like the Tina Rae Jones I'd met at all.

She reached into the pocket of those size-four jeans and jammed a small leather card case under my nose. Pinned to its cover was the badge of the D.C. Metropolitan Police Department.

"You're a cop?" I croaked.

"You'd better believe it. Tank—make that Detective Bernie Younts—and I are members of a special task force assigned to trace the source of the pot that's been killing some people and turning others into out-and-out maniacs. If Duck had come to us back in March when he recognized the tainted pot, we could have been working together instead of sneaking around behind each other's backs and tailing him all summer."

"You mean, he was under surveillance?"

"As squirrelly as he was acting? You bet, especially after it looked like he had a line on where the stuff was coming from. We just didn't understand why he wasn't reporting what he'd learned. After he skipped town and you came back, we switched our focus to you, figuring he might get in touch."

It was easier to deal with this moment's primary concern than the implications of what she was saying. "Where is he? Is he still alive? He was in shock when we found him."

"Oh, shock, my ass. If you'd been in that chilly basement as long as he had, you'd be cold and clammy, too. As for his pulse, it was strong enough a few minutes ago. He was unconscious because he got whacked over the head with his own gun. He kept demanding to know where some piggy bank had come from. They got tired of it, so they put him out of their misery."

"He told you that?"

"No, the Cleveland character. He's spilling his guts so fast, you'd think he'd downed ipecac. Of course, he's blaming everything on his partner. Typical, since his partner can't tell us otherwise, unless he does it from the great beyond."

"Joe's dead?"

"As a doornail. Never made it out of the house. But Cleveland says it was all Joe's idea. Joe paid his college tuition by mixing up designer drugs in the school's chem lab. They kicked him out, but he's been dabbling in concoctions ever since."

"Well, Chunky and I can unsnarl a few of Cleveland's lies. We heard him admit to killing Debbie."

"Debbie? Who's Debbie?" she asked.

I explained and told her where the young woman's remains would be found.

"Good. We've got him, then. Hey, you're smart, Warren, getting me off the subject. Let's get back to you. Talk about playing fast and loose with the law! Why didn't you go to Narcotics with what you knew?"

I wasn't certain I could articulate it. "Because so many things pointed to conclusions I found difficult to accept. I had to prove them wrong."

"In other words, love scrambled your brains. And if your conclusions hadn't been wrong, what then? Would you have turned him in?"

She had understood more than I'd thought. "I've never been sure precisely what the expression means, but I'd have turned him in in a New York minute."

Speculation yanked one brow in an upward tilt. "Well, we'll never know, will we?"

"Where have they taken him?" I asked again.

"Same place we're going, to some local doctor's

clinic. It's the best we can do for the time being. Cleveland, of course, will be transferred to the county jail as soon as they've taken care of his wounds."

"How'd he get hurt?"

She cackled mischievously. "Running through the field trying to outrace the fire. Set off one of his own booby traps. Wound up with an arrow through a leg."

The ambulance slowed and began to reverse.

"Two more questions," I said hurriedly. "Who got me up those steps?"

"Chunky. He's trying to talk the county boys into letting him have his truck tonight. He said if he didn't see you before you left to tell you the two of you are even now."

We most certainly were. "Second question: how'd you two trace me to Sanctuary?"

"Well, we didn't," she said, and grinned. "We wound up in some two-by-four burg called Fellows Ridge yesterday because of the homing beacon we left in your car."

"What?" I squawked.

"Spare me your indignation. We had permission to do it. One of the gas jockeys at the service station told us the owner of the car was in Sanctuary. We drove back down, and it was simply a matter of hitting every single studio until we found you. To tell you the truth, it was fun. I bought lots of stuff."

How nice for her, I thought. "And Tank's a quilter? He made your vests?"

She scowled. "How'd you find out? He only admits it to other quilters."

It was my turn for a sly smile. I'd tell her later. Maybe.

A small building with rooms for five beds in the back, Doc Williams's clinic was a long way from being a hospital, but it probably more than filled the bill for non-emergency problems. A county cop was stationed outside the room on the end. I just hoped there were bars on the windows of that room or we could kiss Mr. Cleveland good-bye.

More than three frustrating and activity-filled hours elapsed before I was left alone—statements taken, scrapes and bruises swabbed, tetanus shot administered, lungs checked, knee examined and wrapped, and, to my chagrin, crutches supplied. I'd had enough experience on them to be fairly comfortable; I just hated the digression. I clunk-clunked from my little room, knocked on the door of the next one and walked into the middle of an argument between an enraged Dillon Kennedy and an implacable and apparently unmovable Detective Bernie Younts. Tank's hand was planted firmly in Duck's chest, holding him down.

"Bitch all you want, buddy," Tank was saying. "You don't get up from here until the man says you can. And he hasn't said it yet."

"Good evening, Detective Younts," I said sweetly.

He had the good grace to blush, an interesting phenomenon, before he scowled at me. "Yeah.

You've got a lot to answer for, Miss Warren." He leaned on the "Miss."

"That makes two of us, Tankie." And I leaned on that. "Duck, how are you doing?" His left arm was supported by a sling.

"I'm fine. I'd be even better if this big ape would get up off me. I've got to talk to Cleveland before they ship him out."

"No dice," Tank said. "And say thank you. This woman risked her life to save your ungrateful ass."

Duck subsided long enough to look at me, his eyes speaking volumes. "I will thank her appropriately the first time we're alone together. She knows how I feel about her."

The door opened, and Doc Williams came in, more grizzled than ever. "Well, Mr. Kennedy, everything looks pretty good. Follow the protocol I gave you, and let your doctor take a look at you as soon as you can schedule it. Here's a prescription for pain. And pay my bill when you get it."

Duck lifted his head from the pillow. "That's it? I can go?"

"Don't see why not. Miss Warren, there's someone to see you in the waiting room."

"Move your hand," Duck said to Tank, "or I'll bite it."

Tank grinned. "Yes, sir."

Assuming that Mrs. Simmons had made the trip over to check on me, I clumped my way out to the waiting room. The young woman rising to greet me wore a nervous and apologetic smile. Her face was familiar, but so much had happened in the past couple of days that at first I couldn't place her.

It must have shown. "I'm Lorna Pike," she said. "From the Peace Station Post Office?"

"Of course. I remember." Well, it was half true.

"I live here in Reedy's Corner, and everybody's heard about the fire and everything. I just couldn't let you leave before I explained why I acted the way I did that night at the post office. I was scared because I remembered who mailed that package to you. It was Mr. Kennedy. I saw him after that with Joe, the white boy I knew was selling drugs. One of my brothers said he'd threatened to kill a cousin of ours who owed him money. So when you asked me what you did, all I could think was, I had to protect my family. And I called my Aunt Clara and warned her, too. Clara Condon, with the rooming house. I was afraid she'd get hurt. I just wanted to apologize."

Ever the defender of justice, I asked, "Would your cousin be willing to testify about Joe's activities?"

"If he isn't, he will be," she said with steel in her eye. "We'll all do whatever we can to help. Maybe that'll make up for how we treated you."

"It's a deal." I thanked her and she left, just as angry voices exploded from the back hall, Duck's among them.

"Come on, man." Tank's tone injected a note of reason. "We're all on the same side," he was saying to the county cop as I swung around the corner from the waiting room. "We're all members of the brotherhood, we all wear a badge." That wasn't accurate, but I wasn't about to correct him. Neither, I noted, was Duck.

"I just want to ask the man one question," Duck said. "I won't touch him, won't go near him. Please!"

Apparently besieged beyond endurance, the cop Doc had called Junior gave in. "All right, but you listen here. This guy is ours. You try any funny business, and brother officer or not, I'll plug you. Am I clear?"

"Perfectly," Duck said with emphasis. Junior looked young and still wet enough behind the ears to do it.

He opened the door, glanced in, and nodded at Duck. "Just you," he said. "Everybody else waits out here."

Duck went in, moving slowly. Junior followed. And closed the door. I could have yanked his hair out. Mine, too.

They were in there for so long, Tank found a chair for me. Tina rushed in, winded. "I found it. It's parked outside. I stopped at a gas station because the oil light was on."

There was no need to ask what she was talking about. She dropped Duck's car keys in my hand.

When Duck finally came out, he looked as if he had expended the last of his physical and emotional reserves. Oddly enough, so did the young cop.

I couldn't stand it. "What did he say?"

I got up to offer him my chair, but he shook his head and leaned against the wall.

"My dad's dead," Duck said, as if, even though

he'd been saying it for years, he couldn't believe it. "His name—my name meant nothing to him! That—that *bastard* found my dad in his rig, parked on the side of the road in upstate New York. Cleveland had abandoned his own car, which, it seems, he'd stolen. He said Dad was in bad shape, chest pains and trouble breathing. Any fool could see he was having a heart attack. He managed to ask Cleveland to drive him to the hospital or use the CB and call for help before he passed out. Cleveland claims no one responded on the radio, and by the time he'd figured out how the gears worked and got to the hospital, Dad had stopped breathing."

"Did he try CPR? Anything?"

"Are you kidding? He had a record and knew he'd have to deal with the authorities if he took Dad's body into the emergency room. He was an opportunist. He stashed Dad's body in one of the containers in the trailer, and kept driving south for two days. He said he stopped one night and buried the container in an old cemetery in the country somewhere in North or South Carolina, he isn't even sure which. He drove all the way to Florida, kept the cab until it broke down and abandoned it in a swamp."

"Oh, Duck, I'm so sorry." I smoothed the back of his neck, feeling ineffectual.

"He says he took the piggy bank because it had money in it and he thought it was cute. If he ever went back home, he'd give it to his girl. He's had it ever since. Toulouse swiped it to hide his stash in. Cleveland hadn't even missed it!"

"How'd he wind up here in the ceramics trade?" I asked.

"He was shacked up with some girl in Key West, and it was her hobby. She hooked him. He's been up and down the Eastern Seaboard for the last five years, making and selling his work and his marijuana crop. He heard about Sanctuary and was trying it for a while. Joe was here as an apprentice. They were a perfect match." Duck's eyes glistened with sudden tears. "And my dad is buried in an unmarked grave somewhere in North or South Carolina!"

"Or Tennessee," Junior added helpfully. "He thought that was a possibility, too."

Doc popped his head out of his examination room. "Not that I haven't enjoyed your company, but I thought you should know I've got a mother coming in with her two children. From the symptoms she describes, it sounds as if they both have mumps. Haven't seen that in years."

"Hell's bells," Tina said, grabbing Tank by the neck of his shirt. "Let's go. I've got to protect the family jewels so we can have some babies."

"Some?" Tank said. "Wait a minute, Tina. How many is some?"

"Don't look so disapproving," she said to me as she towed him toward the door. "We're married. And we'll expect to see you both Monday at headquarters. Prepare to make a full report. 'Night, everybody." And they were gone.

"Duck," I asked, "did you know Tank was a cop?"

"Sure," he responded, but his mind was clearly

elsewhere. "Why do you think I asked him to keep an eye on you?"

"Uh, Doc," Junior said, "what did she mean? Do I need to worry about my—" He glanced at me and flushed radish red. "My you-know's?" he finished lamely.

Doc grinned. "Wait in the room with Cleveland if you're that concerned about your 'you-knows.' Kennedy, are you all right?"

Duck pushed himself upright. "I'm fine. I'm going home."

"No, you aren't." Doc stepped into the hallway, arms akimbo. "You're not up to that. Miss Warren, I'd suggest you take him over to Vangie's. She has the room, and there's nothing she'd like more than to feed him. What he needs now is some tender, loving care. I suspect you could use some as well."

I was past the point where I knew what I needed. We said our thank-yous and good-byes, gathered our belongings and left the doctor to await the mumps.

Outside, Duck gazed at me. "We make one hell of a pair. You're stove up on your right, me on my left. Looks like I'll have to drive. Don't worry, I can make it as far as Sanctuary."

I didn't argue. If he had to concentrate on driving, it would keep his mind occupied until he could be alone and deal with the things he'd learned.

We'd settled in the Duckmobile, a process that had taken longer than normal, given our various encumbrances, and were about to pull out of the diminutive parking lot when Duck slammed on the brakes and jerked the gearshift into Park.

"He's dead, Leigh," he said softly. "He's really dead. He was my idol, my buddy. I couldn't have wished for a better father. How could I have doubted him? I've been practically blind with hatred all these years!"

The anguish in his face and voice was numbing. I fumbled around for some way to help and finally said the only thing I could think of. "You were hurt, Duck. But now you know he didn't walk out on you and your family. He had no control over what happened. If he had survived the heart attack, sooner or later he'd have come home. He didn't abandon you after all."

He rubbed his eyes, digging in with his knuckles. "No, he didn't. And I don't know how, but I'm going to find him and bring him back so he can be buried next to Christopher. That's for some day. Tonight, all I want to do is sleep. Tomorrow, I'd like us to go on home."

"Home," I said, wondering if Neva had finished my apartment yet.

"To *our* place. Yours and mine. As Mr. and Mrs., Mr. and Ms. or Miss, it's up to you. I can't tell you how much I've missed you. Wherever I live, I want you with me. What do you say?"

"Oh." Well, this was an interesting turn of events, the last thing I'd expected. I opened my mouth to tell him I'd think about it. So no one was more surprised than I was when Miss Leigh Ann-Needs-Her-Space Warren looked over at him and said, simply, "What the hell. Okay."